Witch Is How Bells Were Saved

Published by Implode Publishing Ltd

Chapter 1

"Morning, Jill." Britt was doing press-ups on their back lawn.

What was the matter with that woman? Didn't she realise it was seven-thirty in the morning? I barely had the energy to open the dustbin.

"Morning."

"Did you know Lovely was back?"

"Yes, I saw her over the weekend. You must be really pleased."

"I am, but—" She hesitated.

"She's okay, isn't she?"

"Yeah, she doesn't seem to be any worse for wear."

"What's wrong, then? I thought you'd be happy now she's returned."

"I'm pleased to have her back, obviously, but she seems to have taken up with that ruffian across the road. Those two are always together now. He even tried to follow her into our house yesterday."

"I suppose that's better than having them fighting."

"I guess so. It's just that my Lovely is a little princess, and Bruiser is a thug."

"You'd better not let Kimmy hear you say that about her *Fluffykins*."

"By the way, Jill, how are you getting on with your instrument? Was it the tuba you went for in the end?"

"No, I couldn't get along with that, so I swapped it for the penny whistle."

"Have you managed to put in much practice?"

"Of course. Every spare minute I get," I lied.

"Good for you. Kit and I put aside an hour every

evening. If you're going to do something, you may as well do it properly, don't you think?"

"My philosophy exactly."

When I got back into the house, Jack was tapping his watch. "Come on, you'd better get a move on if you want me to give you a lift to the breakers' yard."

"Sorry, Britt kept me talking out there."

"Did she have anything interesting to say?"

"Not really. She was asking if I'd managed to put in much practice on the penny whistle."

"What did you tell her?"

"That I had, of course."

"So you lied?"

"No. I have been practising."

"I haven't seen you."

"I prefer to do it when I'm in the house alone."

"You realise the next meeting is on Wednesday, don't you?"

"That soon?"

"I'm looking forward to seeing how everyone else has progressed."

"You'll be the only one there who's bothered to practise."

"No, I won't. Kit told me that he and Britt spend an hour practising every day."

"Okay, no one except for you and the Liveleys, but they're crazy."

"You're wrong. Everyone seemed really enthused on the night."

"That's what people do. They get all excited about something, but when it comes down to putting in the hours, they flake out."

"I assume you're talking about yourself."

"My case is different. I'm too busy with work."

"What about yesterday when you spent all evening watching that awful box set on Netflix?"

"It was educational."

"It was a comedy western, and you fell asleep while you were watching it."

"I thought you said we were running late."

***

Jack pulled up outside Washbridge Breakers' Yard.

"Shall I come in with you?"

"There's no need. You'd better get going or you'll be late."

"Tell me again how much you have to pay to get your car back?" He smirked.

"Bye, Jack." I slammed the car door.

The spotty young man behind the counter was covered in oil. Or grease. Or maybe it was some new wonder acne cream. He was staring at his phone and he didn't seem to register my presence.

"Are you Wally Bridge?"

"Me? No, I'm Rodney."

"Is Mr Bridge in?"

"He's cleaning out the meerkats."

"There's no need to be sarky."

"I'm not. He is cleaning them out." He pointed to a large wood and glass structure across the yard. "Wally's into meerkats, big time. He's got half a dozen of 'em. I can't see the appeal myself. All they do is stand on their back legs and look around."

"Could you ask him to come over here?"

"He won't come until he's done with the meerkats."

"How long will that take?"

"Another half-hour, at least."

"I can't wait that long. Maybe you can help. It's about a car that you picked up on Saturday by mistake. I spoke to Mr Bridge about it on the phone yesterday."

"I'm just the labourer. I'm only in here until Wally comes back."

"Can I go over there to speak to him?"

"I suppose."

Bridge, an overweight, red-faced man in his fifties, was sweeping out the meerkat enclosure while the occupants peered out of various man-made tunnels.

"Mr Bridge." I knocked on the glass.

He turned to me, shrugged, and mouthed, "What?"

"I'm Jill Maxwell. I called – "

He shook his head and pointed to the door. He surely didn't expect me to go inside, did he?

When I hesitated, he walked over to the door. "If you want to talk to me, you'll have to come in here."

"Couldn't you come outside for a minute?"

"No, I have to finish what I'm doing here first. Are you coming in or not?"

What choice did I have? I couldn't afford to hang around there all day.

"Do they bite?"

"Not usually."

Very reassuring. "I'm Jill Maxwell. I rang yesterday."

"Oh yeah." He grinned. "You're the one who asked us to collect your car *by mistake*."

"I thought I'd explained that yesterday. There was a mix-up over which day my new car will be delivered. It isn't going to come for a few weeks now."

"Like I said on the phone, it'll be fifty quid if you want it back. You're lucky to have caught us before it was crushed."

"That's outrageous. I paid you a tenner to take it away because you said it wasn't worth anything."

"It wasn't then, but now it's worth fifty quid."

"How about twenty?"

"Fifty quid, take it or leave it." He stared at me. "Where do I know you from?"

"I—err—I don't—"

"I remember. You were the one who won the Washbridge lottery, weren't you? I saw it on TV."

"That was me."

"What a great prize. I love clowns—always have."

"Really? In that case, I have a proposition to put to you."

***

Mrs V was at her desk, holding an umbrella over her head.

"We have a leak, Jill." She gestured to a damp patch on the ceiling. "I've called the landlord. He said he'd get someone over here this morning."

"You can't sit there holding an umbrella all day. Let's move your desk out of the way. Can you take that end?"

After we'd moved it, Mrs V placed the metal waste bin

under the drip.

"Did you get your new car on Saturday, Jill? What's it like?"

"No, there was a bit of a mix-up with the prizes. I didn't win a car after all."

"What did you win?"

"A voucher for a course at Clown."

"Oh dear, that must have been disappointing."

"Not really. I never actually believed it would be a new car."

"You seemed so sure."

"I was just joking. Anyway, I'd better make a start. New week, new challenges."

Winky was looking through his telescope.

"Jill, quick! Come and look at this!"

"What is it?"

"If I'm not mistaken, it's a brand new Jag coming up the road." He laughed.

"You've heard, I take it?"

"I saw the presentation on YouTube. Your face! It was a picture."

"I didn't actually think I'd won a Jag."

"Of course you did. You might be able to fool the old bag lady, but you can't fool me. When they announced what you'd won, you looked like someone had just stabbed you through the heart."

"Rubbish."

"Still, you do have the consolation of a course of clown lessons. Oh, wait. You're scared of clowns."

"I'm not scared of them. That's just a vicious rumour."

"When will you be taking the lessons, then?"

"As it happens, I've swapped the Clown voucher."

"For what?"

"That's none of your business."

***

Just when I thought that Winky couldn't get any more annoying, he started making a weird brum, brum sound.

"Do you have to make that noise?"

"Brum, brum."

"What are you doing, anyway?" I stood up to get a better look. "Is that a toy car?"

"Not just any toy car. It's a Jag." He ducked just in time to avoid the stapler. "Hey, that could have hit me!"

"It was supposed to. How come you always kick me when I'm down? Why not try to be supportive for a change?"

"Where would be the fun in that?"

Mrs V came through the door. "You really shouldn't leave these on the floor, Jill." She kicked the toy car under the sofa. "I could have tripped on it."

"But it wasn't—err—sorry. Is Macabre's repair man here?"

"No. It's Daisy Flowers. She wondered if you could spare her a few minutes."

"Sure, send her in, would you?"

"I'll tell her to watch out for the toy cars."

"What brings you here, Daze? Can I get you a drink?"

"No, thanks."

"Have a seat. Is everything okay?"

"I'm afraid this isn't a social call, Jill."

"Oh?"

"There have been reports."

"What kind of *reports*?"

"About you."

"What do you mean? What about me?"

"You're aware that I've turned a blind eye to the situation with Jack."

"Yes, and I'll always be in your debt."

"The thing is, I've gone out on a limb for you, and that's okay, but not when this kind of thing happens." She held out her phone and played a video. "That is you and Jack, isn't it?"

"Err—yeah."

"In the car park near the cinema?"

"That's right. Jack and I were—" What I saw on-screen stopped me mid-sentence.

"And that is you, turning that man into a rat, isn't it?"

"Yes, but I can explain."

"I'm listening."

"He pinched my parking space."

"And?"

"And, err—that's not really a good excuse, is it?"

"No. It isn't. What you did was unforgiveable, Jill."

There was something about an angry Daze which gave me flashbacks to being told off by Mrs Preston at junior school.

"I'm sorry."

"It's bad enough that you did it at all, but to do it in front of Jack makes it ten times worse. What were you thinking?"

"I—err—"

"You weren't thinking! You can't have been. You've put

me in a very difficult position."

"I really am sorry, Daze. What are you going to do?"

"What I *should* do is take you back to Candlefield and let the powers that be decide your fate. And I can pretty much guarantee what they would do."

"You said, *should do*. Does that mean you aren't going to send me back?"

"You've been a good friend to me and the rogue retrievers. I've lost count of the number of times you've helped us."

"I'm pleased I've been able to."

"That's why I won't do anything this time, but this can't happen again."

"It won't, I promise."

"I'm not stupid. I don't kid myself that you're never going to use magic in the human world, but you can't do this sort of thing again. Having a hissy fit and turning that guy into a rat is precisely the kind of thing your grandmother would do. I expected better of you."

"I do. I have. I promise I'll never do anything like that again."

"And please try not to use magic in front of Jack. At least, not while you're out in public."

"I won't. I promise."

"Okay." She smiled for the first time. "Let's never have this discussion again."

"We won't. And, Daze, thanks. I know I messed up, and I really do appreciate what you've done for me."

After she'd left, I gave a great sigh of relief. I'd been a complete idiot by putting everything I treasured at risk. And for what? Just because someone had pinched my parking space.

"Who's been a naughty girl?" Winky pushed the toy car across the floor.

"Shut up, you. And get that car out of my sight before I—"

"Be careful. Don't forget what happened the last time you lost your temper over a car."

***

I'd been summoned to Ever. Grandma wouldn't say over the phone why she wanted me, just that I should get down there straight away.

"What's up with you, misery guts?" she greeted me.

"I've just had a telling off from Daze."

"Daisy Flowers?" She scoffed. "Who does she think she is? Puffed-up little nobody, that's who."

"She's a rogue retriever, as well you know. And please don't call her names. She's done me a big favour by not reporting me."

"Pah! You worry too much. You're more powerful than that lot put together. There's nothing they could do to you."

"You don't know that."

"Of course I do. Why do you think I get away with what I do? It's not because I'm everyone's bestie. They can't touch me, and they know it. The same goes for you."

"Even if that's true, I wouldn't want to let Daze down. She's been a good friend."

"Oh please." Grandma mimed putting a finger down her throat. "Excuse me while I throw up."

"You said you wanted to see me about something."

"I want an update on your investigation into Belinda Cartwheel."

"An *update*?"

"Yes, please."

"Actually, there isn't any update."

"Why not?"

"The thing is—err—I—err—"

"You have been investigating Belinda, haven't you?"

"Not exactly."

"Why not? You promised you would."

"I've been really busy. I've been working on some important cases."

"What could be more important than someone trying to stage a coup d'état and remove me as chairman of W.O.W?"

"I—err—"

"Nothing, that's what."

"Sorry. I'll get straight onto it."

"You'd better. I'll expect a full report."

"You can leave it with me." I started for the door. "Isn't your new beauty salon supposed to open next week?"

"It isn't *supposed* to open. It *is* opening, a week on Friday."

"It's just that I haven't seen any promotions so far."

"Don't worry your little head about it. Everything is in hand. Now, off you trot. I have a rash that needs my attention."

Chapter 2

I'd been hoping that Grandma had forgotten about the W.O.W. business, but I should have known better. I'd declined invitations to the last couple of events, but if I was going to find out what Belinda Cartwheel was up to, I would have to accept the next one that came my way. Fingers crossed it didn't turn out to be another beetle drive.

It was definitely coffee time, so I magicked myself over to Cuppy C where I found both of the twins behind the counter.

"Where are Lil and Lily?"

"Upstairs with Jemima and the other kids."

"I'm gagging for a coffee."

"Latte?"

"I think I'll have an Americano for a change."

"Whoa! Steady on. And a muffin?"

"Actually, I fancy toast with jam."

"Are you sure you're the real Jill Maxwell?" Pearl grinned.

I glanced around. "Where are they?"

"Where are *what*?"

"The cats. I thought they'd be out here by now."

"We've given up on the cat café idea," Amber said. "It's more trouble than it's worth. At least we're not out of pocket, though, because we got a full refund from Cat City. Thanks to you."

"Does that mean this is on the house?"

The twins looked at one another, and then said with one voice, "No."

"You two are so mean."

"Guess where we were on Saturday," Amber said, as she popped two slices of bread into the toaster.

"Weren't you working here?"

"No, we treated ourselves to a day off. Mindy is quite capable of taking charge of this place for a day now."

"Where did you go?"

"To Washbridge."

"Really? You never mentioned you were coming over."

"We wanted to surprise you. We were at the town hall for the prize giving."

Oh bum! "I didn't see you there."

"We only just got there in time to see them announce the main prize-winner. You'd left before we had the chance to fight our way through the crowd to you."

"I was feeling a bit peaky, so Jack and I shot off home."

"In your new Jag?" Amber giggled. So did Pearl.

"That's it, go on, have a laugh at my expense. You might as well. Everyone else has."

"You did rather ask for it, Jill," Amber said. "You were going around telling everyone about your new car."

"I was deceived into believing I'd won it."

"By who?"

"I really don't want to talk about it."

"Still, you did win a course of lessons at the clown school." Pearl was practically in hysterics now.

"It's a pity you're scared of clowns, isn't it?" Amber wiped a tear from her eye.

"I think that toast is burning."

While Amber watched the counter, Pearl joined me at a window table.

"Did Aunt Lucy go with you to Washbridge on Saturday?" I took a bite of the charcoaled toast.

"No. Mum would have cramped our style."

"I assume you spent most of the day shopping?"

"Naturally. While we were there, we dropped into Ever. We thought we might get free drinks and cakes."

"Did you?"

"Of course not. Grandma wouldn't even give us a discount."

"What did you expect?"

"While we were in Ever we did have a brilliant idea."

"Have you forgotten the cat café debacle already?"

"That wasn't our fault. We were conned. And, anyway, this is something really simple but effective." She beckoned Amber to come and join us. "I was just telling Jill about our visit to Ever."

"Don't you think it's a brilliant idea, Jill?"

"Pearl hasn't told me what it is yet, but the chances are that the answer is no."

"Uniforms!" Amber beamed.

"Do you mean those horrible canary yellow things that Grandma makes the Everettes wear?"

"We wouldn't want yellow, but they did make the staff look really smart."

"Very professional," Pearl said.

"So, you're thinking of buying uniforms for your staff?"

"And for us of course. What do you think?"

"It's certainly better than the conveyor belt idea. And the chocolate fountain. Won't it be expensive, though?"

"It will be money well spent in our opinion."

"Hmm." Just then, I was distracted by the sight of a young man who'd taken a seat at a table across the room.

"Stop ogling the customers," Amber said.

"I wasn't. I was looking at his t-shirt."

"Isn't that your face on it?" Pearl raised her eyebrows.

"It looks like it."

"Why on earth would anyone want a picture of you on their t-shirt?" Amber said.

"I'll have you know that mine is the second best-selling witch merchandise at Candlefield Icons. Second only to Magna Mondale."

"And you expected us to give you your breakfast for free? You must be coining it."

"I wish. I haven't received a penny."

"You should complain," Pearl said.

"I tried to, but when I visited Candlefield Icons, the owner wasn't in. Apparently, he's rarely there."

"I know that store," Amber said. "The guy who owns it often comes in here for a coffee."

"Does he?" Pearl looked at her sister. This was obviously news to her.

"You know him. He's that flashy guy with the chequered trousers."

"The one with the hair and the brogues?"

"Yeah, that's him."

"I never did like him. He never smiles and he looks at you like you're something he just found on the bottom of his shoe."

"I heard him on the phone once. His name is Songspindle, or something like that."

"It's Sylvester Songspinner," I said. "Would you do me a favour? Give me a call the next time he's in here?"

***

Back at the office, Winky was sulking because I'd confiscated his toy car. It served him right for being so annoying.

My first clients of the week were a young brother and sister, called Adam and Katie Bell. If I hadn't known, I would never have guessed they were siblings. She was tall and slim; he was shorter and bordering on plump.

"How can I help you?"

Each of them seemed to be waiting for the other to speak—eventually it was the young woman who took the lead.

"Our parents have gone missing."

"Both of them?"

"That's right. Our father's name is Walter, and our mother's is Jean."

"When and how did they go missing?"

"They'd been on holiday in their caravan," the young man piped up. "At the Cliffs Caravan Park near Filey."

"Let me make sure I've understood this correctly. Did they disappear from the caravan park?"

"No, it was after they came back." Katie hesitated. "At least, we think so."

"The caravan made it back home, but they didn't," Adam said.

"Did this happen recently?"

"No." Katie shook her head. "It's just over a year ago now. The reason we're here is because the police have scaled back their investigation."

"They've shut it down, more like!" Adam snapped.

"Is there anything else you can tell me about the day they went missing?"

"There's the burglary," Katie said. "When I hadn't heard from Mum and Dad, I went around to their house. The car and caravan were on the drive, so I assumed they must be home but they hadn't heard my phone calls. When I let myself into the house, the living room had been ransacked."

"Katie called me, and I went straight over there," Adam said. "The police think that Mum and Dad must have disturbed burglars."

"That's a bit of a stretch, but if that is what happened, it still doesn't explain your parents' disappearance."

"Unless the burglars forced them to go with them."

"I suppose that's possible. Did the police come up with any other theories?"

"They never came out and said it, but I got the distinct feeling that they thought Mum and Dad had chosen to disappear." It was clear from her tone that Katie didn't agree.

"There's no way our parents would have done that," Adam said. "They'd never do anything to worry us like this."

"Do you have any theories as to what might have happened?"

"Not really." Adam sighed. "But we've pretty much prepared ourselves for the worst now."

"We just need to know where they are, what happened to them, and if necessary, make sure whoever is responsible is brought to justice." Katie took her brother's hand. "Don't we?"

He nodded. "Do you think you'll be able to help?"

"I hope so. I have a pretty good track record on missing person cases."

***

My clients had not long since left when I received a call from Kathy, asking if I could pick Lizzie up from school. Kathy and Peter had already found themselves a cash buyer for their house, which meant they would be able to move into their new place by the end of the week, but only if everyone exchanged contracts today. She and Peter had to go to the solicitor to sign the paperwork, which meant she wouldn't be able to collect Lizzie. Obviously, being the good sister that I am, I'd agreed. Fortunately, Mikey was staying late for sports practice, so I didn't have to worry about him.

"Auntie Jill!" Lizzie came running across the playground and threw herself into my arms. "I didn't know you were picking me up today. Where's Mummy?"

"Your mummy and daddy have to sign some papers for your new house. Come on, my car is parked around the corner."

All the way back to Kathy's house, Lizzie talked my ears off about the school play.

"I'm a pixie called Wendy."

"That's great. Is Mikey in the play too?"

"No. He says plays are rubbish, but that's only because he can't act. I want to be an actress when I grow up. I'll be on the TV and in movies."

"Good for you."

I was about to unlock the door when Lizzie grabbed my hand and dragged me around the back of the house.

"Come and see Flopsy the bunny."

"I thought Mikey said his name is Jake."

"Jake's a stupid name. Look!"

"He really does have floppy ears, doesn't he? They're big too."

"You're no oil painting yourself, lady," the rabbit said, somewhat indignantly.

"Sorry, I didn't mean anything by it."

"Didn't mean what, Auntie Jill?" Lizzie gave me a puzzled look.

"I—err—nothing. I was just talking to myself. Shall we go inside? I'm ready for a cup of tea."

I brewed myself a cuppa, poured Lizzie some orange squash, and then helped myself to a piece of Victoria sponge.

What? It was the least I deserved for services rendered.

"Are you looking forward to living in your new house, Lizzie?"

"Yeah! My new bedroom is much bigger. It's giant!"

"You have a big garden too."

"Daddy said he'll build a tree house for us. Mikey said he wanted his own because he didn't want to share with a girl. Mummy said we'll have to go to a new school too because this one will be too far away."

"Are you okay with that?"

"Yeah, I don't mind because Mummy said I'll make lots of new friends."

"That'll be nice for you."

"There'll be more ghosts to talk to at the new house, too."

"Oh? Have you seen them?"

"Yes, when we were looking around."

"You're not scared of them, are you?"

"No, of course I'm not. They're all nice, but—" She

frowned.

"But what?"

"They seemed scared."

"Of you?"

"No." She giggled. "Why would they be scared of me?"

"What were they scared of, then?"

"I don't know. We had to leave before I could ask them."

Kathy, Peter and Mikey arrived home about an hour later.

"Have you seen Jake, Auntie Jill?" Mikey came charging into the lounge where Lizzie had been showing me her dolls' house, complete with Jack's furniture.

"Yes, Lizzie showed him to me."

"Auntie Jill was talking to the rabbit," Lizzie said.

Kathy gave me a look.

"What? You're supposed to talk to your pets. It's good for them. I'm always talking to Winky." More's the pity. "How did you get on at the solicitors?"

"All done and dusted," Peter said. "He said it was the quickest sale they'd ever processed."

"When do the current owners move out?"

"They've already left."

"Wow, they must have been keen."

"We move in on Saturday." Kathy couldn't hide her excitement. "I can't believe it's actually going to happen."

"If you need any help, just let me know, and I'll send Jack around."

"Where's your car, Jill?" Peter said.

"It's parked right outside your house. Didn't you see it?"

"Oh right, sorry. I was looking for a Jag." Both he and Kathy burst into laughter.

"Very funny. I expected better from you, Peter."

"Sorry. It was Kathy's idea for me to say it."

"I should have known."

***

Back home, I'd just climbed out of the car when I heard Bessie's whistle. If I was quick, maybe I'd be able to get inside before Mr Hosey spotted me.

"Jill! Yoo hoo!"

Foiled again.

"Hello, Mr Hosey. I was just about to—"

"I have big news!"

"Are you moving house?"

"No? What made you ask that?"

"Err, nothing." Just wishful thinking. "So what is this big news of yours?"

"It's the Washbridge annual Model Train Rally on Saturday, and I've been invited to show Bessie in the main arena."

"That's—err—"

"A great honour? Yes, I know. I'll have to spend all week getting her ready, but it'll be worth it."

"I'm really pleased for you, but I must get going."

"Here." He took a wad of tickets out of his waistcoat pocket and pressed them into my hand. "One of the perks of being invited to show Bessie is that I get lots of free tickets."

"I'm not sure we'll be able to make it."

"Haven't I seen some youngsters at your house?"

"That would be my nephew and niece."

"You can bring them too. There's enough tickets there for all of you."

"Thanks."

As soon as he'd driven away, I dropped the tickets into my bag. Go to a model railway rally? No, thanks because I actually have a life.

Chapter 3

Watching Britt and Kit limbering up in their back garden, ahead of their morning run, was so depressing. Especially as I barely had the energy to pour the milk over my cornflakes.

"What are these?" Jack called from the hall.

"I've no idea. I left my x-ray specs at the office."

"These." He walked into the kitchen, brandishing the tickets that Mr Hosey had given me.

"What were you doing in my bag?"

"Looking for my pen. The one my mother bought me. The one you promised to return the same day. Two weeks ago."

"Whoops! Sorry about that. Did you find it?"

"Yes." He was holding it as though it might be radioactive. "It's covered in some kind of sticky gunk."

"That's probably jam. I put a donut in there yesterday."

"You didn't tell me we'd got free tickets for the model train rally."

"Hosey gave them to me last night. I was going to bin them."

"Why would you do that? It could be fun. I bet Mikey and Lizzie would enjoy it."

"They won't be able to go. Kathy and Peter are moving house this weekend."

"Exactly. They'd probably appreciate it if we took the kids off their hands for a few hours, and this rally would be perfect."

"*Really*? It'll be full of train nerds like Mr Hosey."

"I think it'll be fun. We should check with Kathy to see what she thinks."

"I'll do it later today." Unless, heaven forbid, I happened to forget.

"That's okay." He took out his phone. "I'll do it now."

Needless to say, Kathy was all over the idea, so that was my Saturday ruined: Trains, kids and more trains.

Great!

"Jack, before you go to work, there's something I need to talk to you about."

"That sounds serious."

"It is, kind of. I was going to tell you last night, but you were working late."

"What's up?"

"I had a visit from Daze yesterday. An *official* visit."

"What did she want?"

"To give me a telling off, basically. She had a video of me in the cinema car park, turning that man into a rat."

"What's going to happen? She isn't going to send you back to Candlefield, is she?"

"It's okay, relax. Daze isn't going to do anything this time, but she made it very clear that it mustn't happen again, and that I had to get my act together."

"I hope you're going to take notice. I don't want to lose you."

"That's never going to happen, but if you see me looking as though I'm about to do something similar again, you have to stop me."

"As if you'd take any notice of anything I said."

"Of course I would. In fact, as I recall, I only changed that man back from a rat because you insisted that I did."

"You have to take this seriously, Jill."

"I am. Mind you, Grandma reckons I shouldn't take any notice of Daze."

"Why would she say something like that?"

"She reckons she and I are too powerful to be held in Candlefield against our will. That's why she's so blatant with her magic over here. She doesn't care."

"It's not worth the risk."

"Don't worry. I don't intend to take her advice. And besides, Daze has been very good to me. I wouldn't do anything to upset or embarrass her."

"Come here." He pulled me in for a kiss. "I couldn't bear it if I lost you."

"You don't have to worry. I'm always going to be here, right by your side."

"Even at the model train rally?"

"Yes, even there, but you're definitely going to owe me one for this."

As I stepped out of the door, I was confronted by two of the scariest things I'd ever seen. The tallest of them was blue, tubular with spiky bits. The shorter one was green and bobbly.

I was just beginning to think that maybe we'd been invaded by space aliens when Tony's voice came out of the blue thing.

"Morning, Jill."

"Hi. You gave me a bit of a shock."

"They're horrible, aren't they?" said green, bobbly Clare.

"What are they supposed to be?"

"Germs. It's GermCon this weekend, and it's our first time there. As always, you and Jack are welcome to come along."

"Thanks for the offer, but it looks like we'll be attending

a model train rally on Saturday."

"Mr Hosey's thing? He invited us, but we had to say no because of the con. It's a pity, it sounds like it'll be fun."

"Doesn't it, just?" I started for the car. "I'd better get going. Lots to do."

"Have you and Jack been practising your instruments for the band?"

"Of course. Every chance we get."

"What did I say, Tony?" said green, bobbly Clare. "I told you that everyone else would be putting in lots of practice."

"It's not like we haven't done any practising," Tony AKA the blue, tubular spiky one said. "But it's not easy what with work and the con to prepare for."

"I'm sure you'll be fine," I reassured them.

I knew it. Jack seemed to be under the impression that everyone else was practising their instruments like crazy, but most people were too busy. Or, like me, they just couldn't be bothered.

***

Mrs V wasn't in the office.

And neither was her computer. At least, I didn't think so, but then I spotted it on the floor next to the filing cabinet.

I was still trying to work out what was going on when the woman herself came through the door. A few steps behind her was Armi, carrying what appeared to be some kind of vintage typewriter.

"Put it on there, my little gingerbread man." She pointed to her desk.

Armi was red in the face, and clearly relieved to put the relic down.

"Morning, you two."

"Morning, Jill," Armi gasped.

"What do you think of it, Jill?" Mrs V held out both arms as though she was showing off a prize on a game show.

"It's a typewriter, isn't it?"

"It's the first one I ever used. I was given this as a leaving gift when I left my very first job at Drake, Cheeseman and Tyler. I think they were planning to replace them anyway, so it saved them buying me a gift."

"Right? So, err—why is it here?"

"I've never really got along with computers. You know that, Jill. They're so fiddly and slow. I'll be much more productive with this, you'll see."

"You're going to use it here? For work?"

"You don't mind, do you?"

"I suppose not, provided you're still able to do your normal work. What about other computery things?"

"Like what, dear?"

"I don't know." It was only then that it struck me: I didn't really have the first clue what Mrs V did all day. There was the knitting of course. And answering the phone. But beyond that, nothing that I could think of.

"It's not like I'm going to throw the computer away. It'll still be here if something crops up that I need it for."

"I'd better be going, my little dewdrop." Armi seemed to have caught his second wind. "I thought I'd pop by the estate agents while I'm in town."

Once Armi was out of the door, Mrs V slipped a sheet of paper into the typewriter and began to tap away on the keys.

"It's rather noisy, isn't it?" I shouted.

"Sorry, dear?" She paused. "What did you say?"

"I just said—never mind. I see the waste bin is back in its normal place."

"Yes, the leak has been repaired."

"Good. Macabre isn't altogether useless, then."

"Come and take a look at this!" Winky was on my desk, looking at my computer.

"What is it? I'm very busy."

"Come and see."

"Why are you looking at pictures of horse-drawn carriages?"

"I thought, seeing as we were going all retro-like, you might like one of these instead of that old rust heap you're driving."

"Get off my desk." I gave him a gentle nudge that somehow resulted in him doing a swan-dive onto the floor.

"I could sue you for that." He put on a fake hobble for my benefit. "That's cruelty to animals."

"Cry me a river."

"Are you seriously going to leave that decrepit old thing in the outer office?"

"I think the typewriter will be okay."

"I wasn't referring to the typewriter. I meant the old bag lady. She's beginning to scare people."

***

My latest case was a peculiar one. Sure, I'd dealt with

my fair share of missing person cases, but this one was plain weird. For a start, if Mr and Mrs Bell had wanted to disappear, why bother towing their caravan all the way home first? Surely it would have made more sense for them to 'go missing' while they were at the caravan park. And as for the police's theory that the Bells had disturbed burglars, that was okay as far as it went, but why would the burglars have forced the Bells to go with them? Why not just do a runner?

My first port of call was to the Bells' next-door neighbours, the Hemsleys.

"Hi. I'm Jill Maxwell. I phoned earlier."

"Are you the ant lady?" The elderly man squinted at me over his reading glasses.

"Err, no. I spoke to your wife, I think. About your neighbours, the Bells."

"Is it the ant woman?" A woman's voice came from somewhere in the bungalow.

"No. She says it's about the Bells, and that she spoke to you on the phone."

A woman, her hands covered in what looked like flour, appeared at the man's side. "I told you she was coming, Eric."

"Did you?"

"I knew you weren't listening to me." She gave an exaggerated sigh, and then turned to me. "Men, they're always the same. Sorry, dear, I know you told me your name, but I've forgotten it."

"Jill Maxwell."

"I'm Cynthia. Come on in. Eric, make yourself useful and get us all a drink. Is tea alright for you, Jill?"

"That would be lovely."

"We're expecting the ant woman," Cynthia said. "We thought we'd got rid of the little blighters, but they're back again. Such a nuisance."

"Do you know the Bells well?"

"Walt and Jean? Yes. We've been neighbours for almost thirty years. We've seen both of their children grow up and leave home. Nice kids. Eric and I never had children, did we, dear?"

Eric was back with the tea and a plate of chocolate digestives.

"No, but Adam and Katie were always around here when they were little. They must be beside themselves with worry." Cynthia offered me the plate of biscuits. "I can't believe it's over a year since they went missing."

"Thanks." I was very restrained and allowed myself only a single biscuit. "What I find really strange is that they towed the caravan all the way back home, and only then went missing."

"Cynth and I said the same thing," Eric said.

"Did either of you see them arrive back from their holiday?"

"No. The caravan wasn't there when we went to bed, but it was when we got up the next morning."

"Do you remember what time that would have been?"

"We're creatures of habit, aren't we, Eric? We always turn in at ten. Ten-thirty at the latest. And we're always up by six-thirty."

"That's very helpful, thanks. You're probably already aware that the police believe the Bells may have walked in on burglars. I don't suppose you saw or heard anything unusual?"

They both shook their heads, and Eric said, "There have been very few break-ins in this neighbourhood while we've lived here. In fact, I can only remember one."

"Two," Cynthia corrected him. "There was the Boswells, and the Greys."

"Oh yes, I'd forgotten about the Greys, but both of those were at least ten years ago."

"Tell me about the Bells," I said. "Did they have any problems that you were aware of? Health, family, money, that kind of thing?"

"Not that I know of," Cynthia said. "And Jean and I spoke most days. The four of us used to have dinner at one another's house at least five or six times a year. Jean and I used to take turns making dinner, but she was a much better cook than me."

"No one makes steak and kidney pud like you, Cynth," Eric said, sweetly.

I came away from the Hemsleys with the impression that Walter and Jean Bell were very much an ordinary, unremarkable couple. Unless they'd been very adept at keeping secrets from their neighbours, there was no obvious reason why they should have wanted to disappear. That left only the burglary theory, but that still didn't ring true with me. The neighbourhood had an incredibly low crime rate, with only two burglaries in the previous thirty years. At least, according to the Hemsleys. If that was true, what were the chances that the Bells would walk in on burglars on the day they returned from holiday?

Something else was bothering me too. Why had the Bells travelled home during the hours of darkness? Wasn't that a bit unusual?

Chapter 4

"I thought you'd given up on the clown thing, Mrs V?"

"I have. There's no point now Armi has lost interest."

"It's just that you have white spots all over your cheeks and chin. I thought it must be face paint."

"Oh dear, I hadn't realised." She took a small mirror out of her handbag. "It's the correction fluid."

"The what?"

She held up what looked like a nail varnish bottle. "It's Liquid Paper. Haven't you seen it before?"

"I can't say I have. What's it for?"

"When I make a mistake, I use this to paint over it. When it's dry, I simply type it again."

"It looks like you made an awful lot of mistakes."

"Sorry?" She looked appalled at the suggestion.

"I'm just going on the amount of white stuff on your face."

"I think the bottle must be leaking."

"Did people really have to do that before computers? It seems like an awful lot of messing around."

"Yes. Young people these days don't know they're born. What with their spell check and their addictive text."

"Addic—? Oh, you mean *predictive* text. Are you sure you wouldn't rather go back to your computer?"

"Definitely not. I think I'm getting back into the swing of it. And besides, this brings back some happy memories for me. It reminds me of when I used to work in the typing pool at Bolt, Nut and Ratchet."

"Engineers?"

"No, they were a firm of accountants. There were thirty of us in the typing pool."

Given how noisy a single typewriter was, the noise in there must have been deafening. No wonder Mrs V was a little hard of hearing.

She continued to reminisce, "There was one particular young man, his name was Malcolm Bagmore, who worked in the mailroom. He used to come into the typing pool four or five times every day, and whenever he did, he always made some excuse to talk to me."

"Was he hot?"

"He was very polite, and always very smartly dressed."

"Yes, but was he hot?"

"People weren't *hot* in those days. He was very handsome, though."

"Did you go out on a date?"

"No. I got the impression that he was building up to asking me out, but Lilian Jones got in first. She pretended to drop a box of paperclips on the floor, just as Malcolm was walking past her desk. Malcolm, being the gentleman that he was, stooped down to help her pick them up. And that was that. Lilian's cleavage did the rest."

"So you never got to go on a date with him?"

"No. He and Lilian were married within six months. Last I heard, they had six kids and about a thousand grandchildren."

"What a shame. By the way, I meant to ask you, Mrs V, what's happening with those new-fangled gloves of yours?"

"The Top Tips? I'm afraid I've had to abandon that particular venture."

"Really? You seemed so gung-ho about them."

"I was until Armi sat down and calculated the production costs. When you factor in the time it would take to create a pair, and the cost of the Velcro, it meant I'd have to sell them at about seventy pounds per pair. And, as my little gingerbread man rightly pointed out, no one would buy them at that price, regardless of how good they were. So, it's back to the drawing board, I'm afraid."

I walked into my office to find Winky dressed as though he was going to a wedding.

"What's with the suit?"

"I'm expecting a visitor."

"Is it your mysterious new lady friend? Am I going to meet her at long last?"

"No, it's my Aunt Wynn, all the way from Somerset. She'll be arriving here this evening, and I want to make a good impression." He glanced around. "Mind you, that won't be easy, given the state of this place. Can you get the contract cleaners in this afternoon?"

"No, I can't. If you aren't satisfied, you'd better dig out the mop, duster and rubber gloves. I've never heard you mention this aunt of yours before."

"We usually Skype one another, but she said it had been far too long since she'd seen me in person, so she's coming up for a couple of days."

"I hope you haven't told her she can stay here because that's not on."

"Keep your wig on. She's booked a nice little cat hotel a couple of streets away. There's no way she'd want to stay in this dump."

"What do you mean, *dump*? There's nothing wrong with this office."

"That's not what the rats thought."

"There are no rats in here."

"That's because they packed their bags and moved out last week."

Before I could respond with a witty rejoinder, the white-faced Mrs V stuck her head around the door. "Your two o'clock appointment, Mr Duyew, is here. He's just picking out a pair of socks."

"Send him through when he's finished, would you?"

"Will do."

I turned to Winky. "You'd better hide behind the screen."

"Why?"

"I don't want to have to explain why my cat looks like he's dressed for Ascot."

"You should be pleased I take such a pride in my appearance. One of us has to."

"Behind the screen."

"Fine, but I want my protest registered."

"Duly noted. Now disappear."

"Your receptionist gave me these." Mr Duyew held up a pair of brown socks.

"All part of the service. Do take a seat. I'm Jill Maxwell."

"Call me Victor."

Once Mrs V had brought the drinks through, we got down to business.

"What brings you here today, Victor?"

"It's a very serious matter, I'm afraid. The penguins have gone missing."

"I see. Do you work at the zoo?"

"No, nothing like that. I'm the manager of the Washbridge Penguins. They're a—"

"Ice hockey team?"

"Actually, they're a junior football team."

"Are you saying that the players have gone missing? Surely I would have seen that on the news."

"Not the players. It's the merchandise that has disappeared, specifically the toy penguins. Someone has stolen them."

"I see. Are they valuable?"

"The toys aren't particularly expensive for us to purchase because we buy them in bulk, but the lost revenue is quite substantial because there's a healthy mark-up on this kind of branded merchandise. Have you worked on cases like this before, Jill?"

"Not penguins specifically, but I do have lots of experience on similar cases."

"Excellent. What do you need from me?"

"Maybe the best place to start would be for me to pay a visit to the club's shop. Could that be arranged?"

"It's open every day between nine and six. Just drop in anytime."

Once Victor Duyew had left, Winky came out from behind the screen.

"*Du yew* think he was serious?" He laughed. "Get it?"

"Whatever you do, don't give up your day job. Oh wait, I just remembered, you don't have one."

"Seriously, though, something's not right with all that."

"All what? What do you mean?"

"Think about it. Who would want to steal a load of stuffed toys, particularly penguins? If you were going to do it, you'd at least go for teddy bears or unicorns. There's a market for those, but no one wants a stuffed penguin."

Much as it pained me to admit it, Winky did have a point. Why would anyone want to steal a load of toy penguins? Hopefully, all would soon become clear.

***

I magicked myself over to Aunt Lucy's house, and found her in the lounge with Lester who was wearing a uniform.

"I don't know why you didn't pick one that fitted you." She was pinning the waist of his trousers which was clearly too large for him. "Hi, Jill. Would you be a love and make us all a cup of tea while I *completely* re-tailor this uniform?"

"I explained the situation, Lucy," Lester said. "They only had three sizes, and this was the best fit."

"If this is the best, thank goodness you didn't pick one of the others. Now, for goodness sake, stand still, will you?"

"What's with the uniform, Lester?" I said. "Have you changed jobs again?"

"No, I'm still with the reapers, but the powers that be have decided we need to wear this."

"It looks like a traffic warden's uniform."

"Civil enforcement officer, if you don't mind."

"A what?"

"That's the new name for traffic wardens."

"That's a joke, right?"

"Nope, I'm deadly serious. And the theory behind the uniforms is that we'll blend in better by wearing these."

"If you don't stand still, you'll have to do this yourself." Aunt Lucy was growing more and more exasperated.

"I'll go and make the tea."

By the time I'd made the drinks and returned to the lounge, there was no sign of Lester.

"Have you finished with the uniform?" I handed her a cup of tea.

"I've finished pinning the trousers. I'll sew them tonight and then start on the jacket. It's ridiculous, Jill. You'd think they would at least be able to provide them with uniforms that fit."

"Speaking of uniforms, have the twins told you about their plans?"

"Yes, they told me when they got back from Washbridge."

"What do you think of the idea?"

"It's one of their less crazy ones, but I've warned them that they'd better get uniforms that fit because muggins here isn't going to re-tailor those too. Have you got over the disappointment of the car?"

"Just about. I should have known better than to believe I'd win anything like that."

"What about next weekend? Do you have anything nice planned?"

"Only if you consider going to a model train rally nice."

"You never know, it could be fun."

"Yeah, and I hear there's a flying pigs display too."

"Before you go, you'd better see that dog of yours."

"Does he need a walk?"

"No, he's not long since been for one. He said he has something to show you."

"What is it?"

"I've no idea. He wouldn't tell me."

I finished the last of my tea. "I suppose I'd better go and see what he wants."

When I opened the door to the spare bedroom, the room was in complete darkness. What was going on?

As I reached inside to try to find the switch, the room was suddenly illuminated by a disco ball, hanging from the ceiling. At the same moment, the music from Saturday Night Fever filled the room. I was still trying to recover from that joint assault on my senses when Barry, resplendent in spandex, stepped into the centre of the floor, and began to boogie. He was cheered on by his mentor, the disco-dancing champion, Rhymes.

"Come and join me, Jill," Barry shouted.

I declined his offer because I didn't want to be shown up by a dog.

When the track ended, Barry took a bow.

"What do you think?"

"That was great."

"I owe it all to Rhymes."

"Oh shucks." Rhymes flushed. Who knew a tortoise could blush?

"You'll come and see me perform, won't you, Jill?"

"Perform where?"

"Don't you remember? I've entered the Candlefield Talented Pets Competition."

"Oh yeah. I'd forgotten about that."

"It's next week, on Wednesday night. Please say you'll come. I need all the support I can get."

I was trying to think of an excuse when Aunt Lucy appeared at my side.

"Of course she'll be there, Barry. Jill told me how much

she's been looking forward to it, didn't you?"

"I—err—yeah, of course I am."

"Thanks for dropping me in it there," I said, as Aunt Lucy and I made our way back downstairs.

"You want to support your dog, don't you?"

"Of course, but for most people that just entails taking them for a walk. I get lumbered with attending art exhibitions and now a talent contest."

"It'll be fun."

"In that case, you'll want to be there too, won't you?"

"I'd love to go, but it just so happens it falls on the same night as my whist drive."

"I've never heard you mention a whist drive before."

"Oh yes. Every month, regular as clockwork. I'd love to see Barry perform, but I just can't get out of it."

She was such a liar.

What do you mean, that's rich coming from me?

***

That evening, I treated myself to a long, hot bubble bath. By the time I climbed out, I was perfectly relaxed, but my skin looked like a prune.

Jack was in the lounge, watching the television, and for once, it wasn't TenPin TV.

"What's that you're watching?" I joined him on the sofa.

"It's a new channel."

"I didn't think you liked horror movies?"

"I don't normally, but these are pretty good. In fact, that's the only thing they show on this channel."

"Spooky TV? Really?"

"It's good."

"I'm not watching that rubbish."

"You're scared."

"Don't be ridiculous. Why would I be scared of a movie when I spend most days with ghosts and all manner of supernatural creatures?"

"Sit with me and watch it, then. There's another movie just about to start."

The truth was, he was right, I really didn't like horror movies, but not because I was scared of their ridiculous portrayal of paranormal creatures. It was the unbearable tension when you knew something was going to make you jump. I spent most of my time with my eyes closed, or pretending to look at the screen when I was actually staring at the floor.

Not that I was about to admit that to Jack.

"Incidentally, Jill, I haven't seen Mum for a few days. You haven't heard from her, have you?"

"Not for a while."

"I hope she's okay."

"I'm sure she's fine. She's probably just busy."

Chapter 5

The next morning, I could tell Jack was still worrying about his mother.

"It's not like anything bad could have happened to her," I tried to reassure him. "She is already dead."

"I just think it's strange because she's made contact almost every day since that first time, but then nothing for several days."

"Would you like me to go over to Ghost Town later, and see if I can find out what's going on?"

"That would be great. I know I'm probably worrying about nothing, but it would put my mind at ease."

"Okay. I'll do that."

"You're so good to me."

"I've been telling you that for ages."

***

I thought I'd just about got used to Mr Ivers' stupid vegetable hand puppets, but what I saw at the toll booth completely threw me. At one side of the window was a carrot hand puppet, and on the other side of the window was a broccoli hand puppet.

What's so strange about that I hear you ask? I'll tell you. The window is at least six feet wide, so even if Mr Ivers had a hand puppet on each hand, there's no way he could be controlling them both at the same time—not unless he had somehow split himself in two.

I was still scratching my head at this conundrum when Mr Ivers popped his head above the counter.

"Morning, Jill!"

"Err, morning. I don't understand." I gestured to the broccoli hand puppet at the opposite side of the window. "How are you doing that?"

Just then, a young woman stood up. It was she who was controlling the other puppet.

"Jill, can I introduce you to my new girlfriend, Ivy. Ivy, this is Jill Maxwell who I told you about."

She came over to stand next to Mr Ivers and then offered me her hand. Let me tell you, shaking hands with a rubbery broccoli hand puppet is not a sensation I'm likely to forget in a hurry.

"I'm so very pleased to meet you, Jill. Monty has told me a lot about you. I understand that you and he have been neighbours twice."

"That's right." Aren't I just the lucky one?

"Ivy and I met at a meeting of the Washbridge Puppeteers, didn't we, my sweetness?"

"We did, Monty." She gave him a peck on the cheek. "That was the best day of my life so far. I'm so lucky to have met you."

"Not as lucky as I am." He gave her a hug.

As always, there wasn't a single sick bag in sight when you needed one.

Mr Ivers managed to tear his gaze away from his beloved for a moment. "And, Jill, you'll never guess what Ivy's main interest is. Apart from puppets, of course."

"Base jumping?"

"See, Ivy, what did I tell you? Jill is so funny. No, she's a big movie fan just like me."

"How fabulous for you both."

"From now on, she'll be helping me with my movie newsletter."

"I'm so excited." She beamed.

And the really sad part? She actually did look excited.

***

When I walked into the outer office, and before I could say a word, Mrs V pointed towards my office door, and then said in a hushed voice, "You have a visitor."

There was only one person who would wait in there rather than in the outer office.

"Grandma?"

Mrs V nodded. "I asked her to wait out here, but you know what she's like."

"Is she in a bad mood?"

"I can never tell. She did make some passing reference to your 'tardiness'."

"I suppose I'd better go and face the music."

Unsurprisingly, there was no sign of Winky. He always made himself scarce whenever Grandma came over.

The woman herself was sitting in my chair, with her feet up on the desk.

"What time do you call this?" She tapped her watch.

"Good morning to you too, Grandma. Isn't it a beautiful morning?"

"Not all of us have time to stand around and notice the weather. Do you know what time I started work this morning?"

"I—err—"

"I'll tell you. A quarter past five, that's what time."

"Yes, but then you did sleep for a couple of days solid recently."

"I was witchbernating, as well you know. Don't just

stand there—take a seat—you're making the place look even untidier than it already is."

"Do you have to put your dirty shoes on my desk?"

"Oh, sorry." Much to my amazement, she took her feet off the desk. Then, she slipped off her shoes and socks, and put her bare feet back on the desk. "Happy now?"

Happy wasn't the word that came to mind because I was now forced to stare at her bunion-infested feet.

"What exactly is it that you want, Grandma?"

"Broom flying."

"Sorry?"

"Have you got wax in your ears?"

That question brought back horrible memories involving candles.

"I heard what you said. I'm just not sure what it means."

"I would have thought it was pretty obvious. There are only two words, after all: Broom and flying. As in the art of flying brooms."

"Yeah, I get that, but we don't fly them, do we? Witches, I mean."

"Not nowadays, but broom flying was once a major sport for witches. The biggest tournaments were almost as popular as the Levels is now."

"What happened to change that?"

"The same thing as always happens: People found newer, more 'shiny' pastimes, but I intend to change that."

"How?"

"By bringing back this lost art. I'm still ironing out the details, but I thought you'd want to hear my news before it becomes common knowledge." She removed her feet from my desk and put her shoes and socks back on.

"Err, well, thank you for dropping by to bring me this breaking news. I'm very grateful." Not!

She started for the door, but then hesitated, "I've been meaning to ask, why do you call Annabel, Mrs V?"

"Sorry?"

"Your receptionist."

"I know who she is. It's the question that I don't understand."

"Unless I'm very much mistaken, she got married recently, didn't she? To that funny little man?"

"Armi, yes."

"Didn't she take his name?"

"To be honest, I'm not sure if she did or not."

"You should probably find out."

After Grandma had left, I decided to do just that.

"Mrs—err—V, I've been meaning to ask. When you got married, did you change your name?"

"No, why would I change it? I like being called Annabel."

"I meant your surname."

"Yes, I thought you knew. I'm now Annabel Armitage."

"Oh?"

"What's wrong?"

"I've been calling you Mrs V. Should I start calling you—err—Mrs A?"

"Definitely not."

"What would you like me to call you, then?" Maybe, after all these years, she was finally going to invite me to call her Annabel.

"I'd like you to carry on calling me Mrs V, dear. That

way, I'll know you're talking to me."

"Right. Okay, then."

When I walked back into my office, there was yellow tape blocking the way to my desk. Standing on the desk was a small figure, dressed in a white biohazard suit.

"What's going on?" I yelled.

The figure jumped down, walked over to me, and then removed his mask.

"Winky? What are you doing?"

"Saving your life, probably. You saw her remove her shoes and socks, didn't you?" He shuddered. "But don't worry; I've treated the area. You should be able to have your desk back within an hour or two."

"You don't think you might be overreacting just a little?"

"You wouldn't say that if you'd seen the reading on the odour meter. It was off the scale."

"Oh. Thanks then, I guess."

"It's a good thing Aunt Wynn isn't coming into the office until later. What would she think?"

"I thought you said she was staying at a hotel?"

"She did last night, but she still wants to see where it is that I hang out."

"Just as long as she doesn't disturb me. I'm very busy at the moment."

"Working on your missing penguin case?"

"Not just that. I also have the missing Bells case."

"Penguins, bells? Do you actually have any cases involving people?"

"The Bells *are* people. That's their name."

"Whatever. Aunt Wynn won't disturb you. And, seeing as how you aren't going to do it, I'd better give this place a once over before she comes."

"You know where the broom is."

"Speaking of which. It sounds like you're going to be flying one."

"How did you hear about that? Where were you when Grandma was here?"

"Out on the ledge with Harold and Ida."

"For your information, I will not be doing any flying of brooms, thank you very much."

***

What can I say about Leonard Bell? He would have made the Grinch look like the life and soul of the party. Supposedly, he was Walter Bell's younger brother, but this guy looked much older than Walter had in the photographs I'd seen. And as for Leonard Bell's dress sense: his trousers were at least two inches too short—and not in a hipster kind of way. More in a *I don't know how long my legs are* kind of way. And then there was his shirt. I think he was going for the lumberjack look, but it wasn't happening.

He didn't offer me a drink, and after seeing some of the crockery left lying around the living room, I was mightily relieved that he hadn't.

"Have you found Walter yet?" He pointed to what I thought was a pile of clothes, but which turned out to be a sofa, *covered by a pile of clothes.*

"It's okay, I'll stand, thanks. No, not yet. That's why I'm here today."

"Me and Walt don't speak much." He treated me to a nicotine-stained grin.

"When was the last time you saw him and Jean?"

"Christmas before last, I reckon. He always invites me at Christmas."

That made sense: Where would Christmas be without the Grinch?

"Not since?"

He thought about it for a moment. "No, wait, I forgot about the hoe."

"*Ho*?"

"He'd lent it to me, and I'd forgotten to let him have it back. That reminds me, I've still got his spade somewhere."

"How did Walter seem the last time you saw him?"

"Angry."

"Why was that?"

"Because I hadn't taken his hoe back."

"Right, but apart from that, did he mention any kind of trouble he and Jean might be having?"

"No, but then we don't talk much. We never have."

"What about their children?"

"Katie is nice. She drew me a picture of a scarecrow when she was little."

I couldn't help but wonder if the picture had really been of a scarecrow or of Leonard—one and the same thing, practically.

"That must have been a long time ago. Have you seen her recently?"

He shook his head.

"What about Walter's son, Adam?"

"He's a waster."

"What makes you say that?"

"It's obvious, isn't it? He doesn't work."

"I understood that he was at college."

"Any excuse not to work. Thinks he's better than the rest of us, he does."

"I take it you and he don't get along?"

"I don't see much of him, which suits me. If I gave him the chance, he'd try to get cash out of me like he does his parents, but I'm not as stupid as our Walt."

"Do you have any idea where your brother might have gone?"

"He's probably dead, I reckon."

"What makes you say that?"

"It's the only thing that makes any sense. Adam probably bumped them both off, so he'd get the house."

"That's a very serious allegation. What evidence do you have to make an accusation like that?"

He shrugged.

I'd had my fill of creepy for one day, so I made my excuses and left.

***

I was on my way back to the office when I got a call from Pearl. At least, I thought it was Pearl, but she was speaking so quietly that I could barely hear her.

"What did you say? Can you speak up a bit?"

"I said." She was still whispering. "That guy from Candlefield Icons is in here."

"Songspinner?"

"You'll have to be quick, though, he only ordered a small Cappuccino."

"I'll be straight over."

Seated next to the window, Songspinner was wearing a white suit, white panama, and an obscene amount of gold on his fingers. He was so busy staring out of the window that he didn't notice me as I approached his table.

"Mr Songspinner?"

"At your service, gorgeous. Why don't you pull up a chair?"

"Thank you."

"I'm sorry. Have we met?"

"No, we haven't."

"Your face seems familiar. Are you sure you weren't at Candlefield Races last month?"

"Positive. I do know how you know my face, though. Think t-shirts."

"Sorry?"

"Or mouse mats. Scarves, towels, water-bottles."

"You've lost me now."

"You are the owner of Candlefield Icons, aren't you?"

"I am indeed. Have you visited the shop?"

"I was in there the other day. Your delightful assistant, Vannie, was kind enough to show me the merchandise."

"Did you find what you were looking for?"

"In a manner of speaking. In fact, I found a mountain of stuff all with my picture on it."

"Oh?" The penny, if rather belatedly, appeared to have dropped. "Aren't you—err—"

I nodded.

"I'm sorry, Magna. I didn't recognise you."

"I'm not Magna Mondale! She's dead. I'm Jill Maxwell formerly Jill Gooder."

"Of course. It's a pleasure to meet you face to face."

"Is it, though? Really?"

"Absolutely. Maybe I could persuade you to drop by the shop sometime, to sign some of the t-shirts."

This guy really was taking the mickey. "Yeah, I won't be doing that. I will, however, be popping around to collect my royalties."

"What royalties?"

"The ones you owe me for using my likeness all over your merchandise."

"I don't pay royalties."

"You do now. The only question is how much."

"What if I refuse?"

"Tell me, Sylvester, why did you choose to print *my* image on your merchandise?"

"Because you're the most powerful witch in Candlefield."

"That's right. And that's precisely why you won't refuse to pay me royalties." I stood up. "I'll be seeing you soon."

Chapter 6

After Sylvester Songspinner had stormed out of Cuppy C, Pearl came over to join me.

"How did it go, Jill? Is he going to start paying you royalties?"

"If he knows what's good for him, he will, yeah."

"You'll be rich; you'll be able to retire."

"That would be nice, but I'd better not count my chickens."

"I didn't realise you kept them."

"Kept what?"

"Chickens."

"I don't."

"You just said that you weren't going to count them?"

"I—err—never mind. Have you ordered your uniforms yet?"

"We have."

"What colour did you and Amber settle on?"

"We didn't actually manage to agree on a colour. Do you like turquoise, Jill?"

"I do, actually."

"Me too. I suggested we should make the uniforms turquoise."

"I take it Amber didn't agree?"

"She wanted pink."

"Pink uniforms might look nice, I suppose," said Jill Maxwell, the diplomat.

"I disagree. They'd portray altogether the wrong image."

"If you couldn't agree on the colour, what have you ordered?"

"Half pink and half turquoise."

"I suppose that's a reasonable compromise. How many in total have you ordered?"

"Eight, I think. They should be here on Monday."

"I look forward to seeing them."

***

I was sure Jack was worrying over nothing, but I'd promised I'd nip over to GT, to check if Yvonne was alright. I deliberately hadn't had anything to eat in Cuppy C because I wanted to see if Cakey C were maintaining the high standard that they'd set on launch day.

I was rather surprised to find my mother serving behind the counter—I'd assumed she intended to be strictly hands-off. I was even more surprised to see who was working alongside her. Judging by how flustered she looked, Yvonne was new to the job.

"Morning, darling." Mum leaned across the counter and gave me a hug. "This is a nice surprise."

"How long has Yvonne been working here?"

Jack's mother was currently staring at the coffee machine and looking rather confused.

"She started a couple of days ago," Mum said, and then realised Yvonne was struggling. "It's the third button on the right."

"Thanks. Oh, hello, Jill."

"Hi." I turned back to my mother. "Would it be okay if I borrowed your new assistant for a few minutes?"

"Sure. She's due a break anyway."

Five minutes later, Yvonne and I were enjoying coffee and cake together. Just for the record, the cakes were still up to standard.

"I didn't expect to find you working behind the counter."

"I'm a little surprised myself. I've never done anything like this before, but I'm sure you'd already worked that out for yourself." She smiled. "That coffee machine is so complicated."

"I know what you mean. I struggled when I first operated one of those, but I soon got the hang of it."

What? I'll have you know I'm now an accomplished barista, just ask anyone. Except Amber or Pearl.

"Jack mentioned that you hadn't been in touch for a few days."

"He hasn't been worried, has he?"

"A little, maybe. You know what men are like."

"I should have told him about my new job, but it all happened so quickly. I was just having a drink with Rhona—she's one of my neighbours—when your mother mentioned she was looking for someone else to work behind the counter. Next thing I knew, I'd agreed to do it. I told your mother that I didn't have any experience, but she said I'd soon get up to speed." Yvonne glanced over to the counter. "She's probably beginning to regret that decision now she's seen how hopeless I am."

"Don't be silly. I hope she didn't pressure you into taking the job?"

"Not at all. I've been looking for something to occupy myself with, and the extra money will come in handy. Tell Jack I'll be in touch soon, will you?"

"Of course. He'll be fine once I've explained what you're doing."

She finished the last of her coffee. "I'd better get back to work. I don't want to get sacked in my first week."

I was just about to leave too when Mad called to me from a table across the room. She must have come in while I was chatting.

"Isn't that Jack's mother?"

"Yeah. She's just started here. I don't envy her, working for my mother."

"Do you want to join me, or do you have to shoot off?"

"I can stay for a few minutes."

"Do you want another drink?"

"No, thanks. I'm fine." I gestured towards the huge brown file on the table. "It looks like you're busy."

"My feet have barely touched the ground since I moved back to Washbridge. I'm beginning to wonder if I made the right decision. The extra money is nice, but so was having a life."

"You'll be fine once you're properly settled in. What's in the file?"

"This is just one of the cases I'm working on at the moment. It's a bit of a weird one, to say the least." Mad glanced around to make sure no one was watching, and then took a handful of photographs from the file and placed them on the table.

"Who are they? What have they done?"

"They haven't done anything—except to go missing, that is. There's another dozen in the file, all of whom have disappeared within the last month."

"*Disappeared*, as in?"

"As in gone missing without a trace. They all have families here in GT, none of whom have a clue what's happened to their loved ones."

"Do you have any leads?"

"We've got absolutely nothing. As far as I can tell, there is no obvious pattern."

"Is there anything I can do to help?"

"I wish there was, but I can't think of anything at the moment. Anyway, enough of my problems. How's that new car of yours?" She laughed.

"Is there anyone who hasn't heard about that?"

"I seriously doubt it. You have to admit that you did rather set yourself up for a fall this time."

"I know. I don't know what I was thinking."

"What are you doing for transport now?"

"Fortunately, I managed to get my old car back. I exchanged the clown course vouchers for it."

"I'm really glad I have you as a friend, Jill."

"That's a very sweet thing to say."

"But only because when I see what an absolute train wreck your life is, I realise I'm doing okay after all."

"Hmm."

***

Winky had company.

The sweet old lady-cat was dressed in tweed. I was just about to introduce myself when she spoke to me.

"Get me another bowl, would you? And make sure it's clean. This one is disgusting."

For Winky's sake, I bit my tongue, and passed her a bowl from the cupboard. "There you go."

"Is this the best salmon you could find? The quality really does leave a lot to be desired."

I could feel my blood pressure rising, and Winky wasn't helping matters with that stupid grin on his face. Still, I felt I owed it to him to at least make the effort.

"I should introduce myself. I'm Jill Maxwell. I—"

"I know who you are. You're the two-legged who my nephew generously allows to share his office."

His office? "Hold on. Did you just say—"

"Come on, Aunt." Winky grabbed her paw. "I promised I'd show you the sights."

And with that, the two of them disappeared out of the window.

He and I would be having words later.

Mrs V was tapping away on the typewriter, her hands and face still speckled with Liquid Paper.

"Are you sure the typewriter was a good idea, Mrs V?"

"I think so. I'm sure I'll get the hang of it again soon."

"Okay. I'm just nipping out to see the Penguins."

"A trip to the zoo? Lucky you. It's ages since I've been there."

"Not real penguins. It's the case Victor Duyew came to see me about. His junior football team is called the Washbridge Penguins."

"I see. Has Kathy set a date to move into her new house?"

"Unless there's a last-minute hitch, they'll be moving in on Saturday."

"How exciting for them."

"How's *your* house-hunting going?"

"Don't ask."

"You mustn't become despondent. You'll find the right property eventually."

"We may already have found it. At least, Armi seems to think so."

"Oh? Either you don't share his enthusiasm or you're hiding it really well."

"I don't, but how can I tell him that, Jill? He has his heart set on this place."

"What's wrong with it?"

She reached into her handbag and produced a photo. "See for yourself."

"Oh dear." I laughed. "Sorry. It looks like—err—"

"A giant cuckoo clock? I know."

"Is this some kind of joke?"

"I wish it was. The house belongs to a member of the Cuckoo Clock Appreciation Society. He thought it would be a good idea to turn his property into this monstrosity."

"Is he married?"

"He wasn't when he did that to the house. The man was a confirmed bachelor until he met someone earlier this year."

"Which is presumably why he's selling it."

"He denies it, but quite obviously that is the reason."

"Have you told Armi how you feel about the house?"

"I don't have the heart to, Jill. He's fallen madly in love with it."

"He may have, but you both have to live there. You have to say something."

"You're right. I'll tell him how I feel tonight."

"Make sure you do."

***

This couldn't possibly be it, could it?

The Penguins' ground was located in Greater Wash. I'd expected it to be a playing field with maybe a couple of

Portakabins: One for the shop, the other for changing rooms.

Boy, was I wrong!

Whilst not exactly Premier League standard, it wouldn't have disgraced most non-league clubs. There were standing areas on three sides of the ground, and a smaller stand with seats, on the fourth side.

A man in overalls, with a penguin logo on the back, was sweeping the path.

"Excuse me."

"Are you looking for the shop, love?"

"Err, yeah, but could I ask you a couple of questions first?"

"Fire away. I'll help if I can." He pointed to his small name badge. "I'm Albert."

"This is where the Washbridge Penguins play, isn't it?"

"That's correct."

"Right." I took another look at the stadium, trying to make some sense of what I was seeing.

"Is something wrong, love?"

"Well, no, yeah. It's just that I wasn't expecting anything quite as grand as this."

"No one ever does. You should see the look on the visiting team's faces when they first play here."

"I can't understand how a junior football club could generate enough money to pay for anything like this."

"They can't. The gate receipts wouldn't keep me in overalls."

"So, how does it work?"

"It's all down to Frank Royston. He paid for everything." The man's pocket buzzed, and he took out his phone. "Sorry, I have to take this."

"No problem. Thanks."

The souvenir shop was deserted except for the woman behind the counter.

"Hi!" She seemed surprised to see someone walk through the door.

"You're doing a brisk trade, I see."

She smiled. "You're only my second customer of the day."

"Doesn't it get rather boring?"

"It can do, but I'm a big fan of the Penguins, so I don't mind." She took out her phone. "That's my Ben. He's a defender."

"He's a handsome little chap. I assume you work here as a volunteer?"

"Yes, a lot of the parents take turns on a rota basis. I do most Wednesdays and the occasional Friday. Were you looking for anything in particular?" She spread her arms. "We have lots of merchandise to choose from, as you can see."

"I've actually been hired by Victor Duyew." I glanced at the shelves. "I didn't think there'd be any penguin soft toys left after the theft, but you still seem to have plenty."

"Only the regular ones. The thieves took all the premium ones."

"*Premium*?"

"They only produce a limited number of those, and they have to be reserved before collection."

"What's the difference between the regular ones and the premium ones?"

"I probably shouldn't say this, but I can't tell the difference. The stuffing on the premium ones is perhaps a little more substantial, but that's about it. I have to be really careful not to get them mixed up."

"Are they popular, the premium ones?"

"Very. They always sell very quickly."

"To kids mainly, I assume."

"You'd think so, wouldn't you? But we get all kinds of people buying them. In fact, I'd say that we sell most of them to adults. I suppose they could be taking them home for their kids."

"How did the thieves get in?"

"They rammed the door."

"I see you have CCTV."

"Yes, but it didn't help because they were wearing masks, and they used a stolen car."

"And they only took the premium penguins?"

"That's right."

***

In order to prepare for the big move on Saturday, Kathy was only working mornings that week—nice work if you can get it!

As I'd finished a little early, I decided to call in, to see if I could help.

What? Why wouldn't I help my sister? Sheesh!

"Jill? What are you doing here?"

"I came to see if I could help with anything."

She laughed. "No, seriously, why are you here?"

"This is precisely why I don't try to be nice. It always gets thrown back in my face."

"I'm sorry. Come on in. There's plenty of stuff that needs packing into boxes, you could help with that if you like?"

"Shall I start with the ornaments?"

"No!" She yelled. "It might be best if you started with something—err—else. Why don't you go and find Pete? He's upstairs. He'll tell you what you can do."

Two hours later, and I was beginning to think that this whole good Samaritan thing was overrated. My back was killing me, and I was exhausted.

"I'd better get going. Jack should just about have dinner ready by the time I get back."

"Thanks for your help, Jill," Peter said.

"Yeah, thanks, Sis. Are you coming around again tomorrow?"

"No chance. That's my good deed of the year done. Where are the kids, by the way?"

"They're with my parents." Peter stretched—I clearly wasn't the only one with aching limbs. "They'll be bringing them back in a couple of hours."

"I hope Mikey has come around by the time he gets back," Kathy said.

"Why? What's the matter with him?"

"Pete and I decided it would be nice to get a family photo taken, professionally at a proper portrait studio. We were going to get it framed and hang it above the fireplace in the dining room at the new house."

"And Mikey's not keen?"

"He's refusing point blank to do it."

"What are you going to do?"

"What can we do? Even if we drag him there, it's not like we can make him pose for the camera."

"You could always bribe him."

"What kind of message would that send? That's not how good parenting works, Jill. You'll realise that when you have kids of your own."

Chapter 7

I arrived home just in time for Jack to serve dinner. I'd texted earlier to let him know that his mum was okay, but I waited until we could speak face-to-face to tell him about her new job.

"Working in a tea room? Mum?" He was even more surprised than I'd been. "I never would have thought she'd want to do something like that."

"She said she was bored, and that the money would come in handy."

"How did she seem to be taking to it?"

"She was still struggling with the coffee machine, but she'll soon get to grips with it. I did."

"I guess so. If you could master it, I'm sure she won't have any problems."

"Cheers for that."

"No, I didn't mean—err—I meant—"

"Jack, now would be a good time to stop digging that hole."

"Right. Sorry. How was work today?"

"It sounds like Mrs V and Armi may have found a new house."

"That's great."

"Not really. From the outside, it looks like a giant cuckoo clock."

"That should please Armi."

"But not Mrs V. I said she should tell him she didn't want to live there."

"Do you think she will?"

"I'm not sure. If her *little gingerbread man* has his heart set on it, she might not be able to bring herself to say anything. In other news, Winky's Aunt Wynn came into the office today."

"Is she nice?"

"No, she's a nightmare. She spoke to me like I was the hired help. From what I could make out, Winky had led her to believe that it was his office, which he generously allowed me to share."

"Didn't you put her right?"

"Winky hurried her out of the window before I had the chance to. Don't worry, though, he and I will be having a long talk when I catch up with him."

We'd finished dinner, and I was loading the dishwasher.

"I'm really excited about tonight." Jack was still at the table, fiddling with his phone.

"Why? Is there something good on TV?"

"Very funny. Like you've forgotten."

Whatever it was he was talking about, I'd definitely forgotten about it. "Of course I haven't. I'm just winding you up."

"I thought I might have a quick strum before we set off."

Oh no! "The community band?"

"You *had* forgotten."

"No, I hadn't. It's just that I thought it was next week. Are you sure it's tonight?"

"Positive. Why don't you put in a few minutes practice before we go?"

"Err, I don't think so. I'm pretty much up to speed." Plus, I had no idea where I'd put the stupid penny whistle.

"I'm going to get changed."

"Okay."

As soon as Jack was upstairs, I began to go through all the drawers and cupboards, but there was no sign of the whistle. How would I explain that I'd managed to lose it?

Jack walked into the kitchen to find me emptying the contents of my bag onto the worktop.

"I found this in the bottom of the wardrobe." He handed me the penny whistle.

"Thanks. I put it there for safe-keeping."

"What are you doing?"

"I seem to have lost my phone."

"It's there." He pointed to the table.

"So it is. Silly me."

***

"I bet no one turns up," I said, as we made our way to the dilapidated scout hut, which was home to the community band.

"I think you're wrong. All the people I've spoken to seem really buzzed about the band. I'm really excited to see how everyone has progressed since the last meeting."

"People start off with good intentions, but I expect most of them won't have had time for any real practice."

"*I* managed to find time."

"Yeah, but you're a—err—"

"A what?"

"An exception. Not everyone has your level of dedication."

"We'll see."

The Liveleys had obviously appointed themselves bandleaders, and it was they who greeted us at the door.

"I'm glad you could both make it." Britt was either exceptionally cold or she was sporting a new blue lipstick. "It's another good turn-out."

She was right. I'd expected there to be a huge drop-off in attendance, but if anything, there were even more people this time around.

"A little bird tells me that you've got in a lot of practice on the ukulele, Jack," Kit said.

"Not all that much," Jack lied. "Only when I had a few minutes to spare."

Who was he trying to kid? I was practically a ukulele widow.

"What about you, Jill?" Kit turned his perfect smile on me. "Have you managed to get in much practice?"

"Not as much as Jack, that's for sure." I glanced around the room. "No refreshments again, then?"

"We considered it, but we figured no one would be bothered."

Was he serious? I was bothered—very bothered.

"Okay, everyone!" Kit called for silence. "Welcome to the second meeting of the community band. If you're anything like Britt and me, you'll have been counting the minutes to this meeting."

I glanced around and saw that everyone else seemed to be nodding, so I did the same.

He continued, "We thought it would be interesting to see how much progress you've all made since our first meeting."

This should be a laugh.

Britt spoke next, "When I call your name, please step forward and give us a demonstration of what you can do. And don't worry if you haven't quite mastered your chosen instrument, no one is going to judge you. Why don't we start with Mr Ukulele himself? Our next-door neighbour, Jack."

He stepped forward, eagerly, ukulele in hand. "Thank you, Britt. I still have a long way to go to master this magnificent instrument, but I hope you'll notice a slight improvement."

Don't you just hate false modesty? *Slight improvement*? He absolutely nailed his performance. When he'd finished, everyone in the room applauded loudly. I was praying Britt wouldn't call me next because there was no way I could follow that.

She didn't. In fact, it was as though I was invisible because she called everyone in the room except for me. Not that I was complaining.

The Normals were now centre stage, playing their evil triangles, and even I had to admit they were really good. When they'd finished, there would be only one person left to call, and that was me.

I honestly didn't think many people would have bothered to practise, but I'd been proven wrong. Everyone had come on in leaps and bounds since the last meeting. Everyone that was except for me. There was no way I could start tooting the penny whistle. Not only would I be a laughing stock, but I would have let down everyone else.

I had three options available to me.

One: Admit that I hadn't practised but promise to do so from now on.

Two: Make a run for it.

Three: Use magic.

Yes, I do realise that I'd promised Daze I wouldn't use magic willy-nilly, but this *was* a real emergency.

While the Normals were still tinkling away on their triangles, I sneaked away to a quiet corner at the back of the room and took out my A-to-Z of spells.

What? I know I haven't mentioned it before. A girl has to have some secrets.

The question was, where was it likely to be? There was nothing under P for penny whistle. There were a couple of entries under W for whistle, but they weren't related to musical instruments. Come on, Jill, think! Finally, I tried C for cheat, and bingo! There were dozens of spells on how to cheat at all manner of things. One of them allowed you to fake being able to play a musical instrument. The instructions claimed it would work for any instrument. I'd just have to hope that included the penny whistle.

"Jill!" Britt called. "It's your turn."

"Coming."

On my way to the front, Jack caught my eye and mouthed the words, "Good luck."

As I faced the crowd, penny whistle in hand, I felt as nervous as a kitten. How was I supposed to play with dry lips? What if the spell didn't work? Maybe whoever had come up with the spell hadn't considered the penny whistle to be a 'real' instrument.

I was about to find out.

"That was fabulous, Jill!" Britt gave me a hug. "I loved every minute of it."

"Thanks."

"I didn't realise a penny whistle could make such beautiful music," Kit said.

Everyone was singing my praises. Everyone, that is, except Jack who was waiting for me by the door. He didn't look happy.

As we walked home, he didn't speak.

"Did you hear me play?" I asked.

"Oh yes. I heard you."

"What did you think?"

He stopped dead in his tracks and glared at me. "Have you forgotten already what Daze told you?"

"I don't know what you're talking about."

"Don't give me that, Jill. On the one occasion you could be bothered to practise, I heard you playing. It was beyond bad."

"I practised when you were out."

"Look me in the eyes and swear that you didn't use magic."

"I—err—"

"I knew it." He stormed off.

"Wait." I had to run to catch up with him. "You heard the others. Can you imagine how bad it would have been if I'd got up there without using a little magic to help?"

"I can, yes. It would have looked like you couldn't be bothered to practise, which is true."

"I'm sorry." I grabbed his arm. "I shouldn't have done it."

"No, you shouldn't. It's not that I care about you

cheating, although that is totally despicable. It's the thought that I could lose you over something as ridiculous as this. Can't you see that?"

"Yes, I'm sorry. It was stupid." I gave him a kiss. "Do you forgive me?"

"You can't do it again. You'll just have to drop out of the band."

"Aww." It took all my willpower not to punch the air. "I suppose you're right. If I must, I must."

Although I felt bad about upsetting Jack, that was more than offset by the knowledge that I'd never have to take part in the community band again. A result if ever there was one.

"I'm bushed, and I have an early start," Jack said, as soon as we got into the house. "I'm going straight up to bed."

"Okay." I gave him a kiss. "I'm going to grab a drink and a snack before I come up."

"Don't overdo the biscuits. You know they give you nightmares."

"I won't." The first thing I did when I went into the kitchen was to drop the penny whistle into the pedal bin. "Good riddance."

I'd just put on the kettle and was trying to decide how many custard creams I should allow myself when Jack came rushing down the stairs and into the kitchen.

"Dandelions! Upstairs! Dandelions!"

"Jack, you aren't making a lick of sense."

"Our bed is full of dandelions."

"Why?"

"How should I know?"

"Are you sure? Did you doze off and dream it?"

"No, I didn't. Come and see for yourself."

And, lo and behold, he was right. Every square inch of our bed was covered in the small yellow flowers.

I turned to Jack who had followed me upstairs. "Did you do this? Because if you did, I have to tell you that roses would have been way more romantic."

"I didn't do anything. It was like this when I walked into the room. I think I will have that drink."

"The kettle has only just boiled. I'll be down in a minute."

"Has he gone?" The tiny voice came from on the bed.

"Who said that?"

"I did." One of the dandelions stood up. Not only had it sprouted tiny arms and legs, but it also had a sweet little face. "I'm Tingle."

"Dingle?"

"No. It's Tingle with a T."

"Are you a—err—what are you?"

"I'm a dandelion fairy." She spread her arms. "We all are."

As if on command, all the dandelions got to their feet.

"What are you doing in my bedroom?"

"We were sent to see you by our queen. She wants us to take you back to her palace."

"I was just about to go to bed."

"It's a matter of the utmost importance."

"Okay. How do we get there?"

"Stand still, please."

I did as she asked, and moments later, I was covered from head to toe by the small dandelion fairies.

"Do I need to use magic?" I asked, being careful not to

swallow any of the fairies perched on my lips.

"That won't be necessary. Just relax and let us do all the work."

"Okay."

"Ladies!" Tingle shouted. "On three, we return to Dandelion Central. One, two, three."

Chapter 8

I'd been expecting the fairies to use magic to transport us all to Candlefield, but I was wrong. Instead, a number of them flew over to the window and opened it. Before I could ask what was going on, I found myself being lifted off the ground.

This was all kinds of weird.

How such tiny creatures could lift me was beyond my comprehension, but I didn't have time to give it much thought because, the next thing I knew, we were headed out of the window and into the night. If I'd realised I was going to be carried across the night sky by a small army of fairies, I would have changed into something warmer.

"Where are we going?"

"It's not far," one of the fairies closest to my ear answered.

For such tiny creatures, not only were they incredibly strong, but they were also remarkably fast. We'd long since left the outskirts of Washbridge, and as far as I could make out, we were travelling south. I tried to get my bearings by looking for landmarks, but we were too high, and most of the time the ground was obscured by clouds. Eventually, we began to descend, and put down in what appeared to be the grounds of a stately home.

Relieved to be back on my feet, but still feeling a tiny bit jittery after the journey, I watched the dandelion fairies assemble in two long lines on the lawn.

"Where are we?"

"The royal family lives here." Tingle was now the only dandelion fairy still on my body; she was standing on my left shoulder. "You might know it as the botanical gardens in Oxford."

"I thought it looked familiar. Kathy and I came here when we were kids. How long has your royal family lived here?"

"For over four-hundred years." She pointed to the far side of the lawn. "The queen is coming now."

The queen and her entourage began the slow walk towards us, making their way along the path created by the two rows of dandelion fairies. As she did, she acknowledged the cheers and waves of her subjects on either side.

"How should I address her?" I whispered to Tingle.

"You say: Your Royal Dandelion."

"Are you sure?"

"Of course I'm sure."

"Sorry, it's just that I was once tricked into calling a king Top Dollop."

"Top what?"

"Never mind."

At last, the queen had reached the spot where I was standing. I suddenly felt huge and wondered if I should have shrunk myself ahead of the meeting, but it was too late now.

"Thank you for coming to see me, Jill Maxwell."

"My pleasure, Your Royal Dandelion."

"Did Tingle explain why I wanted to see you?"

"I didn't, Your Royal Dandelion," Tingle said. "I thought you'd want to do that yourself."

"Very well. Am I right in thinking that you can make yourself smaller, Jill?"

"Yes, I can, Your Royal—"

"Enough of the Royal. You must call me Dandy."

"Okay, Dandy. Would you like me to shrink myself now?"

"Yes, please. Then we can both take tea and cake inside."

It was rather late in the day for cake, but I had been interrupted before I'd been able to eat my custard creams, so I didn't feel too guilty.

Dandy's place was much smaller than royal residences I'd visited before. It was, though, beautifully furnished with fixtures and fittings which all had the dandelion theme.

"How's the cake, Jill?"

"It's delicious. What is it?"

"Dandelion cake, of course. And that's dandelion tea. You're probably wondering why I had you brought here."

"I am rather curious."

"We have a situation in Washbridge. I wasn't sure who to turn to for help, so I asked some of my fairy cousins back in Candlefield, and your name kept cropping up. Everyone I contacted spoke very highly of you."

"That's always nice to hear. What exactly is the situation you referred to?"

"How familiar are you with dandelions?"

"Not very. I mean, I like them with burdock, and we always have lots of them in our back garden, but that's about it. I take it you're named after them?"

"Actually, that's a bone of contention. We would argue that we had the name first."

"I see."

"Anyway, the point is that we live amongst the dandelions. They provide the perfect camouflage. Are you familiar with how the dandelion spreads its seeds?"

"Yes, my sister and I used to play dandelion clocks when we were little."

"That's right. The method is extremely effective. Normally."

"Has something gone wrong?"

"Yes, but only in Washbridge, and specifically in Washbridge Park. Are you familiar with it?"

"Yes, I know it."

"For reasons we cannot fathom, the dandelion seeds in that park refuse to disperse."

"I see. Has that ever happened before?"

"No. There's no record of anything like this in any of the history books. The park is one of the largest grassed areas in Washbridge. Without those seeds, the number of dandelions will be drastically reduced, leaving far fewer opportunities for us to hide. That's why I got in touch with you. I'm hoping you may be able to find out what's going on and resolve the problem."

"I have to be honest. This case is very unusual, and a touch out of my comfort zone. Are you sure there isn't anyone better equipped to help you?"

"I've made numerous enquiries, and the truth is, there's no one who has any experience with this kind of problem. You're pretty much our last hope. Please say you'll help."

How could I say no?

"Okay, I'll do my best."

"That's wonderful! Thank you so much."

The dandelion fairies flew me back to the house and put me gently down in the bedroom. After bidding farewell to Tingle, I went in search of Jack, who I found pacing around the living room.

"I thought you'd be tucked up in bed by now." I yawned.

"How was I supposed to sleep? I've been worried sick about you. When I got back to the bedroom, all the dandelions had gone, the window was wide open, and you'd disappeared."

"They took me to see their queen."

"Who did?"

"The dandelions—err, well, the dandelion fairies, actually."

"Don't you think you should have told me what you were doing, so I wouldn't go out of my mind with worry?"

"Sorry. I assumed they were going to take me to Candlefield in which case, time would have stood still here for you. In fact, they flew me down to Oxford. The botanical gardens down there are beautiful. We should pay them a visit some time."

"What did the fairies want?"

"It's rather complicated. Let me grab a shower, and I'll tell you when we're in bed."

***

The next morning, Jack was buttering his toast, and was clearly deep in thought.

"Penny for them."

"I was just thinking about the dandelions."

"What about them?"

"If what you said is true, does that mean every time I see a field of them, they're actually fairies?"

"Not all of them. The fairies mingle with the real

dandelions."

"Fascinating. It's stuff like this I wish I could share with my friends."

"They'd have you locked up if you did."

"You're probably right. Where do you even start with a case like this?"

"I wish I knew. In Washbridge Park, I guess, but I have no idea what I'll do when I get there."

Jack left the house before I did. When I stepped out of the door, I was greeted with the sight of Lovely and Bruiser smooching on next-door's lawn.

"Why don't you two get a room?"

"Sorry, Jill?" Britt shot me a puzzled look. I hadn't realised she and Kit were standing on their doorstep.

"Err, not you two. I was—err, never mind."

"That was an excellent performance you gave last night, Jill," Kit said.

"Thanks, but it wasn't anything special."

"You shouldn't be so modest. It was magnificent, wasn't it, Britt?"

"Absolutely fabulous."

"Thanks, but I'm not sure I'll be continuing with—"

"Tell Jill our big news, Kit."

"I thought we said we'd wait until the next meeting."

"I can't wait that long. Tell her now! Please!"

"Alright, then. We've entered our little community band in the Washbridge battle of the bands."

"Isn't that for rock bands?"

"Not this one. It's specifically for small, local bands such as ours. You haven't heard the best part yet. Each band has to perform as a group, but also has to nominate one member to perform a solo piece."

Oh no! Please no!

"Needless to say, we had no hesitation in putting your name forward as our soloist."

"That's very kind of you, but—"

"Kit, come on." Britt grabbed his arm. "Have you forgotten that you're dropping me at the station? Sorry, Jill, we have to sprint."

Oh bum!

***

"Morning, Mrs V, did you speak to Armi about the cuckoo house last night?"

"Almost."

"What does that mean?"

"I was going to tell him how I felt after dinner, but all through the meal all he did was wax lyrical about the house. By the time we'd finished, I didn't have the heart to burst his bubble."

"You have to say something. You can't allow him to talk you into living somewhere you won't be happy."

"Would you come with me to take a look at the house? I'd really appreciate your opinion. Maybe I'm just blowing this whole cuckoo clock thing out of proportion."

"Okay, if you think it will help. We could go late this afternoon unless something urgent crops up."

"That would be lovely. Thanks, Jill."

"Can I come too?" Winky was on the sofa.

"Come where?"

"To look at the old bag lady's joke house."

"No, you can't. You can stay here in my—or should that be *your* office? I don't think I ever thanked you properly for allowing me to share it."

"I thought you might be a little upset about that."

"You think. That auntie of yours practically accused me of sponging off you."

"She just got the wrong end of the stick."

"What you mean is that you lied to her."

"I may have been a little economical with the truth, but that's all."

"When your auntie comes back, I'm going to tell her the truth."

"No, please don't do that. Aunt Wynn is so proud of everything I've achieved."

"Everything she *thinks* you've achieved, don't you mean?"

"Okay, but what good is telling her the truth going to do? I'm begging you to do this little thing for me."

"What I don't understand is why you care what she thinks about you."

"She's an old lady."

"What's that got to do with the price of fish?"

"She probably doesn't have much longer on this mortal coil."

"I still don't—wait a minute—are you expecting her to leave you something in her will?"

"She has hinted that she might."

"I should have known."

"The thing is, she's worth a bob or two, so if I play my cards right, I could be in for quite a windfall."

"You're so mercenary."

"Will you do it? Will you lie for me?"

"I want half of whatever she leaves you."

"And you said I was the mercenary one."

"Is it a deal or not?"

"What choice do I have?"

"None. Where is your auntie, anyway?"

"She's gone into town to do some last-minute shopping before she goes home. She's going to pop in to say goodbye before she leaves."

***

Never let it be said that I don't learn from my mistakes. If you remember, the last time I wanted information from the police station, I came up with the bright idea of using the 'doppelganger' spell to make myself look like Sushi. You may also recall how spectacularly pear-shaped that went when the woman herself returned to the station early. What a nightmare!

To avoid a repeat of that farce, this time I took the easy option by using the 'invisible' spell to get in and out of the police station. My brief visit proved to be very fruitful because I learned a number of things from their file on the Bells.

Curiously, the Bells hadn't been captured on any of the CCTV cameras located along their main route home.

The police had spoken to Walter's brother, Leonard, and had concluded that although there was no love lost between the siblings, there was no obvious motive or proof that he had been involved in their disappearance.

As part of the investigation, a number of police officers had visited the Cliffs Caravan Park, somewhere I also planned to visit. The report showed they had spoken to the site owner, a Mr Norman Chase, who'd insisted the Bells' time there had been incident free. While at the park, the police had also interviewed two other couples who'd been staying there at the same time: Esme and John James had apparently known the Bells for a number of years. The other couple, the Nightingales, had been staying in the pitch adjacent to the Bells. Neither couple had been able to throw any light on why the Bells might have disappeared.

There was one item in particular in the file that caught my attention: A year before the Bells' disappearance, another couple had apparently gone missing from the caravan park. On this occasion, though, the couple's bodies had been found the next day, at the bottom of the cliffs.

The final noteworthy piece of information concerned the Bells' house. It appeared that some jewellery had gone missing from the property, which gave further weight to the theory that they may have walked in on a burglary.

All in all, I now had much more to go on. In particular, I was keen to visit the park and speak with its owner, to try to find out more about the other couple who had died there a year earlier.

Chapter 9

My phone rang.

"Get yourself over to the Range."

"Hello, Grandma. Yes, I'm very well, thanks. How about you?"

"Never mind all that jibber jabber. I need you at the Range now. This is urgent."

Over the last couple of years, I'd come to realise that Grandma's idea of urgent and mine were light years apart. But I'd also learned that you ignored her 'requests' at your peril. So, with a heavy heart, I magicked myself over to the Range.

When I arrived, there was no sign of Grandma, but waiting there, looking every bit as perplexed as I was, were the twins.

"Did Grandma summon you too?" Amber said.

"Yeah. Any idea what this is all about?"

"Whatever it is, it won't be good," Pearl said, in a hushed voice. She was no doubt aware that Grandma wouldn't be far away. "It's a good job Alan was at home, otherwise I'd have had to bring Lily with me."

"I'm supposed to be behind the counter in Cuppy C," Amber said. "We were just starting to get busy when she called."

"Over there." I pointed to the opposite side of the Range. "Is that her?"

"I think so." Pearl nodded. "What's that she's carrying?"

"I'm not sure." Amber strained her eyes to get a better look.

"Aren't they brooms?" My heart sank as I remembered

what Grandma had said earlier in the week. "Oh no."

"What's going on, Jill?" Amber turned to me. "Do you know something about this?"

There was no time to recount the conversation I'd had with Grandma about broom flying because the woman herself was now only yards away. "Don't just stand there. Come and take one of these."

"Who are you talking to?" I said.

"All of you. Why do you think I brought three of them?"

"What's happening, Jill?" Pearl whispered.

"Trust me, it's better you don't know."

Once we each had one of the brooms, Grandma threw a critical eye over us. "Those are a perfect fit, even if I do say so myself."

Pearl looked around the arena. "You can't possibly expect us to clean this place with these. It'll take forever."

Grandma shook her head. "No, Pearl, I don't want you to clean the Range."

"You might wish she did when you hear what she does want," I whispered.

"Is there something you'd like to say, Jill?" Grandma fixed me with her gaze.

"Me? No, absolutely nothing."

"Good, in that case, to the business in hand. Or should I say the *broom* in hand." She cackled at what I could only assume was meant to be a joke.

Both Amber and Pearl laughed, but it was quite clearly false. Those two were such suck-ups.

Grandma continued, "Many years ago, broom flying was a major sport in the witch community. Unfortunately, like many other things, it's been allowed to fall by the wayside."

"Why would we bother with a broom when we can just magic ourselves from place to place?" Amber blurted out.

"Have you never heard of tradition, young lady? Today's younger generation is too busy with their phones and UPods to appreciate what's important."

"It's 'I'." Pearl corrected her. "They're IPods."

"IPods, UPods, who cares? There's nothing quite like the excitement of flying through the sky, astride a broom."

"I'm not very good with heights," Amber said.

"Keep your eyes closed, then."

"Aren't there any instructions with these?" Pearl eyed her broom.

"Yes, I have them here." Grandma mimicked taking a sheet of paper from her pocket and read out loud. "One: Get on the broom. Two: Fly it."

"There must be more to it than that," I said.

"Why would there be more? Broom flying is an instinctive thing. Come on, we've wasted enough time. Climb on them."

"What about you, Grandma?" Pearl said. "Aren't you going to be flying one?"

"No. I need to stay on the ground so I can watch you. Are you ready?"

"Hold on!" I said. "What do we do to start—"

Before I could finish the question, the broom soared skywards, with me holding on for dear life. The twins were doing likewise.

I had no idea what had just happened. I hadn't cast a spell, so either Grandma had cast one or the brooms were enchanted. Either way, I didn't feel as though I had any control.

"How are we supposed to steer these things?" I yelled at Grandma, as my broom swooped so low that I thought I was going to crash into the ground.

"You control it with your mind," she said. "It's very simple."

That was easy for her to say while she was standing on solid ground. It was all I could do to stay on board the stupid thing. But if I thought I was struggling, that was nothing compared to how the twins were faring. Somehow, Pearl had ended up facing the wrong way on her broom. Amber was in an even worse spot: She was hanging upside down with her arms and legs wrapped around the broom in a desperate attempt not to fall off.

"Come on, you three! That's rubbish!" Grandma shouted. "Focus! Remember, it's all about focus."

I knew she was right. Magic always came down to focus, and this was no different, but it wasn't easy to focus when you felt like you were about to throw up. I did eventually manage to get some small level of control over the broom, and it started to go where I wanted it to. That was more than I could say for the twins who were already back on the ground, looking more than a little green around the gills.

"Okay, Jill, bring her down." Grandma waved a crooked finger at me.

Although I say so myself, the landing was pretty smooth, and I was beginning to feel a little more confident.

"You three are probably wondering what inspired me to revive this long-lost tradition."

The twins clearly couldn't have cared less, and neither did I, but I thought I should at least feign some interest.

"Why do you want to?"

"I'll tell you why. Because I plan to start Candlefield's first ever synchronised broom flying troupe. We'll be putting on displays at galas and the like."

"I'm not doing that." Amber still looked as though she was about to throw up.

"Nor me," Pearl said. "It'll take me all day to get over this."

"I guess that just leaves me." I stepped forward. By now, I quite fancied the idea of leading a troupe of broom flying witches.

"Forget it!" Grandma waved me away. "None of you are even remotely good enough."

"I thought I was getting the hang of it towards the end," I said.

"You know what *thought* did, don't you? If I put any of you into the troupe, I'd be a laughing stock." She took back the brooms. "I'll just have to find someone who is worthy of my time and tutelage."

And with that, she disappeared.

"I feel sick," Amber moaned.

"Me too," Pearl said.

"Actually, I'm feeling quite peckish."

"Shut up, Jill!" Amber yelled. "Don't mention food."

"Sorry. I'll leave you two to it. I hope you feel better soon."

***

I hadn't said I was peckish just to wind the twins up. All that soaring through the air had left me feeling quite hungry. On balance, I decided it was probably best not to go to Cuppy C, so I magicked myself back to Washbridge, and Coffee Games.

When I walked through the door, my ears were assaulted by the sound of—err—what was that noise? It reminded me a little of those racing car sets. The only difference was that the volume in the shop was a hundred times louder.

"What's going on, Sarah?"

"It's today's game of the day: Beetle drive."

"I've played beetle drive before. It shouldn't make that much noise."

"See for yourself." She pointed to one of the nearby booths.

On the table, was what appeared to be a racing track, but instead of racing cars, they seemed to be racing motorised beetles.

I turned back to Sarah who was already pouring my coffee. "That isn't beetle drive. It should be played with a dice, pen and paper."

"I thought it was a bit weird, but the manager seemed to think he knew what he was doing."

Thankfully, I managed to find a table some distance from the racing beetles. After the broom flying ordeal, I needed a little quiet downtime.

"Hi, Jill."

Oh bum! Deli was the last person I wanted to see; she was even louder than the motorised beetles.

"Hi, Deli."

"You don't mind if I join you, do you?" she said.

"I—err—"

"Thanks." She was staring at my face. "What type of

foundation do you use, Jill?"

"Sorry?"

"Choosing the right foundation is really important. It's kind of the—err—thingy of your beauty regime. What's the word I'm looking for?"

"Foundation?"

"That's right."

"I'll bear that in mind."

"What you need, Jill, is a personal beauty audit."

"A what?"

"I took what you said to heart."

"You did? Remind me again what that was."

"That I shouldn't worry about what your grandmother was doing, and that instead I should focus on my own business. Just like your sister did."

"Right, yeah, that's definitely the way to go."

"That's why I've introduced the beauty audit service." She took a handful of vouchers from her bag. "These entitle you to a free audit. There's one for you, and some for you to give to family and friends."

"Right, thanks."

"Make sure you book your place soon because the offer is only good until the end of the month."

"I will."

"I'd better get going, Jill. People to go, places to meet."

"Okay. Great."

***

I didn't hang around Coffee Games for very long because the sound of the motorised beetles was just too annoying. Before heading back to the office, I had a few things I needed to pick up in town. As I headed towards the pharmacy, I spotted a familiar face.

A familiar *feline* face.

Winky's Aunt Wynn went dashing down the street, and around the corner out of sight. Where was she going? What was she up to?

Curiosity got the better of me, so I set off in pursuit.

At first, I thought I must have lost her, but then I spotted her slipping into a jeweller. By the time I reached the shop, and peered in through the window, Wynn was sitting at one side of the counter. The shop was quite busy, and no one seemed to have noticed the cat.

At the counter were a young couple who, judging by their ages and the way they were gazing into each other's eyes, were shopping for an engagement ring. The young woman pointed to one of the trays in the locked cabinet, and watched eagerly as the sales assistant took it out for them to get a closer look.

After that, everything seemed to happen very quickly.

The assistant had no sooner put the tray down than Aunt Wynn jumped onto the counter, and knocked it off, spilling the rings all over the floor. No one reacted for a few seconds, but then the sales assistant rushed around the counter, to shoo the cat out of the door, but not before I'd spotted Wynn do something very interesting.

Half an hour later, shopping done, I headed back to the office.

"Are you still okay to come and look at the house this afternoon, Jill?" A white-spotted faced Mrs V said.

"Yeah. Give me about an hour and then we'll go."

In my office, Aunt Wynn and Winky were both sitting

on my desk.

"Do you mind, young lady." She shot me a look. "I'd like to have a few words with my nephew in private before I leave."

"Of course, but I do have an urgent message for Winky."

"Oh?" he said.

"Yes. While I was out, Gemma the Gems asked me to tell you that Gavin the Grub needs to speak to you immediately. It's a matter of life and death, apparently."

"What's it about?"

"She wouldn't say."

"Is this on the up and up?"

"I'm just the messenger. If you don't believe me, that's not my problem."

He turned to Wynn. "Do you mind if I nip out for a few minutes? This could be important."

"Of course not. Off you go."

As soon as he'd disappeared out of the window, she turned on me. "Are you still here? I thought I asked you to leave."

"That's right, you did, but here's the thing, I'm not going anywhere, and certainly not because some jewel thief asks me to."

"What did you just call me? How dare you?"

"You come here with your prim and proper, butter-wouldn't-melt act, but you're nothing but a common thief."

"This is outrageous! Just wait until my nephew comes back. After I've told him what you said, he'll—"

"He'll do what?" I reached out and lifted her fur flap, to reveal a haul of rings. "Hmm, what do we have here?"

That seemed to knock the stuffing out of her. "Please don't tell Winky. He looks up to me."

"Why would you steal when you're already minted?"

"Why would you think I'm minted? I can barely keep the wolf from the door."

"Winky thinks you're rich. That's why he's—"

"Why he's what?"

"Nothing. It doesn't matter." Despite the way she'd treated me, I couldn't bring myself to tell her that her favourite nephew was only sucking up to her for her money.

"Are you going to tell him about the rings?"

"Not if you promise to take them back."

"I will. As soon as I've said goodbye to Winky."

"Okay. I won't say anything."

"Thanks, Jill. I told Winky he was lucky to have you staying here with him."

"Hmm."

Chapter 10

I made myself scarce, long enough for Winky and his auntie to say their goodbyes. By the time I returned to the office, Winky was all alone, and if the look on his face was anything to go by, he was about to blow a fuse.

"What was that all about?" he demanded.

"What was *what* all about?"

"That rubbish with Gemma and Gavin. They hadn't spoken to you. They don't even know who you are."

"Really? Sorry, my bad."

"Is that all you have to say for yourself? What did you say to Aunt Wynn while I was gone?"

"Nothing."

"Don't give me that. When I got back, it was like she was a different cat."

"I'm sure that's just your imagination."

"I don't think so. She was even singing your praises to me."

"That's nice."

"You're up to something, and when I find out what, there'll be trouble."

"Do you mind if I give you one small piece of advice, Winky?"

"Would it make any difference if I said no?"

"Don't rely too much on the inheritance from your auntie. I wouldn't want you to be too disappointed."

"Excuse me. I'm sorry to interrupt." Harold was standing on the window ledge, peering into the office. "Do you have a minute, Jill?"

"You aren't interrupting anything, Harold," I reassured him. "Winky and I had just finished here, hadn't we?"

Winky gave me a look, said, "I know you're up to something," and then skulked off under the sofa.

"What can I do for you, Harold?"

He lifted his wing to reveal a tiny white box. "It's Ida's birthday tomorrow, and I've bought her a cake."

"How romantic."

"I'd like it to be a surprise, so I wondered if you could hide it somewhere. Just until tomorrow."

"Sure, no problem." I took the box from him.

"Take a look at it, Jill. Tell me what you think."

I lifted the lid to reveal the cutest little cake with a picture of two pigeons kissing. "This is gorgeous, Harold. Do you mind if I take a photo to show my husband? Maybe it will motivate him to buy one for my birthday."

"Go ahead."

I snapped a photo, put the lid back on, and then put the box in the bottom drawer of my desk for safe keeping.

"What kind of cake is it? Is it some kind of special pigeon food?"

"No, it's just an ordinary cake."

"Okay, well it's safe with me."

"Thanks, Jill. I'll pop back to collect it tomorrow."

***

On our way to the cottage, I drove and Mrs V navigated.

Or at least, that had been the plan. Mrs V wasn't exactly Google Maps. In fact, she seemed to have little grasp of the geography of Washbridge and the surrounding area, despite the fact that she'd lived there all of her life.

It didn't come as much of a surprise to learn it was

called Cuckoo Cottage, and even though I'd seen a photo of it, nothing could have prepared me for the real thing.

Weirdly, though, I wasn't as repulsed as I'd expected to be. It was true that the front of the house did resemble a giant cuckoo clock, but if you could get past that (and yes, I do realise that wouldn't be easy), then the rest of the package was really superb.

The cottage was located on the very edge of a wood. Its wild country garden was delightful—as pretty as any I'd ever seen.

"What do you think of it, Jill?" Mrs V said. "Have you ever seen anything quite like this?"

"I can safely say that I haven't." I hesitated. "It is very pretty, though. How difficult would it be to remove the cuckoo clock features? It's only a couple of doors and a long chain."

"But that's the whole point. Armi wouldn't want to remove them."

"The location is fantastic. And this garden is beautiful."

"It is, isn't it? It's even better around the back. Do you want to take a look inside the house?"

"What about the owners? Will they mind?"

"They've already moved out—emigrated, actually. The sale is being handled by the man's sister. She said we could look around anytime."

"We're here now. You may as well give me the whole tour."

"The keys are in my handbag in your car. Is it locked?"

"No. No one is going to steal that thing."

I waited by the back door while Mrs V went to retrieve her bag.

"Oi!" The voice came from somewhere behind me, but I

couldn't see anyone. "Over here!"

Someone, very small, was waving to me from behind one of the trees on the edge of the wood.

"Hello? Who's there?"

"Are you a witch?" The tiny creature, dressed from head to toe in green, stepped out from behind the tree.

"Err, yes, I am. Who are you?"

"William. William Twigmore."

"I'm Jill. Do you mind if I ask what kind of creature you are, William?"

"I'm a wood nymph. I live here with my two brothers. They're back there, but they're too shy to say hello."

I glanced at the car where Mrs V was reaching into the back seat. "I can't talk just now, I'm afraid. My friend will be back in a minute."

"Are you going to buy this house?"

"Me? No. My friend might, though."

"Does she like pink marshmallows?"

"Marshmallows? I don't know."

"I hope so. The previous occupant never ate them. It's been years since we've had any."

"Is that a wood nymph thing? Liking marshmallows, I mean?"

"Only the pink ones. The white ones are horrible." He pulled a sour face to illustrate his point.

"I've got it!" Mrs V held up the key.

"Sorry, William. I have to go."

"What were you doing over by that tree, Jill?" Mrs V said, as she unlocked the door.

"Nothing. I thought I saw a squirrel. Incidentally, Mrs V, do you like marshmallows?"

"Sorry?"

"I was just wondering if you were partial to marshmallows. Particularly pink ones?"

Thirty minutes later, after we'd finished the tour of the cottage, I came away wishing that Jack and I could somehow afford to buy it. The interior was as cute as a button, and the previous owners were including all the furniture with the sale.

"You like it, then, Jill?" Mrs V clearly hadn't expected my reaction.

"I love it. I'd snatch their hands off."

"What about the cuckoo clock thing?"

"Honestly, I wouldn't even care about that. The rest of the house more than makes up for it. And besides, if you use your womanly wiles, I'm sure you'll be able to persuade Armi to remove that, or at least to tone it down."

"It is beautiful. I'll have to give it some serious thought. Thanks, Jill, I do appreciate you taking the time to come with me today."

***

Little Jack wasn't behind the counter in The Corner Shop. Instead, it was Lucy Locket who served me.

"Where's Jack today?" I asked.

"It's the National Corner Shop Symposium in Bognor Regis. Jack's gone down there for a couple of days."

"I guess that means you're in charge, then?"

"Yes, but I'll try not to let the power go to my head." She smiled. "Have you had your free drink?"

I was feeling quite thirsty, so I walked over to the free

vending machine, and chose tropical fruits tea. By now, I wasn't in the least surprised to find that it tasted just like regular tea.

"Would you like any scratch cards, Jill?"

"No, thanks. I never win on those things."

"These aren't the National Lottery scratch cards. These are Corner Shop's own. It's Jack's latest brainwave."

"I hope he's thought this one through. It's been one disaster after another recently, what with the shopping app and loyalty card."

"You can't really go wrong with these. They're only ten-pence each."

"That's remarkably cheap. How much can you win?"

"There are no cash prizes. You can win things we sell in the shop. You have to scratch off five windows, and if three of the pictures match, you win whatever the picture is."

"For ten-pence a shot, it's worth a go. Give me six, would you?"

I resisted the urge to scratch the cards there and then, so that Jack and I could do it tonight. With three cards each, we could have our own mini competition to see who won the most prizes.

And yes, I do realise how sad that sounds, but thanks for pointing it out anyway.

***

As part of my investigation into the missing penguins, I was headed to a mid-week match. Much to my surprise, Jack had decided to accompany me.

"I didn't think you liked football?"

"What made you think that? I was known as Jack the Dribble when I was young."

"You always have been a messy drinker."

"Very funny. If things had been different, I could have been a professional footballer."

"By that, I assume you mean if you'd actually had an ounce of talent."

"Cheek. What time is the kick-off?"

"Six-thirty."

"That's rather early, isn't it?"

"It is a juniors' team remember. They probably all have to be tucked up in bed by nine."

"We'd better be making tracks, then."

"Before we go, I got these from the corner shop."

"Scratch cards?"

"It's Little Jack's latest initiative. I got three for you and three for me. I thought we could see who wins the most prizes. Whoever loses has to buy the tickets for the game tonight."

"Okay, you're on. How do they work?"

"You have to scratch off five of the twelve windows. If you get three matching pictures, then you get to claim whatever that picture is."

"Okay, let's do it. Prepare to lose."

"Dream on, buddy."

I took a few seconds to decide which windows to scratch off on the first card.

What's wrong with that? With these things, it's all about the strategy.

"Yes!" Jack punched the air. "I've won a steak and kidney pie."

I scratched my card. "I've won a prize too."

"What did you win?"

"The same. A steak and kidney pie. I'll try another one."

Five minutes later, Jack and I had won a total of six steak and kidney pies.

"I don't think that's supposed to happen." Jack had a knack of stating the blindingly obvious.

"What's the betting that those windows we didn't scratch off have a picture of a steak and kidney pie too? Let's see."

"If you do that, your winning card will be void."

"So what? I don't even like steak and kidney pie." I began to scratch off the rest of the windows. "See, what did I tell you? Every window, on every card has a picture of a steak and kidney pie under it."

"I don't reckon that's how it's meant to work."

"You think?"

***

"Are you sure you have the right day?" Jack glanced around the stadium. "There aren't many people here."

"Positive. I double-checked the website this afternoon.

The man behind the turnstile was fast asleep.

"Excuse me." I tapped the counter. "Two tickets, please."

"Sorry, love. I must have nodded off."

"There doesn't appear to be many people here tonight?"

"This is one of the best turnouts we've had so far this season."

That was a depressing thought because there couldn't have been more than forty people in the stadium.

"Hi!" A woman seated two rows in front of us gave us a

wave.

"Hello."

"I'm Trish. This is my husband, Jacob. Our Wesley is the goalkeeper for the Penguins."

"Do you come to many matches?"

"We never miss one, do we, Jacob?"

"No, we're always here—same seats every match. We're season ticket holders. What about you two? I don't think I've seen you here before. Is your boy in the team?"

"No, we—err—just fancied a night out."

"I hope they do better than their last home match," Trish said. "We lost twelve-one. Wesley was really upset afterwards."

"Poor little mite," I said. "This stadium is incredible. I believe it was financed by Frank—err—"

"Royston," Jacob said. "That's right. It must have cost him a small fortune."

"Does his son play for the team?"

"Not as far as I know."

"Is Royston here today?"

"I doubt it," Trish said. "I don't think he ever comes to the matches."

"Here they come now!" Jacob got to his feet to greet the teams. "Go Wesley!"

The diminutive goalkeeper gave his parents a wave, and then the teams lined up. Tonight's opponents were The Chippers from West Chipping.

When the final whistle blew, we said our goodbyes to our new friends.

"I hope Wesley is okay," Jack said. "At least he let in one goal less than he did in the last match."

"We'd better go and try to cheer him up. I hope we see you two here again."

Once we were out of the stadium, I breathed a sigh of relief. "Thank goodness that's over. Was it just me or were the Penguins awful?"

"They really were. I felt sorry for little Wesley. Letting in twenty-three goals in two matches can't have been fun. If we have a little boy, we mustn't let him play in goal."

"What about if we have a little girl?"

"She'll want to do ballet or netball, won't she?"

"I can't believe you just said that. Why shouldn't she play football?"

"Err, no reason. I just meant—"

"Girls can play football every bit as well as boys. In fact, it's hard to imagine how they could be any worse than the Washbridge Penguins."

Chapter 11

Jack had got up early so he could nip to the corner shop before he headed out for work. So keen was he to claim his steak and kidney pies. I'd warned him that the cards would be void because we'd scratched out all the windows, but he was adamant that we should still be entitled to a prize.

He was to be disappointed.

"They're all out of pies." He came back, still clutching the 'winning' scratch cards.

"Quelle surprise. I wonder why that could be."

"There are dozens of people down there, all trying to claim their free steak and kidney pies."

"Who could have seen that coming?"

"It's that young woman I feel sorry for."

"Lucy?"

"Yeah, she's having to explain to everyone why they can't have a pie. Little Jack is in Bognor Regis, apparently."

"At the National Corner Shop Symposium, no doubt."

"How do you know that?"

"I like to keep abreast of all things retail."

"Lucy said we should hold onto our tickets until Little Jack gets back."

"She's not still selling them, is she?"

"No, she had the good sense to stop. It's all very disappointing because I was really looking forward to a steak and kidney pie for dinner."

"Them's the breaks, buddy."

"So it seems. Oh yes, I almost forgot, I bumped into Britt and Kit on my way back."

"I bet they were doing something obscenely sporting, weren't they? Had they just run a marathon before breakfast?"

"Actually, they were telling me about the Washbridge Battle of the Bands."

Oh bum! "I really ought to be going to work."

"Before you do, is there something you'd like to tell me, Jill?"

"Err—no—I don't think so."

"Are you sure? Something about a solo performance?"

"Oh that." I forced a laugh. "I'd totally forgotten about that little thing."

"I bet you had. Kit really fancies our chances in the competition, particularly—and these were his very words—particularly as we have such a strong solo performer in Jill."

"It's not my fault. It's not like I volunteered. It was presented to me as mission accomplished."

"You can't go on stage in a competition and use magic."

"What am I supposed to do, then? I can't pull out now. The Liveleys are relying on me to do it."

"I guess that leaves you with only one option, doesn't it?"

"What's that?"

"You'll have to get in some practice on the penny whistle."

"You're surely not proposing that I go on stage and play it without the help of magic?"

"That's precisely what I'm proposing."

Oh bum and double bum!

Later, as we were both leaving for work, I remembered

the photo I'd taken the previous day.

"Hey, Jack, would you like to see something really cute?" I took out my phone.

"I'm already looking at something really cute."

That husband of mine could be a charmer when he tried.

"Just look at that cake. Isn't it something?"

"Are those doves on there?"

"No, they're pigeons. I told you about Harold and Ida who live on my window ledge, didn't I?"

"Probably. It's hard to keep track of all the crazy stuff you come out with."

"It's Ida's birthday today, and Harold gave me the birthday cake for safekeeping."

"That's so sweet. Is it made out of some kind of special pigeon food?"

"That's what I thought, but apparently, it's just a regular cake."

"Nice."

"I don't remember you buying me a cake for my birthday."

"I couldn't find one big enough to hold all the candles."

"Cheek."

***

As I walked up the stairs to my office, I realised something was different, but it took me a few moments to work out what it was. Then it clicked: there was no sound of typewriter keys being thumped.

"Mrs V? How come you're back on the computer?"

"It was a silly idea to try and use the typewriter. I don't

know what I was thinking. I'd convinced myself that the good old days were better, but that simply isn't true. Carbon paper? Correction fluid? There's nothing fun about all that. And those keys were ruining my nails."

"What have you done with the typewriter?" I glanced around the outer office, but there was no sign of it.

"I couldn't bear to look at it for another minute. I took it through to your office, so I wouldn't have to see it. I hope you don't mind."

"No, that's okay."

"I've put it out of sight, in the bottom drawer of your desk."

"Okay, I'll just—hold on, did you just say bottom drawer?" I dashed through to my office, and over to my desk. There were drawers on either side of it, so there was a fifty-fifty chance the cake would be okay. Surely, if she'd opened the drawer with the cake box in it, she would have spotted it, wouldn't she?

Oh no!

I lifted the typewriter out of the drawer and put it onto my desk.

"Is everything okay, Jill?" Mrs V had followed me into my office.

"Err, yeah. Everything's great."

"Are you sure? You're looking very pale."

"I'm fine. How long ago did you put this in here?"

"Last night before I left the office. Why?"

"No reason." That blew any chance I might have had of using the 'take it back' spell.

Once she'd left the room, I took the squashed cake box out of the drawer. Maybe it was only the box that was damaged? Who was I trying to kid? It was practically flat.

"Oh dear." Winky jumped onto the desk. "Whatever has happened here?"

"There's been a slight accident."

"*Slight*?" He laughed. "That's like saying that cutting your throat is just a small nick."

"What shall I do?"

"Change your name and leave the country?"

"You aren't helping."

"Didn't you take a photo of it?"

"Yes! Yes, I did. You're a genius, Winky!"

"I've been telling you that for years."

"All I have to do now is find someone who can make me an identical cake. That shouldn't be that difficult."

Famous last words.

My first thought had been to contact Aunt Lucy, but she and Lester had gone out for the day. That was okay because there were any number of cake shops in Washbridge. One of them was bound to be able to help.

Two hours later, my feet were aching, after trudging from one shop to another. No one could make the cake. At least, not within the required timescale. There was now only one shop left for me to check. I'd deliberately put this one at the bottom of the list because they were clearly the most expensive option. They did, however, offer a super-fast express service. But at a price.

"Hello, madam, how can I help you?" The woman behind the counter was wearing a blue and white striped apron with the words 'Cake Pronto' on the front.

"Hi. Exactly how quick is your express service?"

"What kind of cake is it you're after? Fruit or sponge?"

"Err, what's the most common for birthdays?"

"Fruit usually."

"Okay, that's what I'll have then."

"That's going to take four hours."

"Can't you do it any quicker than that?"

"Not if you want it to be edible."

"Okay, that should work, but I'll need you to start straight away."

"Of course."

"I want it to look like this." I showed her the photo.

"Are those doves?"

"No, they're pigeons."

"You want a cake with *pigeons* on it?"

"Yes, can you do it?"

"Of course."

"Great! I'll come and pick it up in four hours." I started for the door.

"Madam, there's just the question of payment."

"Don't I pay on collection?"

"I'm afraid not. What would happen if you didn't come back? I don't think we'd be able to find anyone else who would want to buy a *pigeon* cake."

"Fine. How much will it be?"

"One hundred pounds."

"*A hundred*?"

"It is our express service."

"Okay, okay." I handed her my credit card. "Just make sure it's ready on time."

By the time I got back to the office, I was shattered.

"Are you okay, Jill?" Mrs V said. "I was worried when you dashed out like that."

"I'm fine. Could you make me a coffee, please?"

"Of course. I'll bring it straight through."

When I walked through to my office, I was horrified to find Winky seated on the windowsill, talking to Harold. If he'd grassed me up, I'd kill him.

"Hi, Jill." Harold gave me a little wave. That was reassuring. If he'd known what had happened to the cake, he wouldn't have done that.

"Morning, Harold."

"Winky tells me you've been taking good care of Ida's cake."

"Of course."

"There really was no need for you to stand guard over it all last night."

"I—err—" I glanced at Winky who was grinning from ear to ear. "I was happy to do it. I didn't want anything to happen to it."

"Like what?" Winky said.

I was going to kill that cat. "Err, like anything. You can never be too careful."

"That's true." Winky nodded. "If you hadn't kept watch, who knows what might have happened? Someone might have opened the drawer and dropped something heavy on top of it. Like a type—"

"So, Harold," I cut across Winky. "When will you need the cake?"

"Not until late this afternoon. I've organised a small surprise party for Ida. Is it okay if I come and collect it then?"

"Absolutely. That would be perfect."

"Okay, I'd better be making tracks. I still have a few things to arrange for the party. I'll catch you later, Jill."

"Later, yeah." I waited until he was out of earshot, and

then turned my glare on Winky. "What were you playing at?"

"Relax. I was only messing with you. Did you get a replacement cake sorted?"

"Yes, but it's cost me an arm and a leg."

"What price friendship?"

***

It was time to pay a visit to the Cliffs Caravan Park near Filey. Driving there and back was out of the question because I needed to be back in time to collect the replacement birthday cake.

As its name suggested, the park was indeed situated close to the cliffs. Some of the caravans were precariously close to the edge in my view. It certainly wasn't the kind of place to take a late night, drunken stroll.

I'd telephoned the park owner, a Mr Norman Chase, but he'd been none too keen to speak to me, and even less enthusiastic about the suggestion that I might pay him a visit. Not one to be put off easily, I figured that if I turned up on his doorstep, he'd have no choice but to engage with me.

"You?" He stepped out of the huge static caravan, which appeared to serve as both his office and home. "I told you on the phone that I had nothing to say to you."

"Really? That wasn't the impression I got. I thought you seemed keen to tell me your side of the story. Were you aware of any issues regarding the Bells during their stay?"

"No, I've already told the police that nothing out of the ordinary happened. And, anyway, as I understand it, their car was found at their house, so whatever happened to them, clearly happened there. It has nothing to do with this park or with me. Now, if you don't mind, I have work to do."

"What about the other couple, Mr Chase?"

"What other couple?"

"The couple who died on this park about a year ago."

"That was a tragic accident. They were walking along the cliff path and got too close to the edge."

"Still, the bad publicity can't have been good for business?"

"Their deaths had nothing to do with the park, any more than the Bells' disappearance does."

A red-haired woman appeared in the doorway behind him. "What's going on, Norman?"

"Nothing, Mary. This young lady was just leaving, weren't you?"

I ignored him. "Mrs Chase? I was asking your husband about the Bells. Did you notice anything unusual during their stay?"

Before she had the chance to respond, Norman Chase had bundled her back inside. "I've told you—we have nothing more to say." And with that, he slammed the door in my face.

His defensive reaction didn't strike me as that of a man with nothing on his conscience. I hadn't really learned anything of interest. Maybe I'd have more joy when I spoke to the two couples, mentioned in the police files, who'd been staying on the park at the same time as the Bells.

***

What with the missing Bells and missing penguins, I'd not been able to give much thought to the dandelion fairies. But I'd made a promise to help them, so instead of magicking myself straight back to the office, I stopped off in Washbridge Park.

Several sections of the huge grassed areas were covered in dandelions, many of which had turned to seed. Unusually, and just as Dandy had said, the seeds didn't seem to be dispersing in the wind. That was very weird, particularly because there was quite a stiff breeze that day. Even when I walked through the hordes of flowers, catching them with my feet, none of the seeds became detached. I'd never seen anything quite like it.

I needed to get a closer look at the flowers, so I went behind one of the larger trees in the park, made sure no one could see me, and then cast the 'shrink' spell. The dandelions now towered above me like giant trees. I was still trying to get my bearings when I heard the sound of footsteps—lots of them—headed in my direction. Moments later, a crowd of creatures came running towards me. They were a strange looking bunch, with long legs, small bodies, and even smaller heads. They all had freckles and white curly hair.

I braced myself for a confrontation, but when they were only a few feet from me, they stopped dead in their tracks. The creature who had led the charge stepped forward, bowed, and said, "We are the Tye."

Before I could respond, I heard more footsteps heading in my direction. Yet another crowd of creatures appeared, and they were every bit as strange as the earlier arrivals. These had small legs, a slightly larger body, and large heads. These weird little guys all had dimples and green hair.

They too came to a halt just a few feet from where I was standing. The creature at the head of this particular group stepped forward and said, "We are the Nees."

Chapter 12

"Let me make sure that I have this right." I turned to the creature who had spoken first. "Your people are called the Tye?"

"That's correct."

And then to the second creature, I said, "And you're the Nees?"

"We are."

"So, together, I guess that makes you the Tye-Nees?" I laughed. "Quite apt really."

They both gave me the same puzzled look.

"Who are you?" the head of the Nees asked.

"Sorry. My name is Jill Maxwell. I'm a witch."

"You're very small for a witch," the head of the Tye commented.

"I shrank myself so that I could get a better look at the dandelions."

"At the *what*?"

"These flowers. I'm sorry, but I don't know either of your names."

"I'm Bill." The head of the Tye took a bow.

"And I'm Ben." The head of the Nees did likewise.

This had to be some kind of wind up. "Where's little weed?"

"Sorry?"

Once again, my dazzling wit had missed the mark.

"Never mind. Have you always lived here?"

"No, we came here from Small Lake," Ben said. "Do you know it?"

"I don't think so. Is it here in the human world?"

"No. It's in Candlefield."

"What about the Nees, Bill? Where do you come from?"

"The same place. The Tye and Nees have always lived side-by-side, so when Ben told me that he and his people were thinking of moving to the human world, we said we'd come along too."

"How long have you been here?"

"Just a couple of weeks," Bill said.

"And how are you finding it?"

"We had a few problems at first, but we seem to have overcome them now. Overall, we quite like it here."

"What kind of problems did you encounter?"

"Mainly the weather. Back in Small Lake, we live in the shadow of the Black Mountains, which means that we don't get too much rain. Over here, though, it always seems to be raining. We spent the first few days soaked to the skin until we found these—what did you call them again?"

"Dandelions."

"Right. Things improved dramatically once we'd taken shelter under the dandelions."

"But then, they started to fall apart," Ben said. "Pieces of them blew away in the wind, leaving us exposed again."

"Fortunately, we had the wherewithal to resolve that problem." Bill tapped the side of his head with his finger.

"How did you do that?"

"With Tye SlowGrowth."

"What does that do?"

"It slows down the dandelion's growth, so it doesn't fall apart so quickly."

"Oh dear." Everything was starting to become much clearer.

"What's wrong?" Ben said.

"The thing is, when you saw the white bits floating away in the wind, the dandelion wasn't actually falling apart. Those are its seeds, which it releases in order that new dandelions will grow."

"We had no idea." Ben turned to Bill. "Did we?"

"None at all. We have no desire to cause any harm."

"I believe you. We'll need to come up with some other solution to your problem that doesn't involve treating the dandelions with SlowGrowth."

"We'd be open to any suggestions," Ben said. "What did you have in mind?"

"Nothing at the moment. I'll need to give it some thought. Let's say I do manage to come up with an alternative, is there anything you can do about the dandelions that you've already treated?"

"We have a solution which will neutralise the SlowGrowth," Ben said.

"Great. I'll go away and have a think, but in the meantime, please don't treat any more dandelions with SlowGrowth."

"We won't." Bill reassured me. "You have our word."

Whenever I think I've encountered every kind of supernatural creature there can possibly be, I come across another. The Tye and Nees were a little on the weird side, but clearly good-natured. They'd appeared genuinely upset when they realised the harm they'd inadvertently inflicted on the dandelions. All I had to do now was to find something else for them to use as shelter from the rain, but how exactly was I supposed to do that?

Answers on a postcard, please.

***

For now, at least, the dandelion problem would have to go on the backburner because I had a cake to collect.

Hopefully Cake Pronto would make good on their promise to have the cake ready in four hours because I couldn't bear the thought of having to explain to Harold why his wife wouldn't be getting her birthday cake.

The same woman was behind the counter.

"Hello again." She certainly didn't have the look of someone who was about to deliver bad news.

"Hi. Is it ready?"

"Only just, but yes. I'll go and get it for you."

Phew! It made a pleasant change for something to go right for once.

When the woman reappeared, she was carrying a white box. A *big* white box. "There you go." She placed it onto the counter.

Maybe they only had the one size of box, and the cake inside was much smaller? With fingers crossed, I lifted the lid. Oh bum!

"It's too big."

"Sorry?"

"This cake is too big."

"It's regular cake size."

She reached under the counter and retrieved the copy of the photo she'd printed off. "It looks identical to me."

She was right—it did look exactly the same as the original. The problem was that the photo gave no sense of scale.

"Is it an issue?" she said. "We can make a smaller one if you wish, but there'll be another charge, and of course it will take some time."

"No, it's okay." I picked up the box. "This one will be fine, thanks."

There was no need to panic; everything was going to be okay. All I had to do was to shrink the cake and box so that it was the same size as the original. I found a quiet spot with no one around, and then cast the spell. Was that the right size? Almost, but maybe still a little too big. I repeated the spell. Now it looked perfect.

At least I hoped so, but the real test would be when I handed it over to Harold.

When I got back to the office, he and Winky were on the windowsill, chatting.

"Harold was beginning to worry that you'd run off with his cake," Winky quipped.

"I didn't say that," Harold said. "I know the cake is safe in Jill's hands."

"Thank you, Harold." I walked over to the window and handed him the cake box.

"Thanks, Jill."

"Don't you want to check it?" I said.

"I'm sure that's not necessary."

"I'd prefer it if you did. Just to be sure."

"Okay, then." He lifted the lid and took a peek at it.

I held my breath while he studied the cake. Was it exactly the right size? If not, would he notice? What about the picture of the pigeons? It looked okay to me, but then I wasn't a pigeon.

He closed the lid and nodded his approval. "It looks great. Thanks again, Jill. I'll go and show it to Ida."

"That was a close call." Winky whistled. "You looked

terrified."

"Rubbish. Of course I didn't."

"How much did the replacement cake cost?"

"Too much, but it was worth it."

"This is why your sister can afford to move to a new house and you're stuck in that little matchbox of yours. She doesn't throw away her money on birthday cakes for pigeons."

Before I left for home, I decided to review my current cases ahead of the weekend. The Bells case continued to frustrate me. If they'd planned to disappear, why had they driven all the way home from Filey first? If they'd disturbed burglars, why hadn't the thieves simply scarpered? Why bother to abduct the Bells?

Walter Bell's brother, Leonard, certainly had it in for the Bells' son. He'd as good as suggested Adam was after his parents' money, but I'd been less than impressed by Leonard, and I wasn't sure I should take anything he had to say at face value.

I'd learned very little from my visit to Cliffs Caravan Park, but it had raised a question mark about the park owner. For someone with nothing to hide, he had acted very strangely.

The other case was proving to be every bit as weird. I couldn't understand why someone would splash out such large amounts of money on a stadium for a junior football team. It would have made more sense if Royston had a kid in the team, but he didn't, and as far as I could make out, he wasn't even interested in football.

I wouldn't be able to work on either case on Saturday because Jack had committed us to looking after Lizzie and

Mikey while Kathy and Peter moved into their new house. As if that wasn't bad enough, he'd also signed us up to go to the model railway rally. The fun just never—started.

I'd just have to try to find some time on Sunday to work on the cases.

***

When I pulled onto the drive, Britt and Kimmy were chatting. With a bit of luck, I'd be able to sneak into the house without them spotting me.

"Hiya, Jill!"

So near, and yet so far.

"Hi." I started to edge towards the door. Maybe I could still make it inside.

"Come and look at this." Kimmy held up what looked like a greetings card.

Resigned to my fate, I went over to join them.

"What do you think?" She handed me the card.

"Love Your Cat day?"

"I've got one for Lovely." Britt handed me a similar card.

I knew there was an international cat day because Winky reminded me of it every year, but I'd never heard of Love Your Cat day.

"Is this for real?" I said.

"Of course it is." Britt sounded surprised by the question. "You have to get a card for your cat. What's his name again?"

"It's Wonky, isn't it?" Kimmy said.

"Winky, actually. I don't believe in buying cards for animals." Or humans, truth be told.

"But he'll be upset if all the other cats get a card and he doesn't."

"He'll get over it."

I could tell by the look on their faces that I'd gone down in their estimation. From now on I'd probably be referred to as the heartless cat owner.

"I'd better get going, ladies."

Kimmy wasn't about to let me get away that easily. "Britt tells me you're going to perform solo in the Battle of the Bands."

"Actually, I wanted to talk to you about that, Britt."

"We put in the final paperwork this morning," she said. "It's going to be great."

"We can't lose with you on our team," Kimmy said. "Go, Jill!"

"What did you want to say to me, Jill?" Britt said.

"I—err—nothing. It doesn't matter. I'd better crack on."

"You've still got time to buy a card for Winky," Britt called after me. "It isn't Love Your Cat day until next Wednesday."

"Okay, thanks."

Not. A. Chance.

***

It was my turn to make dinner, and I simply couldn't justify ordering another takeaway. Much as I hated to admit it, Winky had a point about my spending. I wasn't nearly careful enough with money. That would have to change if I wanted to move to a bigger house.

"Hi, beautiful." Jack gave me a kiss. "Something smells

good."

"Dinner should be ready in about ten minutes."

"I bumped into Britt on my way in."

"Was she doing press-ups again?"

"No, she showed me the card she'd bought for Lovely."

"Ridiculous, eh?"

"I think it's a nice idea. Have you got one for Winky?"

"Of course I haven't. I don't have cash to burn."

"He'll be upset."

"He'll get over it, and besides, I've been thinking about our spending. We need to start cutting back."

"What prompted this?"

"I just thought that if we were more careful with our money, we'd be able to buy things."

"Such as?"

"I don't know. A new house for example."

"I might have guessed. And what cutbacks are you proposing to make?"

"For starters, I won't be buying a Love Your Cat card."

"You'll have to come up with something much more radical than that if you want to make a real impact."

"I'm willing to do that."

"You could start by cutting out custard creams and buying budget brand plain biscuits instead."

"Are you insane?"

***

After dinner, I spent a little time checking to see if there was anything in the house that I could sell, but I pretty much drew a blank.

When I joined Jack in the lounge, he was watching

Spooky TV.

"Why are you watching that rubbish again?"

"It's not rubbish. There are some quality movies on here."

"Says you."

"You're just scared."

"Don't be ridiculous. Of course I'm not."

"Okay, come and watch a movie with me."

"What's on?"

"You'll be sorry to hear that you just missed Killer Clowns."

"That's very disappointing."

"The next one up is called The House On Gravestone Hill."

"Sounds unmissable."

"Sit next to me." He patted the sofa. "I have popcorn."

"Okay, then, but if it's as bad as it sounds, I'm going up to bed."

Twenty minutes in, Jack stood up. "This is dire. I'm going to call it a day."

"I might watch it for a bit longer."

"You said you hated these movies."

"I do usually, but this one isn't bad."

"I'll never understand you, Jill." He gave me a kiss. "Goodnight."

"Goodnight."

What Jack had said was true: The movie was beyond awful, but I'd spotted something that had caught my attention. Once I was sure Jack was upstairs, I made a phone call.

"Mad, it's me."

"Jill? You're lucky to have caught me. I was just about to turn in."

"Do you have that file with you? The one with the missing ghosts?"

"It's in the kitchen. Why?"

"Could you snap a few of the mugshots and send them over to me?"

"I already have digital versions of them. I can let you have all of them if you like. What do you want them for?"

"I'd rather not say just yet. Not until I've had the chance to check something."

"Okay. I'll ping them over to you in a few minutes."

Chapter 13

Jack had bought himself a new brand of muesli, and he was clearly excited at the prospect of his first bowlful.

"What time did you come to bed last night?" he said.

"Just before one o'clock."

"I thought you didn't like horror movies."

"I don't. I hate them."

"And yet you stayed up to watch the worst film I've seen in a very long time."

"I had my reasons."

"You fell asleep down here, didn't you? Go on, admit it."

"No, I didn't. I was helping Mad with something."

"Doing what, exactly?"

"When I was watching that movie, I recognised one of the ghosts."

"One of the actors, you mean?"

"That's just it. He isn't an actor—he's a real ghost."

"I don't understand."

"The other day, when I went over to Cakey C to check on your mother, I got talking to Mad. She mentioned that a lot of ghosts had disappeared from Ghost Town."

"Disappearing ghosts?" He laughed. "Isn't that what ghosts are supposed to do?"

"Hilarious. Anyway, they've been disappearing off the streets, and no one has any idea what's happened to them. When I watched that movie last night, I saw a face I recognised. It took me a while to work out where I knew him from, but then I remembered the photos that Mad had shown me."

"And he was one of them?"

"That's right, so after you'd gone to bed, I gave Mad a call, and she sent over photos of all the ghosts who have gone missing. And bingo! Another four of them were in that movie."

"Okay, so what does that mean?"

"I'm not entirely sure. Isn't that TV station relatively new?"

"Spooky TV? Yes, it's only been on air for a few weeks, but they already have a lot of new movies online."

"If my hunch is correct, they're able to produce the films much more cheaply than their competitors by using what is essentially slave labour."

"Are you saying the ghosts are being made to take part in the films against their will?"

"It's a definite possibility, so I need to speak to Mad to see how she wants to play this."

As Jack popped the first spoonful of the all-new sawdust into his mouth, there was a knock at the door.

"Morning, I have a letter for you." The man was wearing the uniform of Candlefield Special Delivery Services.

"Hello, again. Your name is on the tip of my tongue. Stream? No. Splash? No."

"It's Puddles."

"Of course it is. Sorry, it's been a while."

"There you go." He handed me the letter.

"Thanks. Nice to see you again, Puddles."

"Who was that?" Jack asked when I got back into the kitchen.

"Candlefield Special Delivery. He brought this for me." I tore open the envelope and took out the card inside. "Oh bum!"

"What is it?"

"It's from Belinda Cartwheel. An invitation to the next WOW event."

"I thought WOW stood for the Witches Of *Washbridge*?"

"It does."

"So how come it was delivered by Candlefield Special Delivery?"

"That's a good question. I assume Belinda must have posted it while she was in Candlefield."

"You don't seem very thrilled about the invitation."

"I'm not. Grandma has been bugging me to find out what Belinda is up to, but I've managed to fob her off so far. I guess I'll have to do something about it now."

"What does your grandmother think the woman is up to?"

"It appears she's trying to unseat Grandma from her position as chairman."

"Your grandmother won't like that."

"Tell me about it. I just wish they could sort it out between themselves, and not involve me."

"When is it?"

"Next Tuesday. At least it's not another beetle drive."

"Isn't that the game where they drive beetles around a racing track?"

Give me strength!

***

By the time we got to Kathy's house, the removal van had already arrived.

"You've made an early start!" Jack shouted.

"The removal men were here at seven." Kathy came

down the drive to meet us. "They haven't taken the kettle yet, so I can make you both a brew if you fancy one?"

"That's okay. We thought we might call somewhere on the way to the park, and pick up some breakfast," I said.

"What Jill means," Jack chipped in. "Is that *she* wants breakfast. I had muesli before we set off."

"Hey, you two." Peter came out of the house, clutching something in his hands. "Look what I've got."

"They're not interested in your silly seeds." Kathy sighed.

She had that at least fifty percent right.

"Where did you get those?" Jack, AKA the other fifty percent, enquired.

"A guy came to the door selling them last night. They were an absolute bargain."

"He's more excited about those stupid seeds than he is about the new house." Kathy rolled her eyes.

"Auntie Jill!" Lizzie came charging out of the house. "Uncle Jack!"

"Hello there, beautiful." I gave her a hug.

"Can we have a ride on the train?" Mikey had followed her outside. He clearly thought he was too old now for hugs and the like.

"We certainly can," Jack said. "The man in charge of the train lives near to us."

"Do you think he'll let me drive it?" Mikey said.

"No he won't!" Kathy stepped in. "Children aren't allowed to drive it."

"Aww!" Mikey scuffed his foot on the ground in protest. "That's not fair."

"Come on, everyone." I led Lizzie to the car. "Your mummy and daddy have lots to do. Let's go and get some breakfast."

While the kids and I tucked into pancakes, Jack pretended not to be hungry.

"Would you like a bite?" I waved one under his nose.

"No, thanks. I'm still full from the muesli."

"If you say so. Hey, kids, who's excited about sleeping in their new house tonight?"

"Me!" Lizzie screamed.

"What about you, Mikey?"

He shrugged. "I'd rather have a go-kart."

"Your new bedroom is much bigger, though, isn't it?"

He shrugged. "Ryan in my class has got a go-kart. It's wicked."

I hadn't been sure how many people would attend the model railway rally. If I'm honest, I'd half-expected it to be just a dozen or so men, dressed in anoraks.

Boy, was I wrong.

The rally had only been open for twenty minutes when we arrived, but already it was crowded, with queues at every turnstile.

"I didn't realise this would be so big." Jack looked out over the numerous marquees.

"When can we have a ride on the train, Auntie Jill?" Lizzie tugged at my hand.

"We'd better go and find it first."

In the centre of the park, surrounded by the marquees, were Mr Hosey and Bessie.

"Look at that queue," Jack said. "We'll be waiting for ages."

"Why don't I get in the queue and keep our place while you take the kids around the marquees?" I offered.

How selfless of me, I hear you say. Much as I'd like you to believe that, the truth was that I'd much rather stand in line, messing around on my phone, than have to look around a dozen marquees full of boring model trains. Plus, it was a beautiful day, so I had absolutely no desire to be inside those stuffy tents.

"Don't you mind, Jill?"

"Of course not. It's better than the kids having to spend hours in the queue. They'll get bored."

"Okay, if you're sure."

"Listen out for your phone. I'll text you when I'm near the front."

"Okay." He gave me a kiss, and then led the kids over to the nearest marquee.

Mr Hosey drove Bessie around the perimeter of the park, tooting his horn as he went. Each ride took approximately ten minutes. The cost of the ride was included in the admission price of the rally, so there was no shortage of customers queuing to go on Bessie.

Just over an hour later, I figured that I would be on the next ride. Thankfully, Jack had been monitoring his phone, so when I texted him, the three of them came hurrying to join me.

"What have you got there?" I pointed to the large box that Jack was holding under his arm.

"I treated myself to a model railway."

"You're kidding."

"I thought they looked like fun."

"Where are you going to put it?"

"There's plenty of room in the spare bedroom." He

lowered his voice to a whisper. "Since you shrank my furniture and gave it to Lizzie. When I've put it together, you can have a go on it if you like."

"Gee, thanks. I can hardly wait."

Mr Hosey was personally supervising the passengers as they climbed into the carriages. He'd started at the back of the train and was slowly working his way to the front.

"I want to drive it!" Mikey shouted.

"Don't be silly," I said. "You can't drive it."

We were almost at the front of the queue, and by my calculations, we would get seated in the front carriage.

"Stop!" Mr Hosey shouted. "You can't go in there!"

I turned around to see who he was shouting at, and to my horror, I saw Mikey climbing into the driver's cab.

"Mikey!" I yelled. "Get out of there, right now!"

To my horror, the engine sprang into life, and the train began to move away.

"Look, Auntie Jill." He leaned out of the cab window. "I'm driving it!"

"Stop it! Right now!"

I wasn't sure if he was ignoring me or he didn't know how. Either way, the train was headed down the park towards a line of trees. The kids onboard appeared to be enjoying the ride, but I could tell from the parents' expressions that they realised something was very wrong.

To make matters worse, the train was going much faster than when Mr Hosey had been driving it. At that pace, it would crash into the trees in less than a minute. I had to stop it.

But how?

I'd promised not to use magic in public, but this was an emergency if ever there was one. After casting the 'faster' spell, I set off in pursuit of the train, but I feared I'd left it too late. Even with the help of magic, I didn't think I would make it in time to prevent it crashing into the trees. A lot of people, including Mikey, were bound to be hurt. And then, Kathy would kill me.

With the train only yards from the trees, I closed my eyes and braced myself for the worst.

But nothing happened.

I'd expected a huge crash, but there was nothing. When I opened my eyes, I saw that the train had pulled up just short of the trees. Everyone was climbing out of the carriages: the parents wearing looks of relief, the kids whooping at the fun of it all.

Mikey was still seated in the driver's cabin.

"You!" I screamed at him. "Get out here! Now!"

"Sorry, Auntie Jill." He couldn't meet my eyes. "I didn't mean to do it. My foot caught the lever."

"Come here." I gave him a huge hug, out of sheer relief. "Thank goodness you managed to stop it."

"I didn't stop it. I didn't know how to."

"Oh?"

"Is everyone okay?" Mr Hosey came hurrying towards us. Jack and Lizzie were a few paces behind him.

"I think so. It's lucky the train stopped when it did though. It must have got caught up in the mud."

"No, that was me." Mr Hosey held out a small metal box. "I had this remote control made for just such emergencies."

"It was you who stopped it?"

"In the nick of time by the look of it."

"You need to put some kind of lock on the driver's cabin."

"Good suggestion, Jill. I'll get onto that."

While Mr Hosey went over to check on Bessie, Jack gave me a hug. "Are you okay?"

"Just about. I'm sorry about—err—you know."

"What do you mean?"

"I had to use magic," I whispered. "I thought it would help me to catch the train."

"Don't be silly. You had no other choice. I thought for a moment there that Mikey was a goner. We really ought to punish him for being so stupid."

"I know, but I'm just glad he's okay."

We spent another couple of hours (which felt more like two days) looking around the rally. By then, even the kids had had more than enough, and were ready to go home.

"We still have one marquee to look around," Jack said.

"I don't care. The kids have had enough, and I certainly have. Let's take them home."

"Okay. I suppose that'll give me time to make a start on my railway layout tonight."

"Whatever floats your boat. And don't forget you need to drive us to the new house."

By the time we arrived, the removal men had left, but Kathy and Peter still had a ton of unpacking to do.

"How was it, kids?" Kathy said.

"I drove a train." Mikey bounced into the house.

Kathy gave me a puzzled look.

"It's a long story. I'll tell you all about it another day."

"What about you, Pumpkin." Kathy ruffled Lizzie's hair. "Did you have fun?"

"It was okay, but it would have been better if there had

been dolls. It was just boring trains. I had a nice pancake, though. Can I go and see my new bedroom, Mummy?"

"Of course you can. Off you go." She turned to us. "Thanks, Jill, and you, Jack. I don't know how we would have managed if the kids had been under our feet."

"Where's Peter?" Jack asked.

"In the kitchen. He's making cocktails."

"*Cocktails*?"

"When we were unpacking, he found his old cocktail shaker. It hasn't been used for ten years to my knowledge. Why don't you go through? You'll be ready for a drink."

"Why not?" I figured I deserved one after the day I'd had.

"I'm driving," Jack frowned. "But I'll take a cola if you have one."

"Hey, you two." Peter was shaking the cocktail maker. "You're just in time for one of my specials. I call it the Pete Powerball."

"Sounds great."

"Look!" Kathy pointed to the glasses on the table. "We even found some old cocktail umbrellas."

Hmm. That had given me an idea.

Chapter 14

It was Sunday morning, and although I planned to work for part of the day, I'd assumed we would both enjoy a nice long lie-in.

Jack clearly had other ideas because when I opened my eyes at just after seven, I was all alone in the bed. I thought maybe he'd nipped to the bathroom, or he'd decided to treat me to breakfast in bed. Fifteen minutes later when he was still a no-show, I reluctantly climbed out from under the covers and went in search of him. I'd no sooner stepped onto the landing than I heard noises coming from the spare bedroom.

"Jack?"

"Morning. I thought I'd make an early start."

The floor was covered in small pieces of railway track.

"What time did you get up?"

"About six."

"You haven't made much progress."

"This stuff is more complicated than it looks. It's the signals which have me confused."

"I thought you'd got up to make me breakfast in bed."

"I would have, but I didn't want to wake you."

Yeah, right.

"I wouldn't say no to a coffee, though." He held a piece of track in each hand. "Would you say these look the same length?"

"It's no good asking me. My eyes can barely focus yet. I'll go and make coffee."

"A couple of slices of toast wouldn't go amiss." He gave me that smile of his—the one he thinks I can't resist.

The trouble is, he's right. More's the pity.

I sat on the windowsill in the spare bedroom, sipping coffee, and watching Jack trying to figure out which piece of track went where.

"You look like you need help."

"No, I don't. I've almost got it figured out."

"If you say so. I told you I'm going to be working part of today, didn't I?"

"Yes!" He punched the air. "That's one of the signals done. Sorry, what did you say?"

"Never mind. I'll see you later this afternoon."

I'd just about got used to the idea of being a ten-pin bowling widow, and a ukulele widow, but it seemed I was now a model train widow too. I really needed to get a hobby of my own. Something I could throw myself into with the same amount of enthusiasm that Jack did.

***

I was going to pay a visit to the two couples who had been at the caravan park at the same time as the Bells, but first I called in at The Corner Shop.

Little Jack was back behind the counter, and he seemed to have something of a spring in his step.

"Morning, Jill, what do you think of my new stilts? They have built-in springs which give me more bounce."

"Ah, that explains the spring in your step. They're very good, but don't they make it a little more difficult to get around?"

"Not now I'm used to them. I hope you aren't here to claim your steak and kidney pie. I'm afraid I've been cleared out of them."

"What went wrong with the scratch cards?"

"It was my own fault. I ordered them online, and it turned out the supplier was a bit dodgy. That'll teach me not to check the reviews first. If I had, I'd have seen he'd done the same thing before. I was lucky that it was only steak and kidney pies. One poor guy got a batch of cards where every one of the pictures was a bottle of champagne. It ended up costing him a small fortune."

"I assume you've stopped selling them now."

"Yes, lesson learned. What can I do for you today, Jill?"

"Actually, I have a rather unusual request."

"Fire away. I enjoy a challenge."

I explained to Little Jack what I needed, and although he was rather surprised, he seemed confident he'd be able to get hold of them by the following morning.

"Thanks, Jack. I'll call in tomorrow to collect them."

***

As my husband was likely to be occupied with his toy train for most of the day, I decided I'd take a leisurely drive rather than use magic. First stop was Mansfield, home of Paul and Sandra Nightingale. Their bungalow was in a cul-de-sac of identical properties.

Sandra was a fussy woman, who had a penchant for frogs. Not real ones, thankfully. The house was full of frog ornaments of all shapes and sizes.

"Wherever we go, I always buy a frog." Sandra handed me a cup of tea. "Interestingly, it all started at Filey, didn't it, Paul?"

"Mmm." He nodded.

"That's when Paul bought the first." She picked up a glass frog from the sideboard. "This is the one that started it all."

If Paul's expression was anything to go by, he regretted ever making that first purchase.

"Thank you for talking to me today. I wanted to ask you about the Bells. I believe you were in the next pitch to them?"

"That's right." It was clear that Sandra did most of the talking in that house. "A nice couple, weren't they, Paul?"

He nodded. A man of few words was Paul Nightingale.

"Did you get the chance to talk to the Bells much during your stay?"

"Yes, they were both very chatty, weren't they, Paul?" She didn't wait for him to reply before continuing. "In fact, we spent a couple of days together—the four of us."

"Doing what?"

"Nothing very exciting. We went for a walk and grabbed lunch one day. And on the day that they left, we'd been out for a drive. We offered to go in our car, but they insisted we take theirs, didn't they, Paul?"

Another nod.

"Did they act any differently on that last day?"

"Not really. They were pretty much the same as always. We went for a drive to Driffield, looked around for an hour or so, grabbed lunch at Wetherspoons, and then went back to the caravan park. Mind you, I didn't think that we were going to make it back."

"Why's that? Did the car break down?"

"No, but the petrol light was on most of the way back. I thought Walt would pull in and get some fuel, but he drove past three or four petrol stations. I was beginning to think he hadn't noticed the warning light, but when I pointed it out, he just laughed, and said that there was plenty of fuel left, and that he never took any notice of the red light. It turned out he was right because we made it back to the park okay."

"Presumably you said your goodbyes to them then?"

"Actually, no, but only because we had no idea that they planned to leave that night. They'd told us that they were going to stay the weekend and leave on Sunday night, so we were surprised when we got up on Saturday to find they'd left during the night."

"Didn't you hear them leave?"

"No, but then Paul is a very deep sleeper, and I always wear earplugs because of Paul's snoring."

When I left the Nightingales, both Sandra and Paul saw me to the door.

"Thank you for your time." I handed her my business card. "Please give me a call if you think of anything else that might help."

"We will."

On my way out, I spotted a small silver cup, standing amongst the frogs.

Sandra must have seen me looking at it because she remarked, "That's Paul's. He came first in the annual competition at his debating club."

Now I was the one who was speechless.

***

From Mansfield, I headed to Newark, which was only about a forty-minute drive. I had plenty of time, and I was starting to feel quite peckish, so I pulled into a roadside diner called Skates.

The first thing I noticed when I stepped inside was the temperature. Someone had clearly gone a little crazy with the aircon because it was freezing in there.

"Wait there, please!" shouted a young woman, dressed in a blue and white striped top and a short blue skirt.

I did as she said, and then watched as she glided over to me.

"Welcome to Skates." She glanced at my feet. "Did you bring your own?"

"Sorry?"

"Do you have your own skates, or would you like to borrow some?"

Only then, did I realise that she was wearing skates. And not roller skates, but ice skates.

"Actually, I was just hoping to grab something to eat."

"That's fine. Take my hand."

I did as she said, and she helped me across the floor, which I now realised was one large ice rink.

Once we reached the safety of a booth, she kept hold of me until I was safely seated.

"Take a look at the menu, and I'll be back in a few minutes to take your order."

"Okay, thanks."

I found it quite difficult to focus on the menu because someone was performing toe-loops only feet from my table.

My waitress returned a few minutes later. "Are you ready to order?"

"I think I'll have the Lutz burger, please."

"And to drink?"

"I don't see any hot drinks on here?"
"That's because we don't serve them. People kept spilling them and melting the ice."
"In that case I'll have the Lasso strawberry milkshake."
The food was surprisingly good, but the experience was marred a little when someone failed to land a triple salchow. Bravely, he managed a smile as the paramedics stretchered him away.

***

Esme and John James also lived in a bungalow. Theirs, however, was not cluttered with ornamental frogs. In fact, there wasn't a single frog to be seen.
Cheese, though, that was a different matter. The whole house reeked of cheese, and the first thing Mr James said when I walked through the door was, "Would you care for some cheese?"
"I'm—err—okay, thanks."
"Excellent." After taking me through to the dining room, he scurried away and returned moments later with a cheeseboard.
I can take or leave cheese, and when I do partake, it's usually cheddar, or if I'm feeling particularly adventurous, Brie. I'd certainly never seen anything quite like the eclectic selection that was now being offered to me.
"What kind of cheese is that?"
"Yak."
"What about that one?"
"Casu Marzu."
"What are those white things?" I flinched. "Are they—

?"

"Maggots? Yes."

"Do you think I could possibly have a biscuit instead?"

"Are you sure you wouldn't like to try any of these?"

"Positive, thanks."

"Very well." Clearly disappointed, he took away the cheese (and maggots). When he returned, he had a packet of biscuits (cheese, naturally) and he was accompanied by his wife.

"Jill, this is Esme." He handed me the packet of biscuits.

"It's very nice to meet you, Esme."

She may have spoken, but it came out as a squeak.

We took our seats around the dining table. Paul at one end, facing me. Esme seated to one side, picking at the pocket of her apron.

"Thank you both for sparing me your time today. I believe you were at the Cliffs Caravan Park at the same time as Walter and Jean Bell."

"That's right, but we were only there until the Tuesday, weren't we, Esme?"

She nodded.

He continued, "We had to leave to attend the Cheese Appreciator's annual awards ceremony, didn't we, Esme?" Another nod from his wife. "I was presented with the Big Cheese award for the second year in a row, wasn't I, Esme?"

She didn't respond at all this time. Presumably, she was all nodded out.

"I understand that you've known the Bells for some time?" I said.

"We have indeed." Paul was nibbling on a piece of cheese. "It must be fifteen years now."

"Did you first meet them at the Cliffs?"

"Yes. We go back there most years, don't we, Esme?"

"Always the same week as the Bells?"

"Not always, but most years."

"How would you say they seemed this year?"

"A little subdued, I'd say, wouldn't you, Esme?"

She nodded.

"Do you have any idea why that might have been?"

He thought about it for a moment. "Nothing I could put my finger on. Although, now I come to think about it, Walt did say something about their son, err—"

"Adam."

"Yes. I got the impression that there had been some conflict between them, but Walt didn't elaborate."

"But you say they seemed quiet?"

"Yes, when I was telling them about my Big Cheese award, I could sense their attention was elsewhere."

"Did they happen to mention how long they intended to stay at the Cliffs?"

"I understood they were going to stay until the Sunday."

"And yet, they left on the Friday night. Don't you find that a little strange?"

"Very, but then the whole thing is rather odd. Do you think something happened to them?"

"That's what I'm hoping to find out."

On my way out, I noticed a small silver plaque in a glass cabinet.

"Did you win that for debating?" I asked Esme.

She gave me a puzzled look but said nothing.

"That's my Big Cheese award," Paul corrected me.

My discussions with the Jameses and the Nightingales had revealed very little. The only thing I'd learned for sure was that both couples had believed the Bells had intended to stay at the Cliffs until the Sunday. What had triggered their change of heart? Why had they suddenly upped and left on the Friday night? According to the Nightingales, the Bells had been in good spirits. Paul James, though, had insisted they'd been subdued and distracted, but that could easily have been a reaction to his boring cheese-related monologue.

***

Unbelievably, when I arrived home, Jack was still upstairs in the spare bedroom.

"You can't possibly still be working on that?"

"There's a piece of track missing. Look!" He pointed to the rail track that now covered over half of the bedroom floor.

"Does it matter?"

"Of course it matters. Watch."

He grabbed a small controller, flipped the switch, and one of the small engines began to trundle slowly around the track. At least, it did until it reached the point where the missing track should have been. Then it derailed and flipped onto its side.

"Is it meant to do that?" I grinned.

"Of course it isn't. I've been swindled."

"What are you going to do?"

"It's okay. I called Mr Hosey earlier. He's going to pop around in a few minutes. He reckons he'll be able to find me a section of track to fill the gap."

"You've asked Hosey to come around here? Are you insane?"

"What else could I do? Oh, and there's something else too."

"What?"

"I kind of suggested he could join us for dinner."

Chapter 15

"How many times do I have to say I'm sorry?" Jack looked at me across the kitchen table. "I made you a fry-up, isn't that enough to get you to forgive me?"

"Not even close. You inflicted Mr Hosey on me for four hours last night. Not just one hour. Not two. Not even three. *Four* whole hours. That's two-hundred and forty minutes. Or fifteen thousand seconds."

"Fourteen-thousand, four hundred, actually."

"Shut up!"

"Sorry. How was I supposed to know he'd stay so long?"

"You invited him for dinner."

"I was just being polite."

"What have I told you about being polite? It's asking for trouble. And did you see the way he eats? Yuk! The man was talking all the time—I could see every mouthful. It turned my stomach."

"He did come up with the missing piece of track for me, though."

"It wasn't worth the sacrifice."

"What can I do to make it up to you?"

"I haven't decided yet. You owe me big time for this, Jack. You have to promise that you'll never invite him over here again."

"Actually—"

"What?"

"He said he'd like to come and see my railway, once I've got it all set up."

"That's just great. I'll expect plenty of warning so that I can make myself scarce."

"Where will you go?"

"Anywhere. Just so long as I don't have to be under the same roof as that man."

Last night had been a whole new level of purgatory. Not only did Hosey have disgusting eating habits, but he had the ability to speak non-stop about trains for hours on end. By the time he left, my brain had turned to mush. The experience had seriously tested my resolve not to use magic in anger. How I'd resisted the temptation to turn him into a bug, and then squash him under foot, is nothing short of a miracle.

***

Even though Little Jack had said he'd be able to fulfil my rather unusual order, I'd had my doubts, but he'd come through for me, big time.

"Thanks, Jack, you're a star."

"My pleasure, Jill. Would you like me to help you take those boxes to your car?"

"It's okay." I lifted all three. "They're not very heavy. Thanks again."

From The Corner Shop, I headed straight to Washbridge Park. At that time of the morning, it was pretty much deserted apart from the occasional dog walker.

Being careful not to squash any of the dandelions, I put the three boxes on the grass. After opening one of them, and taking out a couple of samples, I shrank myself.

"Bill! Ben! Are you there?"

There was no answer, and I wondered if maybe I'd called too early in the day. Perhaps the Tye and Nees were late risers.

"Jill?" Ben yawned. His heavy eyes suggested I'd just woken him. "Good morning."

"Hi. I'm sorry if I woke you."

"It's okay. I was about to get up anyway."

"Morning, Jill!" Bill came to join us." He too looked half asleep.

"I have something to show you." I brought my hands out from behind my back.

"What are those?" Ben said.

"Umbrellas." I put one up and handed it to him. "And there's one for you, Bill."

"These are fantastic." Ben twirled the umbrella around and around.

"And so colourful." Bill looked equally impressed.

"Will you be able to use these instead of treating the dandelions with SlowGrowth?"

"Definitely." Ben nodded. "But we'll need a lot of them."

"I have two-thousand with me today, and I can get more if you need them."

"That should be more than enough. How can we ever thank you, Jill?"

"You can start by neutralising the SlowGrowth that you've already spread on the dandelions."

"No problem. We'll get straight onto it."

"Do either of you have a phone?" I asked.

"Of course. Who doesn't have one these days?"

"I'll give you my number. If you need any more umbrellas, just give me a call."

"What about the cost of these?" Bill said. "You have to let us reimburse you."

"You have money, too?"

"Of course we do. How else would we have bought the phones? Will this be enough?" He reached inside his pocket and brought out a wad of banknotes.

"That's way too much."

"Hold the rest on account for us. That way, when we do need more umbrellas, you'll already have the cash."

"Okay, thanks."

After saying my goodbyes to Bill and Ben, I reflected on how curious it was that the Tye and Nees should have phones and cash, and yet have never heard of umbrellas. There wasn't time to dwell on that, though, because I needed to pay a visit to the Oxford Botanical Gardens.

"Good morning, Jill," Tingle said. I'd called her earlier to say I'd be coming over.

"Morning, Tingle."

"Her Royal Dandelion is expecting you. Would you follow me, please?"

As I sat and chatted to the queen, dandelion tea and cake were once again the order of the day.

"And you say they're called Tinys?" Dandy took a small bite of cake.

"Actually, there are two separate—err—tribes, I suppose you'd call them. There are the Tyes and then there are the Nees. They look very different, but they do seem to live alongside one another."

"Interesting. And you're sure we won't have any more issues with them?"

"I don't think so. The cocktail umbrellas seem to have done the trick."

"All the good things I heard about you are true, Jill." She picked up a small silver bell and rang it.

Almost immediately, Tingle came rushing into the room. "You rang, Your Dandelion?"

"Bring me the gift, would you?"

"Of course, Your Dandelion." Tingle scurried out, and returned moments later with a small gift-wrapped box, which she handed to the queen.

"Thank you, Tingle. That will be all." The queen handed the present to me. "This is just a little something to show our gratitude."

"There really was no need for you to do that."

"There was every need. Open it, please."

Inside was a beautiful necklace with links in the shape of tiny dandelions.

"It's beautiful, thank you."

"I'm glad you like it. I designed it myself. I should also mention that it comes with three wishes."

"Really?"

"Yes, but I must urge caution in their use because these necklaces are ultra-sensitive. If they hear the words *I wish*, they will react immediately, so be very careful what you say out loud."

"Okay. I will. Thanks again."

How very kind of the queen. Not only was it a beautiful necklace, but I also had three wishes. All I had to do now was to decide what I should use them for.

Decisions, decisions.

***

Mrs V was busy at work on her computer.

"Morning, Jill."

"Hi. Did you come to any decision about the house?"

"I didn't, I'm afraid. *I wish* I could make my mind up."

I almost jumped out of my skin as the dandelion necklace began to vibrate. Fortunately, it stopped as quickly as it had started. All very weird.

"That's it!" Mrs V announced. "I've decided. We're going to buy the cuckoo house."

"You are? I thought you weren't sure."

"I am now. There's no doubt in my mind."

"Good for you."

There was no sign of Winky, but there were some strange mechanical noises coming from behind the screen.

"Winky? Is that you behind there? What are you up to?"

"I'm busy."

I didn't like the sound of that. Given recent events (for which, read: zip wires and tunnelling machines), I didn't feel comfortable not knowing what he was up to, so I took a peek behind the screen.

"What's that?"

"It's a printing press."

"What's it doing in here?"

"Don't you have some work you should be doing? I'm up against a deadline here."

"A deadline for what?" I walked around the machine to find out what he was printing. "Love Your Cat greetings cards? I should have known! I didn't think I'd heard of it before. You invented the whole thing, didn't you?"

"I'm only looking after the interests of my fellow felines."

"Don't give me that rubbish. You've done this so you can sell these overpriced cards. You must be making a small fortune."

"A *big* fortune, actually. At least, I would be if I could get them printed quicker." He kicked the printing press. "This thing is just too slow. I'll never have them all printed in time. *I wish* it would go ten times faster."

The necklace vibrated again. What was wrong with the stupid thing? This was starting to freak me out.

"Yes!" Winky punched the air. "That's what I'm talking about."

It took me a moment to figure out what had caused him to get so excited, but then I realised the printing press was now churning out the cards much faster. He must have found a way to adjust the speed.

I'd no sooner taken a seat at my desk than Harold appeared on the window ledge. "Morning, Jill."

"Morning, Harold." I crossed my fingers and asked, "How was the cake?"

"Very nice, thanks. Ida really enjoyed it. I think I must be losing my marbles, though."

"Why do you say that?"

"I could have sworn I'd ordered a sponge cake, but it turned out to be fruit."

"Oh? You must have been mistaken."

"It wouldn't be the first time." He shivered.

"Are you okay?"

"Yeah, I'm just a little cold. *I wish* the sun would come out for a change."

The stupid necklace vibrated again. I couldn't possibly live with this—it was way too distracting, so I slipped it off my neck.

When I turned back to speak to Harold, he was basking in the sun, which had just broken through the clouds. "This is more like it. I'll go and see if Ida fancies a trip out somewhere. Bye, Jill."

"Bye."

"What's that ugly thing you're holding?" Winky said.

"It's a necklace. It was a present from the dandelion fairies."

"It looks like it just fell out of a lucky bag."

"I think it's pretty."

"So why aren't you wearing it?"

"It keeps vibrating."

"It's probably radioactive."

"Don't be stupid. I'll have you know that this can grant me three wishes."

"And I have a goldmine you can buy a part-share in if you're interested."

"It's true. I'll prove it to you."

"Go on, then."

"What should I wish for? I know: a year's supply of custard creams."

"Is that the best you can come up with? You can wish for anything in the world, and you choose custard creams? Pathetic."

"It's only the first wish. It'll be like a test run. I can use the other two for something more meaningful."

"Okay, go on." He sighed. "It's not like it's going to work anyway."

"You'll see." I gripped the necklace tightly, and said, "I wish for a year's supply of custard creams."

Nothing happened.

"Three wishes?" Winky laughed. "They saw you coming, didn't they?"
"Maybe it takes a while for the wish to be processed."
"Sure."
I waited, but five minutes later, there was still no sign of my custard creams.
"Maybe I have to be wearing it for it to work?" I put the necklace back around my neck. "I wish for a year's supply of custard creams."
Nothing! Not so much as a crumb.
"Entertaining as this is, I have cards to print." Winky disappeared back behind the screen.
How very disappointing. I'd totally believed Dandy when she'd said the necklace would grant me three wishes. It just goes to show you can't trust anyone these days.

***

I'd heard from more than one source that there had been some friction between the Bells and their son, Adam. That didn't necessarily mean he'd had anything to do with his parents' disappearance, but it was worth further investigation, so I'd arranged to meet with his sister, Katie. Hopefully, by speaking to her alone, I'd get a better picture of the relationship between her sibling and their parents.
I'd barely got through the door of her apartment, which she shared with a single flatmate, before she was demanding answers.
"Do you have any news about Mum and Dad?"
"I'm afraid not."

"Nothing at all?"

"Not really."

"Why didn't you want Adam to be here today?"

"Could we have a seat, and I'll explain everything."

"Sorry, yes, come through to the lounge. Milly is out."

"That's your flatmate?"

"Yeah. Do you want anything to drink?"

"No, thanks. Look, Katie, this isn't easy for me to ask, and I don't want you to read too much into it, but what kind of relationship does Adam have with your parents?"

"Has someone been saying something about him?"

"Do you and he both get on well with them?"

"I guess I've always been closer to them than Adam."

"Had there been any kind of falling out between him and your parents just before their disappearance?"

She looked as though she was going to say something but then changed her mind.

"It's important you tell me everything, Katie."

"Adam had had a few money problems. Several of his credit cards were maxed out."

"Did he ask your parents for help?"

"Yeah. He seemed to think they should bail him out. They had done a few times before, but—" her words trailed away.

"Katie? Did they refuse to help him this time?"

"Yes. Dad said he had to learn to stand on his own two feet. There was a massive bust up over it."

"When was this, exactly?"

"About a week before they disappeared."

"Right."

"Adam didn't have anything to do with their disappearance if that's what you're thinking. He would

never do anything to hurt them."
"Whose idea was it to come and see me?"
"Err, both of us."
"One of you must have floated the idea initially."
"Adam did."
"What reason did he give?"
"He wanted to find Mum and Dad obviously."
"Okay." I could see she was getting upset. "Thanks."

Although I hadn't said this to Katie, there was another reason why Adam might have wanted to hire me. Perhaps he'd hoped that my investigation would provide the necessary proof to declare his parents dead. If that happened, he and Katie would no doubt stand to inherit their estate.

Chapter 16

I fancied coffee and cake, so I magicked myself over to Cuppy C, but I was out of luck because the shop was full to bursting. What was going on? Were the twins running some kind of promotion? They hadn't mentioned anything to me about it. Even if I'd been prepared to hang around long enough to get served, there would have been no chance of getting a seat, so I bailed and took a walk over to Aunt Lucy's.

There was something very weird going on. Everywhere I looked, people were out on the streets in numbers, and there seemed to be a general carnival atmosphere about the place. Was today some kind of public holiday? If so, no one had bothered to send me the memo.

"Hi, Aunt Lucy, it's only me."

"We're in the kitchen, Jill!"

We? Hopefully, she meant herself and Lester.

No such luck!

"Hello, Grandma."

"If it isn't my sleuthing granddaughter. I assume you're here to give me your report on Belinda Cartwheel?"

"Err, no, I didn't even realise you were here." If I had, wild horses wouldn't have dragged me there.

"What exactly am I paying you for?"

"You aren't paying me. As a matter of fact, I've just received an invitation from Belinda to attend a function at her house. Hopefully, I'll have something to report afterwards."

"I sincerely hope so. At this rate, I'll have retired from WOW before that woman gets the chance to oust me."

"Would you like a drink, Jill?" Aunt Lucy said.

"Yes, please. A cup of tea would be nice. I called in at Cuppy C, but it's packed in there. Is something happening in Candlefield today? All the streets are full of people, and they seem to be celebrating something."

"I take it you haven't heard the news?" Grandma said.

"What news? What's happened?"

"Braxmore is dead."

"How do you know?"

"The fact that his body was found in the marketplace was kind of a clue."

"Here in Candlefield? When?"

"Last night."

"Are they sure it's him?"

"It's ninety-nine percent certain. They're doing a few final tests, apparently."

"How did he die?"

"No one knows, and from the look of it, no one cares." Aunt Lucy passed me the tea. "Would you like something with that? I made some cupcakes yesterday."

"Do you really need to ask her?" Grandma rolled her eyes. "Have you ever known her to refuse cake?"

Ignoring the jibe, I took a moment to decide between the various flavours. In the end, I plumped for the lemon.

"You haven't forgotten that it's Barry's competition on Wednesday, have you, Jill?" Aunt Lucy said.

"I've been trying to. Are you sure you wouldn't like to go in my place?"

"Obviously, I'd love to, but I'm going to bingo."

"*Bingo*? I thought you said it was a whist drive."

"Did I say bingo? I meant whist drive."

Wow, she was such a terrible liar.

"It looks like it's down to me, then. How's his dancing

coming along?"

"I don't know. Barry won't let me watch him practising. He insists it would be bad luck. I can tell you one thing, though, I won't be sorry to hear the last of that music. I'm all discoed out."

"I can't hear anything up there at the moment."

"Hmm, there's a reason for that." Aunt Lucy shot Grandma a look. "Isn't there, Mother?"

"What did you do, Grandma?"

"I'm too old to have to listen to that awful noise, so I put that soft dog and his little friend to sleep for a while."

"That's a horrible thing to do."

"You should be thanking me for stopping that terrible racket. Anyway, I have something I want to show you."

"It's not made from wax, is it?"

"No. It's under here." She began to unbutton her cardigan.

"What are you doing? You can't strip off in here!"

"Don't get your knickers in a twist." She pulled the cardigan open. "Look!"

"Is that—?" I stared in disbelief at the t-shirt. "That's me on there, isn't it?"

"They were selling them off cheaply on the market. Five for a tenner."

"Why do I have a moustache in that picture?"

"I think it kind of suits you. That wasn't the only thing they were selling. There was all kinds of stuff."

"With my picture on it?"

"Yeah, complete with the moustache. I've got a mug back at the office."

"Great." I drank the last of my tea. "I'm going to have words about this."

"Jill!" Grandma called after me. "If they have any of those tea towels left, get one for me, would you?"

It took me much longer than usual to get to the marketplace because there were now even more people on the streets. Once there, though, it didn't take long to find the stall I was looking for.

"Excuse me!" I tried to catch the eye of the stallholder, but it wasn't easy because he was doing a roaring trade.

"Yes, love. What can I get for you? If you're after one of the t-shirts, you'd better look sharp. I only have a few left."

"Do you recognise me?"

"I—err—I don't think so. Are you the woman from the tripe shop?"

"No, I'm not! That's me on the t-shirts, and the towels, and the mugs, and—"

"Well I never. So it is. I didn't recognise you without the moustache. When did you shave it off?"

"I didn't shave it off. I've never had one."

"Oh?" He scratched his head. "Did you wear a false one when you posed for this photo?"

"No, I didn't. Someone must have added the moustache. How come you've got all of these, anyway?"

"It's not my normal line. I usually sell decorative boomerangs, but I was offered these at a fantastic price, so I figured why not? The boomerang business has been very slow lately, but it's bound to bounce back eventually. In the meantime, this has proved to be a nice little earner."

"I'm very pleased for you, but where did you get these from?"

"I don't suppose it will do any harm to tell you now. It's

a one-off deal anyway. Do you know that shop near the rescue centre?"

"Candlefield Icons?"

"Yeah, that's the one. The owner approached a few of us here on the market to see if we'd be interested. I took one look and snapped up the lot. Are you sure you wouldn't like a towel? What about a mouse mat?"

"No, thanks."

"Here." He handed me a handkerchief. "You can have this for free."

Before I could tell him where he could shove his hanky, he'd moved on to serve another customer.

How dare Songspinner put a moustache on my photograph?

It took me ages to fight my way through the crowds in the market, and I was still seething when I burst into Candlefield Icons where Vannie was pricing up a consignment of Magna Mondale mugs.

"Is he in?" I demanded.

"Hello again. Sylvester? No, I haven't seen him for a couple of days."

Vannie was sporting an ensemble similar to the one she'd worn on my previous visit. Today, though, the tutu was blue, the tights green, and the DMs white.

"I don't suppose you know how I can get hold of him?"

"Sorry, no. Is this about the—" She ran a finger under her nose.

"*Moustache*? Yes, it most certainly is."

"I told him you wouldn't be very happy about it, but he wasn't in the mood to listen. He was really angry. He kept saying something about—err—royalty, I think."

"Royalties."

"Yeah, that was it. He said he wasn't paying royalties to anyone. He got me to move all of your stuff into the back."

"I can understand him clearing it out of here, but why add the moustache?"

"He said no one would recognise you that way."

"The man's an imbecile. How did he add the moustaches?"

"I don't know. I think he used magic, but he was by himself in the back when he did it. He sold it all as a job-lot to someone, but I don't know who."

"The next time you see Mr Songspinner, will you give him a message for me?"

"Sure."

"Tell him not to buy any green bananas."

***

I'd carried out some research into Frank Royston, the generous benefactor of the Washbridge Penguins. He was a multi-millionaire who had made his money from a chain of furniture stores. The head office, plus the chain's first-ever store, were based in Washbridge. Although I'd found a number of articles about Royston's business, there had been precious little coverage of the man himself. Apparently, Frank Royston did not court publicity. Undeterred, I figured Royston would probably be willing to spare me some of his time once he knew it was about his beloved Penguins.

I was wrong. Despite numerous calls, I couldn't get past his many gatekeepers.

"But I've been hired by Victor Duyew, the Penguins' manager, to try to find—"

"Yes, and as I've already told you, I've explained that to Mr Royston, but he still isn't able to spare you any time. I'm very sorry."

"But, if I could just—"

I was wasting my breath because the gatekeeper had already hung up.

I wasn't defeated just yet, though. Maybe, if I could speak to some of Royston's employees, that might throw more light on the top man. Getting to speak to someone in the busy head office might prove problematic, so I decided to start with the furniture store.

Over the years, I'd bought my fair share of furniture, so how come I'd never come across Royston Furniture Superstores? The answer soon became apparent—its location on one of the older, run-down retail parks was doing it no favours. At least half of the other units were vacant, and the car park was less than ten percent full.

The shop was deserted except for a solitary middle-aged man who scrambled to put on his jacket when I entered the store.

"Good morning, madam."

"Afternoon."

"Is it?" He glanced at his watch. "Goodness me."

Under other circumstances, I might have assumed he'd been so busy that he'd lost track of time, but judging by his dishevelled hair, I was more inclined to think that he'd been asleep.

"I'm Richard." He adjusted his tie. "Are you looking for anything in particular today? Sofas? Beds? Carpets, maybe?"

"Actually, I'm not here to buy anything."

"Oh." I could practically hear his heart sinking.

"I wonder if I could ask you a few questions about the owner, Frank Royston."

"You can ask, but you'd be wasting your time. I know nothing about him."

"You've met him, though?"

"No." He smiled. "I hardly move in the same circles as Royston."

"But he must have visited the store?"

"No, he never has."

"How long have you worked here?"

"Fifteen years."

"And he's never once visited this store in all that time?"

"Nope."

"Wow!" I glanced around. "Quiet day you're having."

"This is pretty much normal."

"What about weekends? It must be busier then?"

"A little. Some weeks. But not always."

"It must be boring."

"It is, believe me. If I was younger, I'd look for another job, but—" He shrugged. "I reckon I've left it too late."

"Thank you for your time, Richard."

"My pleasure. Are you sure there's nothing that takes your fancy?"

The more I learned about Frank Royston, the less sense it made. The man had spent a small fortune on a stadium for a junior football team, which he appeared to take little or no interest in.

If this store's performance was indicative of the rest of his retail operation, he was in big trouble. But maybe this was an isolated case. After all, this store had been the first one he'd opened, so maybe he only kept it open because it had a special place in his heart. The newest store in the chain opened two years ago in Leeds. I felt sure that store would be doing much better than the one in Washbridge.

I was wrong.

The solitary salesman in the Leeds branch was called Stephen and was bald. His experience and story were practically the same as Richard's. Once again, I was the only customer in the store.

"And you say it's always as quiet as this?" I said.

"Yeah. Week in week out."

"What do you put that down to? It can't be the location."

The Leeds store was on a newer, much busier retail park.

"I shouldn't be saying this, but it's the prices. Just look at this sofa for example."

"Wow, you weren't joking." The sofa in question was nothing special. "No one is going to pay that kind of money for that."

"Tell me about it. Even when we do get customers through the door, they take one look at the prices, and leave."

"I assume you've given feedback to your head office."

"I used to, but I soon realised they didn't want to know. The prices never changed. It's almost like they don't want to sell anything."

"What about the man himself? Frank Royston? What's his reaction when he visits the store?"

"Royston, come here?" Stephen snorted with laughter. "He's never set foot through that door all the time I've worked here."

"Which is how long?"

"Almost eight years."

"Do you ever talk to the managers at any of the other stores?"

"Yeah, most weeks."

"Do you get the impression that any of their stores are faring better? Could it just be that this is still a relatively new store?"

"It's not that. All the other managers tell exactly the same story: Anaemic sales due to overpricing."

"Do you recall anyone saying that Royston had visited their store?"

"No. If he has, then no one has ever mentioned it to me."

Chapter 17

I gave Mad a call.

"Where are you, Mad?"

"In my apartment. I have to stay in because the carpet man is coming."

"Is he like some kind of superhero?"

"I wish. He's going to fit a new bedroom carpet. I thought you might have called me back about those photos I sent over to you."

"Sorry, I've been crazy busy, but that's why I'm calling now. Can I pop over?"

"Sure, I could do with the company."

"Okay, see you in ten."

When I arrived at Mad's apartment block, there was a van parked close to the main entrance. The sign on the side of it read Hush Carpets. Was someone winding me up? That was practically the same name as the one I'd made up for Mrs V's benefit.

"Hey, Jill, you spend more time here than I do."

"Hi, Charlie. I'm just on my way to see Mad."

"Are you still doing that private investigator stuff?"

"For my sins, yeah."

"A friend of mine has been having a few problems recently, so I mentioned your name to him, and I told him that he should think about contacting you."

"What kind of problems?"

"He runs his own business here in Washbridge: singing telegrams, that kind of thing. He suspects that one of his competitors has been trying to sabotage him."

"Okay, well, if he does need my help, you know where I

am."

"Thanks."

"The carpet man is here," Mad said, as she let me in. "He arrived a few minutes ago."

"Hi!" The ginger-haired man nodded at me.

"Hush Carpets? That's kind of a strange name, isn't it?"

"It's named after me. I'm Tony Hush."

"I'd keep quiet about that if I were you." I laughed.

"Sorry?"

"Take no notice of her," Mad said. "She has a weird sense of humour."

"Okay, anyway, I'd best get started." He headed towards the bedroom.

"Mad, I'm sorry I haven't been back to you before now, but things have been a little crazy."

"No problem. Did the photos I sent across help?"

"They certainly did. Let's take a seat at the table, and I'll show you." I took out my phone. "I think I know where at least some of these missing persons are. Him, him, her, him and her were all in a movie called The House On Gravestone Hill."

"*Movie*? I don't understand."

"There's a new TV channel that started up recently. I wouldn't have known anything about it if it hadn't been for Jack. He's pretty much obsessed with it."

"And this film, Gravestone Whatever, was on this new channel?"

"That's right. The TV station is called Spooky TV. The only thing they show is horror movies. Jack talked me into watching one on Friday night. It was terrible, and I was on the point of going to bed when I spotted a face I recognised. It was one of the ghosts in the photos you'd shown me. That's when I called you. There were five of them in that single movie."

"What does that mean? That they've all quit GT to seek fame and fortune in the movie business?"

"That's one possibility, I suppose, but I doubt it. I don't imagine Spooky TV has much of a budget to make the movies they're producing, so it's much more likely that they've come up with a way to do things on the cheap. Instead of paying actors, I believe they're snatching people off the streets of GT, and forcing them to take part in their terrible movies."

"Human trafficking? Is that what you're suggesting, Jill?"

"Strictly speaking, I suppose it's *ghost* trafficking, but yes, that's what it amounts to."

"The lowlife slime balls!" Mad spat the words.

"Pretty much."

"I need to find out who's behind this, rescue the ghosts they're holding, and then put the lowlifes behind bars."

"I've been giving that some thought, and I've come up with an idea if you're interested."

"Of course. Fire away."

After I'd explained what I had in mind, Mad declared herself one-hundred percent behind my plan, and she was able to provide me with the equipment I needed to put phase one into action.

***

I'd arranged to meet the colonel in Cakey C.

Yvonne was busy behind the counter, and she appeared

to be much more confident now with the coffee machine.

"Hi, Jill, what can I get for you?"

"I'll pay for these," the colonel insisted.

"Thanks, I'll have a latte, please."

"And something to eat?"

"No, thanks. Just the drink will be fine. Why don't you grab a table, Colonel, and I'll bring the drinks over?"

"Will do. I'll be over there by the window."

"Did you tell Jack why I hadn't been in touch?" Yvonne handed me the drinks.

"I did, yes. He was rather surprised to hear you were working in a tea room."

"I'm rather surprised myself, but now that I've mastered that machine, I'm actually quite enjoying it. It's nice to get out and meet more people. I'll still be able to chat to Jack in the evenings, provided I can stay awake long enough because after a shift here, I'm usually dead on my feet. *Dead on my feet*, get it?" She laughed.

I could see now where her son had got his terrible sense of humour from.

"Yeah, that's—err—anyway, I'll let Jack know what's happening."

"I thought Priscilla might have joined us." I handed the colonel his drink.

"It's her day for basket weaving."

"I didn't realise she was into that."

"Oh yes. To the point of obsession." He grinned. "We can barely move in our house for baskets. Still, she really enjoys it and that's all that matters. I'm quite intrigued to know why you wanted to see me. You said something about movies?"

"It's related to the movie business, but more importantly, it involves ghost trafficking."

"A despicable practice. I hoped we'd seen the last of that."

"Unfortunately not."

I told the colonel about Spooky TV and my suspicions that ghosts were being snatched from GT, and made to work in low-budget, straight-to-streaming horror movies.

"I saw at least five ghosts on Mad's missing persons list in a single movie."

"That's terrible. What can I do to help?"

"I need to find out where the people behind this are operating from. To find out where they are making these movies."

"It's in the human world, I assume?"

"I'm pretty sure it is. The problem is there's no easy way to track them down—that's why I need your help." I took out the small components that Mad had given to me.

"What are those?" the colonel studied them carefully.

"Tracking devices. It isn't easy for me to ask this, but essentially, I need volunteers who are prepared to put themselves in harm's way. Normally, I wouldn't dream of asking anyone to do that, but I can't think of any other way to find the missing persons."

"What exactly do you need them to do?"

"I'm hoping that some of the people on your books will be prepared to wear these devices, and then deliberately put themselves in a position where there's a strong likelihood that they may be snatched by the traffickers. We know the area where they generally operate, and that they usually snatch their victims in the early hours of the morning, so there's a good chance it could work."

"That's a lot to ask."

"I know, and I wish there was another way."

"Don't worry. Once my people have heard what's happening, I'm sure you'll get a few volunteers."

"There is of course no guarantee that the traffickers will take the bait, but we have to give it a try."

"Let me have those." He took the tracking devices. "As soon as I get back to the office, I'll put the word out, and ask for volunteers. I'll let you know how I get on."

***

I'd no sooner magicked myself back to the human world than I received a call from Myrtle Turtle.

"Jill, can you talk, or have I caught you at a bad time?"

"It's okay. Go ahead."

"Do you remember when you were over here recently that I mentioned the problem with the church bells?"

"I do, yes. Didn't you say they needed replacing?"

"That's right, but we've had an expert take a look at them, and he reckons they can be restored for a fraction of the price of new ones."

"That's good news, isn't it?"

"It is indeed, and it's inspired us to mount a big push to raise the necessary funds. Which brings me onto the reason for my call."

"I'm a bit short at the moment, but I suppose I could let you have a few quid."

"I'm not after a donation."

"Oh?"

"We're having a fundraiser this Saturday, and I wondered if you and your husband might like to come over. All of your friends and relatives are welcome too. Everyone in the village is phoning around, trying to drum up interest, so I thought I should do my bit."

"Yes, we should be able to make it. And, I'm sure my sister and her family would be up for it too."

"Fantastic, I'll see you all on Saturday."

"Okay, I'll see you then."

As I walked to the car park, I spotted a man dressed in a uniform identical to the one I'd seen Lester wearing. The man was clearly pretending to be studying a car number plate, but he wasn't fooling me.

"Hi, there."

The man seemed surprised that I should speak to him.

"Is this your car, lady?"

"No. Mine's in the car park." I glanced around to check no one was listening. "It's okay, I know what you're really up to. My uncle is in the same line of business."

"I wondered why you'd stopped to speak to me. So few people do unless it's to complain that I've given them a ticket."

"You're actually issuing parking tickets, then?"

"Of course. That's what I do. That's my job."

"Of course." I gave him a knowing wink. "I guess it helps to maintain your cover."

"Sorry? I don't understand."

"I just meant that no one will realise you're waiting around for someone to pop their clogs if you're handing out parking tickets."

"What do you mean by *pop their clogs*?"

"It's okay." I gave him another wink. "I understand you have to be discreet about the bodies."

Just then, I spotted Lester, standing across the road. I was about to point him out to my new friend when I realised that Lester was gesturing frantically and mouthing something to me. It took him a few attempts, but I eventually worked out what he was saying.

He's not a grim reaper.

Oh bum!

"What do you mean *bodies*?" the not-a-grim reaper said.

"Sorry, did I say *bodies*? I meant tickets. Anyway, it was nice speaking to you." I hurried across the road to where Lester was now hiding behind a lamppost.

"What were you doing, Jill?"

"I thought he was—err—one of you."

"What did you say to him?"

"Nothing really."

"You didn't mention grim reapers, did you?"

"Of course not. I may have said the word *bodies*, though, but I think I got away with it."

"You didn't mention my name, did you?"

"No. I don't think so. Well, maybe just the once."

"Oh boy. I hope word of this doesn't get back to my bosses."

"I'm really sorry, Lester. Is there anything I can do?"

"I think you've already done quite enough."

***

"Let me get this straight." Jack laughed. "You walked up to a traffic warden and asked how many bodies he'd processed."

"No, I didn't say that. It was just a simple misunderstanding. And they aren't called traffic wardens now. They're called civil enforcement officers."

"Seriously? I didn't know that. What did Lester have to say?"

"He wasn't impressed."

"I bet."

"I was over at Aunt Lucy's earlier today, and it seems like the whole of Candlefield is in carnival mode."

"How come?"

"Braxmore is dead."

"Who? I've never heard of him."

"I thought I'd mentioned him before. Basically, he was the evillest dude the paranormal world has ever known."

"What happened to him?"

"No one knows. His body was found in the marketplace. All of the streets were full of people celebrating."

My nose began to tickle, and I sneezed.

"What's that?" Jack laughed.

"What's what?"

"That, in your hand."

I'd instinctively reached into my pocket for a tissue, and without realising it, I'd brought out the handkerchief that the market stallholder had given to me.

"It's nothing."

"That's your picture on there, isn't it?"

"No." I shoved the hanky back into my pocket.

"Yes, it is. I saw it. What's that all about?"

"If you must know, they're actually selling all kinds of merchandise with my photo on it, in Candlefield. T-shirts, towels, mouse mats, all sorts of stuff."

"But, why?"

"Because I'm considered something of an icon over

there."

"No, I meant why do you have a moustache in the photo?"

Chapter 18

"Go on, spoilsport." Jack grinned.

"The answer is still no. And for goodness sake, wipe that marmalade off your chin. How old are you? Ten?"

"Just one t-shirt, please. I promise I won't wear it in public."

"I am not buying you a t-shirt that has a picture of me with a moustache on it, and that's final."

"Aww." He sighed. "So, what are you going to do about the guy who did this?"

"I've not decided yet, but you can bet your life it will cause him every bit as much embarrassment as he's inflicted on me."

***

I'd barely got through the door of the outer office when Mrs V came dancing around her desk.

"We've done it, Jill. We've put in an offer for the new house."

"Good for you. You seemed so unsure there for a while."

"I know. It's very strange. I was going backwards and forwards on whether we should do it or not, but then yesterday when I was talking to you, it all became very clear, and I realised I wanted to live there."

"When do you expect to hear back from the seller?"

"I'm not sure. Armi is going to give me a call if he hears anything."

"Fingers crossed, then."

"Would you like a drink?"

"Not just now. I have to nip out in a few minutes. I need to do some work on the Bell case."

"You haven't forgotten what day it is tomorrow, have you?"

"It isn't your birthday is it?"

"No."

"Jack's birthday? No, that's not for a while. It isn't my wedding anniversary, is it?"

"Of course not, dear. I'll never like that cat of yours, but I know you have a soft spot for him, so I wouldn't want you to forget Love Your Cat day. Have you got him a card?"

"Don't worry, Mrs V. That's all in hand."

Winky was on the sofa, and thankfully, the printing press had fallen silent.

"Well, have you?" he asked.

"Have I *what*?"

"Bought your darling feline a Love Your Cat card?"

"No, I haven't, and what's more, I don't intend to."

"That's not very nice." He sulked. "In fact, it makes me quite sad."

"If you think that pathetic little act is going to bother me, you can think again. There's no way I'm buying a card just to line your pockets." I walked over to the screen. "Where's the printing press gone? I thought you would have had it going full pelt today."

"There's no need. I've fulfilled all my orders already. There was a moment yesterday when I didn't think I was going to make it, but then the machine seemed to find another gear, and in the end, I managed to get all of the orders out last night."

"And how much have you made from this little escapade?"

"It's so vulgar to talk about money, don't you think?"

"I should at least get a share for allowing you to use my office as your print room."

"Much as I'd love to give you a share, all the money is tied up now."

"How very convenient."

"There are still plenty of cards in the shops, though, so if you change your mind, you can still pick one up later today."

"Yeah, that's never going to happen."

I'd only been at my desk for a few minutes when I had an unexpected visitor.

"I have Mr Duyew out there," Mrs V said. "He doesn't have an appointment, but he says he needs to speak to you urgently."

"You'd better send him through."

"Sorry to barge in like this, Jill." He looked more than a little stressed.

"That's okay, Victor. Have a seat."

"I won't if you don't mind. I can't stay. I just came to give you this." He reached into his pocket and fished out a wad of twenty-pound notes, which he placed onto my desk.

"What's this?"

"It's payment for the work you've done so far. It's quite a bit more than we agreed."

"I don't understand. The case is still on-going, and I didn't ask for an interim payment."

"I need you to stop all work on the case. Straight away,

please."

"Are you sure you wouldn't like a seat, Victor?"

"No, thanks, I really can't stay."

"Won't you at least tell me what's prompted this sudden change of heart?"

"It's—err—we just decided not to pursue it." He was already backing towards the door. "Thanks again." And with that, he was gone.

I counted the cash; there was double what I was owed.

"I think you've just reached an all-time low." Winky grinned.

"What are you talking about?"

"You're obviously so bad at your job that your clients have now taken to paying you extra *not* to work on their case." He ducked just in time to avoid the hole punch. "Oi, that could have hit me."

***

I didn't have time to dwell on Victor Duyew's sudden and unexplained change of heart because I needed to focus on the Bell case, which was still very much alive. Two people had now pointed the finger at Adam Bell, on the basis that he was desperate to get his hands on his parents' cash. And yet, I still wasn't convinced that he was behind it. Maybe he was a brilliant actor, but when he'd visited my offices, he'd seemed genuinely concerned about his parents.

One of the other things that still bothered me about this case was the Bells' journey home. There were several things which didn't make any sense. First, why had they decided to travel overnight on the Friday when they'd told the Nightingales and Jameses that they would be staying until the Sunday? What had caused that sudden change of heart, and could whatever it was be connected to their disappearance?

How come there was no trace of them on CCTV on their journey home? If they'd travelled their normal route, along the main roads, they would inevitably have been picked up on camera at least once. And finally, what had happened when they arrived back at the house? Did they really walk in on a burglary? What were the chances of that? Pretty remote, I would have thought.

Something the Nightingales had said was playing on my mind. They'd mentioned that the fuel warning light had been illuminated on the journey back from Driffield. That being the case, the Bells would have had to call at a petrol station not long after they left the caravan park on the Friday night. The police had checked roadside cameras for sightings of the Bells, but had they checked the petrol stations? I had no way of knowing, so I intended to pay them a visit. I figured the Bells would have had to call in at a petrol station within twenty miles of the caravan park, and a quick check on the map narrowed that down to just seven. There were others, but to have visited any of those would have meant the Bells having to head in entirely the wrong direction.

So, with that in mind, I took another drive to Filey.

It was a sunny day, and the interior of the car was like a sauna because it didn't have aircon. If I hadn't been cheated out of that Jag, it would have been a much more enjoyable excursion.

An hour later, and of the petrol stations I'd visited so

far, two had no CCTV, and the other three didn't retain the recordings for long enough. That left just one petrol station on my list. I wasn't feeling very optimistic, particularly when I pulled up on the forecourt and couldn't see any trace of cameras. Still, I needed a cool drink anyway, so I might as well ask about the Bells, just in case.

"No petrol?" The middle-aged man behind the counter had discarded his shirt, which should have been illegal with a beer belly like his.

"No, thanks." I put the ice-cold can of orange on the counter. "Just this, and a bag of salt and vinegar crisps, please."

He had to stand up in order to take my money because the cash register wouldn't open until he moved his belly out of the way. "Ten pence change."

"Thanks. Do you have CCTV?"

"Nah, we used to have it, but someone nicked the cameras. Why?"

I took a drink of the orange and then held the can to my forehead. "It doesn't matter. I'm just trying to trace someone who may or may not have called here in a blue Volvo on the fifth of June last year."

"The *fifth* of June? That's my wedding anniversary."

"That's nice. Congrats."

"A blue Volvo, you said?"

"That's right. Why? You can't possibly remember that far back, can you?"

"I wouldn't normally, but the Mrs and I had booked to go on holiday the following day, by way of celebration. I was just about to lock up for the night when a woman pulled up in a blue Volvo, towing a caravan. She didn't have the first clue how to get the petrol cap off, so she came and asked me to help. By the time she'd filled up and left, I was thirty minutes late. Nora, that's the missus, wasn't impressed because we had to be at the airport at four in the morning, and we almost didn't make it."

"And you're sure it was a woman?"

"Positive. If it had been a bloke, I wouldn't have been so accommodating."

"Was there anyone else in the car?"

"No, it was just her."

"What time would this have been?"

"It was a couple of minutes before eleven. That's when I normally close."

"Do you happen to remember what she looked like?"

"Not really. She was a redhead, that's all I remember."

I took out my phone, did a quick Google search, and then showed him a couple of photographs. "Is that her by any chance?"

"Yeah, it is."

"Are you sure?"

"One hundred percent."

***

I'd just arrived back in Washbridge when my phone rang.

"Colonel?"

"Jill, I wanted to give you an update. I spoke to our people as soon as I got back, and much as I'd expected, several volunteers came forward."

"Do they understand the risks?"

"They do, but like me, they're disgusted by what's

happening, and they want to do whatever they can to help. In fact, I had more volunteers than I had tracking devices, so I was forced to disappoint a few of them."

"That has really restored my faith in human nature."

"I think you'll find that should be *ghost* nature." He laughed.

"When will they be able to start?"

"They already have. A few of them were out on the streets last night, but there were no reported incidents. They all returned safe and sound."

"That's good, I guess, but it doesn't help us to catch the traffickers."

"Maybe we'll get lucky tonight. I'll keep you posted, Jill."

"Thanks, Colonel, and please be sure to pass on my thanks to all the volunteers."

***

Since breakfast (a thrilling bowl of cornflakes) I'd only had a can of pop and a packet of crisps. I needed something substantial, so I magicked myself over to Cuppy C for a muffin.

What? I challenge you to name anything more substantial and nutritious than a blueberry muffin. Everyone knows that fruit is good for you, right? Add to that all the muffinness, and you can't go wrong.

What the—? I couldn't believe my eyes.

The twins had been unable to agree on the colour for the uniforms, and my understanding was that they'd compromised by ordering a number of each colour. Clearly, I'd given the twins way too much credit because it turned out that the left half of the uniform was pink, and the right half was turquoise. They looked ridiculous. I couldn't believe the twins had gone ahead and ordered such monstrous things.

Wait, scrub that. Of course I could believe it.

The two ladies in question were seated at the window table, deep in conversation.

As I approached the table, Pearl spotted me, and said something to Amber that I clearly wasn't supposed to hear.

"Shush, she's here!"

"Hello, you two."

It was a toss-up which of them looked the more guilty.

"Hi, Jill." Amber forced a smile.

"Hey, Jill," Pearl said. "Do you like the new uniforms?"

Telling the twins that I thought they were awful wouldn't do any good now, so despite my true feelings, I felt I should be supportive.

"They suck bigtime."

What? I know what I said about being supportive, but I couldn't help myself.

"They do not!" Amber protested. "Everyone says how unusual they are."

Unusual, clearly being a euphemism for ugly. "Pink and turquoise don't go together."

"Like we're going to take fashion advice from you." Pearl scoffed.

"It doesn't matter what I think, anyway. As long as you two are happy for your staff to look like jesters, that's all that matters."

"We like them, don't we, Pearl?"

"Yes, we do. They look great."

"Okay. What were you two talking about when I came over just now?"

"Nothing." Pearl shrugged.

"Yes, you were. I heard you tell Amber to shush."

Pearl was squirming in her seat. "It was nothing—just private business talk."

"Yeah," Amber said. "We were just discussing the accounts. It's nothing to concern you."

I'd seen some poor liars in my time, but these two were the worst.

Chapter 19

Back in Washbridge, I was still trying to make sense of what I'd learned from speaking with the petrol station owner. Even when he'd told me that he remembered the Volvo and caravan, I couldn't be sure it was the Bells' car, but then he'd mentioned that the driver was a woman—a redhead. When I'd shown him a photo of the caravan park owners, he hadn't hesitated in identifying the driver as being Mary Chase.

Although this was undoubtedly a breakthrough, it raised more questions than it answered. Why had Mary Chase driven the Bells' car and caravan back to their house? How had she managed to avoid being spotted on camera on that journey? Where was Norman Chase when his wife was driving the Bells' car? And, most importantly, what had happened to the Bells?

Frustrating as it was, those questions would have to wait because I was due to attend the WOW function being hosted by Belinda Cartwheel. I would have gladly given it a miss, but Grandma was already giving me grief, and she'd no doubt continue to do so until I found out exactly what Belinda was up to.

"Jill, I'm so pleased you could make it." Belinda greeted me at the door. "We haven't seen you for a while. I was beginning to think you were avoiding us."

"Not at all. I've just been very busy. I'm sure you know how it is."

"Of course. Is your grandmother coming?"

"I'm afraid not. She's very busy too. Her new shop opens on Friday, so that's occupying a lot of her time, as you can imagine."

"Another shop? My oh my. What's this one going to be?"

"A beauty salon."

"Really?" Belinda scoffed. "I wouldn't have thought that was her forte. Still, I'm sure she knows what she's doing."

"She usually does."

"Do go through and mingle. I'll catch up with you later."

I couldn't quite put my finger on it, but there was something about that woman that gave me the creeps.

All the usual suspects were present, and the majority of them seemed to be genuinely pleased to see me. I'd been worried that there might be some carryover from when Grandma had taken it upon herself to impersonate me, but no one mentioned it. One big plus was that there wasn't a single beetle to be seen. In fact, there didn't appear to be any theme to this particular meeting. It was just an excuse for everyone to drink, eat and chat. Although I wasn't a big fan of WOW, I could see how it could be helpful, particularly to witches new to the human world. Having other witches to talk to would be a godsend to those who were feeling isolated and missing the paranormal world.

After an hour or so, I went in search of the loo. As I walked past the kitchen, I noticed that the door was slightly ajar. Inside, Belinda appeared to be refreshing the punch bowl, which was almost empty. I was just about to move on when I saw her take a small bottle from her pocket and pour the contents into the punch. What was I to make of that? Maybe it was just a little something to put the 'punch' in punch. Whatever it was would have to wait because I was practically plaiting my legs.

I got back to the living room just in time to see everyone raising their glasses to make a toast.

"To WOW!" Belinda said.

Her words were chorused around the room, and then everyone downed their drinks.

"Jill?" Belinda had spotted me. "You missed out on the toast."

"Sorry, I was in the loo."

She took a glass, filled it with punch and handed it to me. "To WOW!"

I glanced at the window and pointed. "What's he doing out there?"

When Belinda turned around to find out what I was looking at, I poured the punch into the flowerpot next to me.

"What did you see?" She turned back to me, puzzled.

"Didn't you see him? It was a man on a unicycle. He's gone now."

It might have been my imagination, but after the toast, the atmosphere in the room seemed to change. Conversations were few and far between, with most people preferring to stand by themselves. I tried to engage a few people in small talk, but all I could get out of them were monosyllabic responses.

Belinda clinked a spoon against her glass. "Everyone, can I have your attention? It's been lovely to see you all today. Before you leave, however, there's one important matter we need to address." She picked up a clipboard from the table. "I know that most of you feel it's time for a change at the top of WOW. This is a petition to remove Mirabel Millbright as chairman. If all of you sign this today, it will make it practically impossible for her to continue. Please line up in single file and add your signature on your way out."

To say I was gobsmacked would have been an understatement. It was bad enough that she should use a get-together like this for political purposes, but to do it while I was present was the height of audacity. Did she really expect everyone to sign her petition without question? Did she think I'd stand by and allow that to happen?

Everyone apart from me had already formed a line. There could be only one possible explanation for their complicity: the punch had been spiked. How should I play this? I made a snap decision and joined the back of the queue. As I waited in line, I thought it significant that no one asked any questions or passed any comment when it was their time to sign. Instead, they simply took the pen and scribbled their signature. Ten minutes later, and I was the only one still to sign. Everyone else had already left, leaving only Belinda and me in the house.

"There you are, Jill." She handed me the petition and a pen. "Even if the number of signatures isn't enough to persuade your grandmother to resign, seeing your name on there should do the trick."

"You could be right." I looked her straight in the eyes. "There's just one slight problem with your plan." I took the sheets of paper off the clipboard and ripped them into a thousand tiny pieces. "Whoops!"

Belinda dropped to her knees and tried to gather

together the shredded pieces of paper. "What have you done?"

"I'm onto you, Belinda. I saw you spike the punch, and I intend to let all the members of WOW know what you've done."

"You'll pay for this." Her face was like thunder, but much more curiously, her voice had changed.

Gone were the sickly-sweet tones of Belinda Cartwheel. In their place was a much gruffer voice—it was a voice I would have recognised anywhere.

"Ma Chivers!"

Discarding the small pieces of paper, she got to her feet, and slowly transformed in front of my eyes. "Get out of here!"

"That will be my pleasure. I'll let the other members know that you've decided to resign from WOW, shall I?"

"Get out of here before I do something I'll regret."

"Your empty threats don't scare me, Ma. You're a spent force."

"The Elite Competition says otherwise."

"That was a hollow victory, and everyone knows it. What's it like to be all alone in the world?"

"You don't know what you're talking about."

"Where's Alicia? Oh yes, she saw you for what you are and left. And what about Cyril? I haven't seen him for a while. It's just you now, is it?"

"Get out of here!"

"Nothing would give me greater pleasure."

Why hadn't I twigged before? Why hadn't Grandma? Ma Chivers was extremely powerful, and if anything, she was growing even more so. It was only her fit of rage that had allowed me to see through her disguise.

What would have happened if I hadn't stumbled upon her spiking the punch? I might have signed the petition, and that would have made Grandma's position untenable. How would I have explained why I'd betrayed her in that way?

If *I* was angry, that was nothing to how Grandma would react when I broke the news to her. I decided it would be best to wait until after the launch of the beauty salon.

***

My phone rang.

"Kathy? Slow down! I can't make out what you're saying. What's wrong?"

"It's Mikey. He's disappeared."

"What do you mean, *disappeared*?"

"He finished school early today because he had a check-up at the dentist. It wasn't worth taking him back to school, so I brought him straight home afterwards. He went to play in the garden, but now there's no sign of him."

"It's a large garden. Are you sure he isn't hiding somewhere?"

"I've looked everywhere. There's no sign of him, Jill. I don't know what to do. Should I call the police?"

"Not just yet. Where's Peter?"

"He's working in West Chipping, but he's not answering his phone, so I've left him a voicemail."

"Do any of the neighbours have kids? Maybe he's gone around there to play?"

"They're all still at school, and besides, Mikey knows he isn't allowed to leave the garden without asking me first. Can you come over?"

"Sure. I'll be with you in about twenty minutes. He'll probably be back by the time I get there."

But he wasn't, and when I pulled onto Kathy's drive, I could see that she was in full-blown panic mode.

"He's gone, Jill. I've looked everywhere. Someone must have taken him. I have to call the police."

"Hold on a minute. Let me take a look around first."

She checked her watch. "I have to collect Lizzie from school."

"Why don't you go and get her, and if Mikey hasn't turned up when you get back, then we'll call the police. Where was he the last time you saw him?"

"Down the bottom end of the garden. He said he wanted to look at the seeds that Pete planted."

"Where are they exactly?"

"Near the far end, behind the tree on the left side of the garden."

"How many trees do you have?"

"Three altogether."

"Cripes. Okay, off you go. And try not to worry."

It was a stupid thing for me to say. How was she not going to worry? I was panic-stricken, but I couldn't let Kathy see that. As soon as she'd gone, I hurried down the garden.

And that's when I saw it.

The stalk of the plant was almost as thick as the tree. This definitely hadn't been here the last time I'd looked around. How come Kathy hadn't mentioned it?

Shielding my eyes from the sun, I looked up to try to see how tall the plant was, but I couldn't see the top of it because it disappeared into the clouds. I was getting all kinds of bad vibes. It couldn't be, could it? It was just a fairy tale. Wasn't it?"

I gave Daze a call.

"Jill, are you okay? You sound kind of weird."

"Listen, Daze, this is going to sound all kinds of crazy, but are you familiar with the story of Jack and the Beanstalk?"

"Of course. Why do you ask?"

"It's just a story, right? It's not real."

"I wish that was true."

Oh bum!

"What's happened, Jill?"

I quickly told her about Mikey's disappearance, and what I'd discovered in the garden.

"This is really bad. You have to act quickly."

"What's going on?"

"The giants are real."

"Giants? As in more than one?"

"Yes, there are lots of them living in the clouds. Most of them are law-abiding and keep themselves to themselves."

"But—?"

"But a few of them develop a taste for—" She hesitated.

"A taste for *what*?"

"Human children. Has your brother-in-law done any work on the garden recently?"

"Yes, Peter sowed a load of seeds that he bought from someone at the door. He said they were a bargain."

"That would have been a Beaner."

"A *what*?"

"They're nymphs who are employed by the rogue giants to distribute the seeds. They work on a commission basis."

"Commission for what?"

"They're paid a fee for every child that climbs the beanstalk."

"I don't understand why Kathy didn't see it. It's huge."

"It's only visible to children."

"How come I can see it, then?"

"That's because you're a witch. Adult humans can't."

"I'd better get up there and find him."

"Wait, Jill. Those giants are very cunning and extremely powerful. You should talk to your grandmother first."

"There isn't time."

"You'll just have to make time because if you go charging up that beanstalk, the giant will squish you. How's that going to help Mikey?"

"Okay. I'll magic myself over to see Grandma now. Thanks again."

"Good luck."

By the sound of it, I was going to need it.

Chapter 20

I magicked myself to an alleyway close to Ever, and then hurried around to the shop. Julie, the head Everette, was wearing the infamous yellow top paired with blue trousers. It really didn't work, and I wondered for a minute if she'd got dressed in a hurry, but then I realised that all the Everettes were sporting the exact same ensemble.

"Morning, Jill." She seemed much brighter than of late.

"Morning. Sorry, I can't stop. I have to see Grandma urgently."

"She's not in a very good mood. She told me off because my fingernails were the wrong colour."

"Okay, thanks for the warning."

"Morning, Grandma."

"Didn't anyone teach you that you should knock before entering a room? I might have been shaving my legs."

"In your office?"

"This had better be important. I have lots to do before the launch of the new shop on Friday."

"It's a matter of life and death."

"What about my report on Belinda Cartwheel?"

"That'll have to wait. Mikey is in grave danger."

"Who?"

"My young nephew. Kathy's boy."

"A human? Why would I care about a human?"

"Because he's just a small boy and he's in grave danger."

"I'm still waiting to hear a reason why I should care about him."

"Because I know what Belinda Cartwheel is up to, and I won't tell you unless you help Mikey."

"That's blackmail."

"Yes, it is, so are you going to help or not?"

"It doesn't look as though I have any choice. What's wrong with the kid?"

"Kathy's husband, Peter, bought some seeds at the door."

"That old con?" She cackled. "There's one born every minute."

"Do you know something about this?"

"Let me guess. The Beaners sold your human brother-in-law a bag of cheap seeds. He planted them, and then your cousin, Spikey, climbed the beanstalk that had miraculously appeared in the garden."

"His name is Mikey and he's my nephew, but essentially yes, that's what happened."

"He'll be a goner, then."

"Don't say that. He's only just disappeared, and according to Daze, I might still have a chance of saving him."

"Why are you wasting time talking to me, then?"

"Daze said you'd be able to advise me how best to deal with the giant. She said you might have some spell or potion I could use."

"Why didn't you say so before?" Grandma pointed to the metal cupboard at the back of the office. "You'll find it in there. Look for the jar marked 'Giant Slayer."

"Great, thanks." I hurried over to the cupboard. "I can see a jar of coffee and four jars of Bunions Away, but I can't see—" I was interrupted by the sound of Grandma cackling.

"You're so gullible. Did you really believe there is such a thing as Giant Slayer?"

"How can you joke at a time like this?" It took all my willpower not to grab her by the throat and throttle her. "A young boy's life is at stake."

"Don't get your knickers in a twist. It was only a joke." She pulled open the top drawer of her desk and took out a small paper bag. "Here, use this on the giant."

"Is it some kind of potion? What does it do?"

"No, it's sneezing powder."

"*Sneezing powder*? Is that the best you can do?"

"You'd better hold onto it. You'll thank me later."

"Thanks for nothing."

I stuffed it into my pocket and was about to magic myself back to Kathy's house when Grandma said, "Have you got any cash on you?"

"You're not actually going to charge me for this powder, are you?"

"Of course not. What do you think I am? You'll need cash to pay the Fly-Me-Ups."

"The what?"

"They're little creatures who live on the beanstalks. They'll get you to the top much quicker."

"I don't need any help from Fly-Me—whatever they're called. I can use magic."

"Good luck with that."

"I have to go."

"What about Belinda Cartwheel? You haven't told me what you found out."

"That'll have to wait. Sorry."

***

Pay some little creature to get me to the top of the beanstalk? I scoffed at the very idea. Why would I do that when magic would do the job?

Standing at the base of the beanstalk, I tried to magic myself to the top.

Nothing happened.

I tried again. And again. Still nothing happened. What was going on? I could only assume that the spell wouldn't function because I was trying to get to some indeterminate destination in the sky.

Not to worry. I could use levitation instead. I cast the spell and began to float upwards. This was going to be so easy.

Famous last words.

Everything was going fine until I reached the clouds, but then I lost sight of the beanstalk. I was floating aimlessly, higher and higher. At this rate, I'd be out of the earth's atmosphere and headed into space. In the end, I had no choice but to reverse the spell, and float back to earth.

There was nothing for it but for me to climb the stupid beanstalk. I'd never been one for climbing trees, even as a kid. It always seemed like a lot of work for no reward. Fortunately, there were plenty of branches sprouting from the stalk, so I was able to move from one to the next without having to over-stretch.

Fifteen minutes later, and I was still only about a hundred feet off the ground. I simply wasn't cut out for this climbing lark.

"Do you need some help?"

The squeaky little voice made me jump, and I almost

lost my grip.

"Who said that?"

"Sorry, I didn't mean to scare you." The little green creature was the shape of a small football, with stubby little arms and legs. "I'm Freddy."

"I'm rather busy at the moment, Freddy."

"You seem to be struggling. I could help you get to the top for a small fee."

"Are you a Fly-Me-Thingy?"

"A Fly-Me-Up? Yes."

"You're rather small. Are you sure you can get me to the top?"

"Of course. It's what we do."

"What would it cost?"

"Ten pounds."

"That's not too bad, I suppose."

"Forty pounds altogether."

"You just said it was ten."

"That's right. There'll be four of us, so four times ten is forty."

"It'll take four of you?"

"Of course. You didn't think I could do it by myself, did you?"

"I—err—no, I suppose not."

"So, would you like us to take you?"

What choice did I have? At this rate, it would take me all day to get to the top. "Okay." I fished the cash out of my pocket and counted out forty pounds. "There you go."

"Thanks." He put two tiny fingers in his mouth and whistled. "Come on guys! We have a punter."

Moments later, three identical creatures appeared. Identical that is except for the colour. One of them was blue, another orange and the third one was purple. Two of them took hold of my feet while the other two grabbed my hands.

"You need to let go of the stalk," Freddy said.

The idea of letting go terrified me. What if these creatures couldn't support my weight? But what choice did I have?

I closed my eyes, let go of the stalk and hoped for the best.

It was the weirdest sensation to be carried by the creatures who had propeller-shaped tails. My weight clearly wasn't an issue because less than a minute later, we'd reached the top of the beanstalk.

"Here we are," Freddy said.

"Don't let go of me."

"Why not? We're here."

"But there isn't any ground. It's just clouds. I'll fall through them."

"No you won't. It's perfectly safe, trust me."

The four of them released me and, thankfully, it turned out he was right because I found I was able to walk on the clouds, which was pretty cool.

"Thanks, guys."

"Our pleasure." And with that, the four of them disappeared.

Walking on clouds was kind of weird; it felt as though I was treading on sponge. Although I'd reached the top of the beanstalk, I had no idea where to go next. Whichever way I looked, all I could see were clouds and more clouds. What was I supposed to do now? Was Mikey even alive or had he already been eaten by the giant? I was almost on the point of despair when I spotted something poking out of the clouds. As I drew closer, I could see it was a road sign which read: Giant's Castle – this way.

At long last, it seemed that I might have caught a break.

The giant's castle was an ugly building with high towers at the four corners. As far as I could tell the only way in was through the huge double wooden doors, which were closed. I tried to magic myself inside, but that spell refused to work, and I didn't fancy trying levitation again. Not after what had happened before.

I was still trying to figure out what to do when I heard the sound of hooves. Moments later, a horse-drawn cart stopped outside the gates. In it was a large cage full of hens, clucking frantically. The weird hooded figure who'd been driving, climbed down and knocked on the castle doors.

This might be the only opportunity I would have, so I hurried over to the cart, climbed into the back, and squeezed into the space between the cage and the side. Not long after the hooded creature had returned to the cart, the gates creaked open. When it came to a halt again, I slipped off the back and then followed the hooded creature who was carrying the cage.

Once inside the huge hall, I slipped behind one of the stone columns. At the far side of the dimly lit hall, which was devoid of all but the most basic furniture, the giant was seated on a stone throne. It's certainly true that I haven't seen many giants in my time, but this guy must have been a contender for the Ugliest Giant Ever award. After the hooded creature had placed the cage of hens on the floor, he bowed, and then backed out of the room.

I'd made it this far, but where was Mikey? Was I too late? Had he already been munched by the monster? If he had, what would I tell Kathy? I couldn't tell her that her only son had been eaten by a giant. It would be kinder to say I hadn't been able to find him, but then she'd spend a lifetime wondering what had happened to him.

And then I heard a sound that made my heart soar.

"Help!" Mikey shouted.

It took a moment for me to work out where the sound had come from, but then I spotted another small cage at the side of the giant's throne. Mikey was looking through the bars, clearly terrified by his ordeal. Although I was relieved to know he was still alive, it broke my heart to see how traumatised he was.

Somehow, I had to get to the cage and get him out, but how? Even if the 'invisible' spell worked, the giant was bound to see Mikey once I'd released him. I needed to create a distraction, and I knew just the thing.

Fortunately, the giant was focussed on the book in his hand, so I was able to creep over to the cage of hens. It was locked, but much to my relief, the 'power' spell still seemed to be working, so I forced the door open. Once freed, the hens flew in all directions, clucking loudly. Just as I'd hoped, that was enough to get the giant's attention. Grumbling to himself, he put down the book, and set about trying to catch them.

Seizing my opportunity, I hurried over to the cage in which Mikey was being held.

"Auntie Jill!" Mikey shouted.

"Shush!"

"I want to go home."

"It's okay. I'm going to get you out of here. Stand back

from the door."

Once I'd forced the cage door open, I grabbed his hand and we legged it towards the door. We almost made it too, but when we were just a few feet from freedom, a giant hand scooped us up.

"Hmm." The giant licked his lips. "Dinner."

"I don't want to be eaten!" Mikey screamed.

"It's okay." I tried to reassure him.

As the giant brought his hand closer to his mouth, I could see his rotten teeth and yellow tongue. What a horrible way to go.

That's when I remembered the powder that Grandma had given me. I reached into my pocket, opened the paper bag and blew with all my might.

"Achoo! Achoo!"

The giant was consumed by a fit of sneezing. As he tried to wipe his nose, he released his grip a little.

"Come on, Mikey." I grabbed his hand, and the two of us jumped onto the giant's arm and slid to the floor.

Once outside the castle, we ran as fast as our legs would carry us back to the beanstalk.

"Quick, Mikey. Climb down."

As I joined him on the stalk, I could feel the clouds vibrating, and in the distance, I saw the giant headed our way. He would be on us in a matter of seconds.

"Do you need any help?" The squeaky voice belonged to another Fly-Me-Up; this one was yellow.

"Yes, please. Can you fly us down?"

"That's what we Fly-Me-Downs do."

"I thought you were called Fly-Me-Ups?"

"They're our cousins. It will cost one hundred pounds for the two of you."

"I thought it was forty pounds per person?"

"That's what our cousins charge. Our service is slightly more expensive."

"Whatever." I took the cash from my pocket and handed it to him. "Just get us out of here!"

Less than a minute later, they put us down in Kathy's back garden.

"Is the giant coming to get us, Auntie Jill?" Mikey was looking up at the top of the beanstalk.

"No, you're safe now."

I quickly cast the 'thunderbolt' spell, which cut through the base of the beanstalk, and sent it crashing to the ground. Next, I cast the 'forget' spell on Mikey and then led him into the house.

"Where's Mum?" he said, clearly still a little disorientated.

"She's gone to collect your sister from school. They should be back in a minute."

In fact, Kathy's car had just pulled onto the drive, so I went out to meet her.

"Have you found him, Jill?" She had obviously been crying.

"Yes, he's in the house. He's okay."

"Where was he?"

"He was in the garden all the time."

"But I looked everywhere."

"There's a lot of thick foliage down the bottom end. He was hiding in there."

"Is he okay?"

"Yeah, he's fine."

"Thank goodness." She broke down in tears.

"Why's Mummy crying, Auntie Jill?" Lizzie looked very

concerned.

"She's okay. She's just happy."

"Why do grown-ups cry when they're happy?"

"Grown-ups are a bit weird. Why don't you come inside, and I'll get us all a drink?"

The kids had gone upstairs; Kathy and I were in the lounge, enjoying a well-deserved cup of tea.

"Hi, you two." Peter popped his head around the door.

"You're home early." Kathy stood up and gave him a kiss.

"I'd finished the job I was working on, so I thought I'd call it a day. Besides, I want to try and do some work in the garden."

"Peter, do you have any of those seeds left?" I said.

"No, I've used them all, but I'm beginning to think I may have been conned. I'm not sure anything will ever grow from them. Why do you ask?"

"No reason."

"I've got something to show you, Jill." Kathy led the way through to the dining room. "Ta da!"

Mounted on the wall was a huge framed photograph of the whole family.

"That's lovely. How did you talk Mikey into doing it?"

"We simply sat him down and reasoned with him. He soon came around once he realised how important it was to me."

"I must say, it's a beautiful photo."

When it was almost time for me to leave, Mikey came rushing down the stairs. "Auntie Jill, come and see my new racing car track."

"I didn't know you liked racing cars?"

"Yes, I do. They're great."

"When did you get the racing track? I didn't miss your birthday, did I?"

"No. Mummy bought it for me for being in the family photo."

"Did she now?" I looked at Kathy who at least had the good grace to blush.

Chapter 21

"An actual beanstalk?" Jack was staring at me, open-mouthed. Fortunately, he'd already finished eating his muesli.

"Yes."

"An *actual* giant?"

"That's right."

"That's so cool."

"There was nothing cool about it. Mikey and I came this close to being his dinner."

"It's a good job your grandmother gave you that sneezing powder. You owe her one big time."

"I know, and if she ever finds out, she'll never let me forget about it."

"You get to do all the exciting stuff while I'm stuck doing paperwork most of the day. Isn't there some way for you to give me magical powers? Then I could go on adventures with you."

"Why didn't you say before? I'll just nip to the corner shop and buy a jar of Turn-Me-Into-A-Wizard."

"You don't realise how lucky you are, Jill. Most people would kill to have your life."

"I do realise, but it isn't all fun and games. It's hard work a lot of the time too."

"Would you prefer to have my job?"

"I—err—"

"That's what I thought. Take today for example. I have to attend a seminar on The Impact of Social Media on Today's Police Force." He yawned.

"It could be interesting."

"Not as interesting as climbing a beanstalk and visiting

a giant's castle."

Jack was right.

And yes, I do realise that's not something I say very often, but on this occasion, he was spot on. Since I'd discovered I was a witch, my life had become so much more exciting. Sometimes I wondered how I used to fill my time B.W. (Before Witch). Life was certainly much simpler back then, but would I choose to go back to those days if I could?

Not likely. I was having way too much fun.

***

"We've got it, Jill." Mrs V was practically dancing around the outer office—she was so excited.

"The house? They accepted your offer, then?"

"Yes, we heard last night. I know I had my doubts, but now I'm really looking forward to moving in."

"Do you have any idea when that will be?"

"It shouldn't be too long. The new house is vacant, and ours is going on the market later today. The estate agent reckons we'll have no problem selling it."

"I'm really pleased for you. It seems like everyone is moving house at the moment." Except for me.

"I meant to ask. How are Kathy and the family settling into their new place?"

"Very well, thanks." Apart from the whole beanstalk/giant incident, that is. "They seem to like it. Mrs V, do you think you could make me a cup of tea before I shoot off?"

"Of course. Will you be gone long?"

"Probably. I'm going to pay another visit to the Cliffs Caravan Park."

"Morning, Winky."

He stared at me for a moment and then, without a word, turned his back to me.

"I said, good morning."

All I got in return this time was a grunt.

"What's wrong with you?"

"Do you know what day it is?"

"Wednesday."

He turned around. "I mean what *day* it is."

"It's too early for your cryptic—oh, wait a minute. Are you referring to Love Your Cat day?"

"Of course."

"You're not sulking because I didn't get you a card?"

"I'm not sulking, but I am very disappointed, and a little hurt."

"Don't give me that load of old cobblers. First of all, Love Your Cat day isn't a thing. Or at least it wasn't until you invented it. And, secondly, you've made a small fortune off the back of this little scam, so if you're expecting me to feel bad, then you, my friend, are going to be very disappointed."

"I've said it before, but I'll say it again, you've become very hard."

***

I was more or less sure that Mary Chase had driven the Bells' car and caravan back to their house on that fateful night, so she must know what had happened to them.

And if she knew, I was pretty sure that her husband did too. The challenge was to get them to divulge that information.

After a leisurely drive to the coast, I parked a quarter of a mile from the caravan park, and made my way from there on foot. As I approached the entrance to the park, a car was just coming through the gates. It was Mary Chase. She was too busy focussing on the road to notice me, so I waited until she'd driven away, and then made my way in. Judging by the number of vacant pitches, I estimated that the caravan park couldn't have been more than fifty percent occupied. For that time of year, that struck me as rather poor.

As I approached the Chases' office/living quarters, the door opened, and Norman Chase stepped out. I considered confronting him there and then, but what exactly would I have said? That some random man at a petrol station reckoned he'd seen Mary Chase driving the Bells' car? He'd just laugh in my face. I was going to need much more than that. Maybe I'd find something in their office.

Chase headed off in the opposite direction, and as soon as he was out of sight, I hurried over to the office. To my surprise, it wasn't locked, so I slipped inside. So far, so good, but what exactly was I looking for? Something that belonged to the Bells, maybe?

Inside, there were two desks—his and hers, I assumed. I started with the one closest to the door and began to go through the drawers. Fifteen minutes later, I'd finished with the first desk, but I'd found precisely nothing. I was just about to start on the second one when I heard the door open.

Oh bum!

"Mary? Why are you crying?" Norman Chase said.

As you're no doubt already aware, I'm a think-on-my-feet kind of person, so in the split second between my hearing Chase at the door, and him walking into the office, I'd been able to come up with yet another cunning plan.

Although he was staring straight at me, he was actually seeing his wife, Mary, in floods of tears. All courtesy of the 'doppelganger' spell.

"That horrible Maxwell woman has been here again," I said, in my best Mary-like voice.

"Where is she?"

"She's gone, but I think she might be onto us."

"Why, what did she say?"

"Something about knowing that I was the one who drove the Bells' car back to their house."

"She can't possibly know that."

"That's what she said. She reckons someone saw me."

"She's bluffing. She doesn't have anything."

"I'm scared, Norman."

"Don't be silly." He came over and gave me a hug, which was pretty gross, but I had to play along with it. "They can't do anything without the bodies."

I very nearly reacted to that awful revelation and gave the game away. *Bodies*? That could mean only one thing: the Bells were dead.

"What if they find them?" I said through fake tears.

"They won't."

"You can't know that. Maybe Maxwell has already found them."

"Don't be silly."

"I'm not. I'm just scared, Norman."

"There's no need to be." He took my hand. "Come on. I'll show you."

He led the way out of the office, and through the caravan park. Based on what Norman had said so far, I wasn't sure if Mary knew the location of the Bells' bodies or not. Had he disposed of them alone or had she been with him?

After leaving the caravan park, we walked along the cliff top for another ten minutes. There were very few people around—just the occasional jogger and dog walker. Eventually, we came to the top of a set of wooden steps, which led down onto the beach.

"What if someone sees us?" I said, as we made our way down the steps.

"They won't. I promise."

Once on the beach, we continued to walk along the sand. After about half a mile, the beach became pebbles, and the going was much more difficult. Norman checked that there was no one else around, and then started towards the foot of the cliffs. When we got closer, I spotted a small cave opening, which was barely visible behind thick shrubbery.

Once inside the cave, he took out his phone, and switched on the flashlight app. Only then did it occur to me that this might be a trap. Had Norman somehow realised I wasn't Mary? No, that simply wasn't possible. Another sup might have seen through my spell, but not a human.

The cave was much deeper than I'd expected it to be, and we'd been walking for almost a minute when he stopped.

"See!" He pointed to an area of ground that had recently been disturbed. "Maxwell will never find them here. No one will." He gave me another creepy hug. "Will you stop worrying now?"

"Sorry."

"It's okay. We just have to keep our nerve, and it will all blow over. The police have already given up on it, and that Maxwell woman will too. You'll see."

The climb back up the wooden steps was exhausting, but at least I had some of the answers I'd been seeking. I now knew that the Bells were dead and where they'd been buried, but I still had no idea why or how they'd been killed. That would be something for the police to determine.

I had a more pressing problem: what to do about the Chases. When the 'real' Mary returned, Norman would soon realise that he'd somehow been conned into revealing the location of the Bells' bodies. Once that happened, he might try to move them, or he and Mary might do a runner.

We were almost back at the caravan park when I pulled up.

"Mary? What's wrong now?"

"Nothing. I'm fine." I quickly cast the 'forget' spell, reversed the 'doppelganger' spell, and then left, leaving Norman confused and somewhat disorientated.

If everything worked according to plan, he would remember nothing about the 'fake' Mary or his trip down to the cave.

***

I really wasn't looking forward to this next part.

"Is Susan Shay in, please?" I was at Washbridge police station.

I could have reported my findings to the local police in Filey, but I figured it would take longer for me to explain to them who I was, and why I was involved with the case. Much as I disliked Sushi, I could at least cut to the chase with her.

"Is she expecting you?" The sergeant behind the desk had a streaming cold.

"No, but if you could tell her that it's Jill Maxwell, and that I know where the Bells are."

"Which bells?"

"Walter and Jean Bell. They went missing over a year ago."

"You'd better take a seat."

A few minutes later, Sushi greeted me with her customary scowl.

"My sergeant tells me you know the whereabouts of the Bells?"

"That's correct. I'm afraid they're dead."

"Are you sure?"

"I haven't actually seen their bodies, but yeah, I'm pretty sure."

"You'd better come with me."

Needless to say, Sushi was the perfect hostess, offering me a choice of drinks and snacks.

What? Of course I'm joking. I got absolutely nothing from her. Zilch. Nada.

After telling her everything I knew, she said, "And the

bodies are buried in a cave near the caravan park?"

"It's a fair walk from the park, but yes."

"How did you find them?"

That was a good question. I could hardly tell her that I'd transformed myself into Mary Chase.

"I—err—followed Norman Chase."

"And he just happened to lead you to where the bodies were buried."

"Yeah. I got lucky, I guess."

"That seems to happen to you a lot, doesn't it, Maxwell? Getting lucky, I mean?"

"What can I say? I avoid black cats, never walk under ladders and I've never broken a mirror."

"If what you say is true, then the implications are that one or both of the Chases killed them. But why?"

"I reckon that's for you to find out. I've done my bit." I stood up. "Now, unless there's anything else you need from me, I should get going."

"Okay, but if this turns out to be a wild goose chase, you'll be very sorry."

"Once again, no thanks are necessary."

***

Despite Sushi's warning that I shouldn't contact the Bells' children, that was the first thing I did once I was out of the police station. The news would be devastating for them, but I figured it would be better coming from me.

"Katie, it's Jill Maxwell. I'm afraid I have bad news for you."

"Oh no." She burst into tears. "They're dead, aren't they?"

"I believe so. You and Adam must prepare yourselves for the worst."

"What happened to them?"

I told her as much as I could. As much as I knew.

"How did they die?" She managed through her sobs. "Were they murdered?"

"I don't know, but the fact that the Chases hid their bodies suggests there must have been foul play of some kind. I expect the police will be in touch with you soon. They'll no doubt be questioning the Chases."

"Thank you for calling, Jill. And for finding them."

"No problem. I'm just sorry it didn't turn out differently."

I'd no sooner finished talking to Katie Bell than I got a call from the colonel.

"Jill, I thought you'd want to know that two of our people were snatched from the streets of GT last night."

"Does Mad know?"

"Yes, she's tracking them now."

"They're in the human world, I take it?"

"That's right. Mad is waiting for the signals to stop moving around before she makes her move."

"Okay. Ask her to contact me before she goes after them, would you? I'd like to be involved."

"Will do."

"Thanks, Colonel."

Chapter 22

Although the end-result wasn't exactly what I'd been hoping for, at least I could mark the Bell case closed. To reward myself, I popped into Coffee Games.

Ever since the shop had made the transformation from Coffee Triangle, I was never quite sure what I might be walking into. I was hoping that it wasn't musical statues day because that always made getting served a tediously slow process.

Once inside, the first thing I noticed was that there were several small groups of people gathered together. One of those groups was standing directly in front of the counter.

"Excuse me, please! Coming through."

There was no sign of Sarah. Instead, I was served by a young man with lip and nose piercings.

"Hi. Is it Sarah's day off?"

"She no longer works here, I'm afraid."

"Oh?"

He whispered, somewhat conspiratorially, "She's gone to work for one of our competitors. I'm Piers, what can I get for you today?"

I was just about to give him my order when one of the men standing in the nearby group screamed in agony and fell to the floor. I expected one of his friends to go to his aid, but they didn't react—they continued to chat as though nothing had happened.

"Are you okay?" I crouched down beside him and checked his pulse, which seemed to be fine. "Can you hear me?" There was no response, so I turned to his 'friends' and said, "Don't just stand there. Call an ambulance."

They didn't. Instead, they all began to laugh. I was just

about to give them both barrels when I realised that the man on the floor was laughing too.

"What's going on?" I stood up.

"It's wink murder day," Piers said, by way of explanation.

"It's what?"

"Wink murder. You get together in groups, and one person is nominated to be the murderer. He 'murders' his victims by winking at them."

"I've never heard of it."

"Neither had I," Piers admitted. "We had to look up the rules online. It's proving to be very popular, though. If you'd like to play, I can put your name down for the next group."

"No, thanks, I'll pass."

Once I had my coffee and muffin, I made my way to the very back of the shop where it was less crowded.

"Jill! Hiya!" Betty Longbottom waved. "Come and join us."

Oh bum! The last thing I needed was Betty Longbottom.

"Jill, this is Rhonda." She nodded to her companion. "We went to school together."

"Pleased to meet you, Rhonda. I won't interrupt. I'm sure you have lots of catching up to do. I only came over here to get away from those winkers."

"No, you must join us," Betty insisted. "Rhonda, this is Jill Maxwell. She's a private investigator."

"Really? How very cool."

"Rhonda has a pretty cool job too," Betty said. "She's in TV."

"I actually work for an independent production

company. We're commissioned to create programmes by the major TV networks."

"She's worked on some of the big reality shows, haven't you, Rhonda?"

"A couple of them, yes."

"Don't be so modest. She worked on Paws For Thought—that series that was set in a pet shop, and Suds—about everyday life in a car wash. You remember those, don't you, Jill?"

"I—err—to be honest, I don't watch much TV these days."

"Rhonda is putting together a proposal for a brand new series." Betty could barely contain her excitement. "And you'll never guess what she's thinking of doing?"

"Something to do with Coffee Games?"

"No. Coffee shops have been done to death. She's going to make a programme based around The Sea's The Limit."

"Nothing has been finalised yet, Betty," Rhonda said. "Not until we get it green-lighted."

"I know, but that'll just be a formality when they see what you have in mind. Just think of it, Jill. Can you imagine how much publicity it'll generate for the business."

"It all sounds great."

Just then, a small group of customers came and stood right next to our table.

"Watch out!" Betty picked up her coffee. Rhonda and I did likewise, but I didn't have time to grab my cake, and the next thing I knew, a man 'dropped dead' onto our table, squashing my muffin.

To be fair to him, the 'murder victim' did offer to buy me a replacement, but before he could, I received a phone call from Mad to inform me that operation 'Takedown Spooky' was about to begin.

***

I'm not sure what I'd been expecting, but it definitely wasn't this nondescript, steel-clad unit on a quiet side road, halfway between Washbridge and West Chipping. If it wasn't for the cars parked outside, you would probably have assumed the building was unoccupied because there was no signage to suggest otherwise.

I met up with Mad in a layby, a quarter of a mile from the isolated factory, and she outlined the plan. I say *plan*, but in all honesty, we would pretty much be winging it.

"You know what you have to do?" Mad looked at me for confirmation.

"Yeah, I've got it, but please be as quick as you can."

"Will do."

Mad was going to head around to the back of the building to try to gain entry, and hopefully, locate the captive ghosts. Meanwhile, my job was to distract the people in the offices at the front of the building.

Here goes nothing.

"Hello?" I was standing in what would normally have been the reception area, but which was empty except for an old desk, a chair, and a filing cabinet. "Anyone home?"

There was a telephone on the wall, but when I picked it up, there was no dial tone.

"Who are you?" A tall man, with criminally poor taste in aftershave, wafted into the room.

"Hi." I engaged my super-duper friendly smile.

"What's going on, George?" A second man appeared.

This guy looked like he'd just dipped his hair into a vat of cooking oil.

"Hello, gentlemen," I said. "My name is Justine."

"Justine who?" Bad Aftershave demanded.

"Justine Case. And you are George and—?"

"George," Cooking Oil snapped.

"George and George? Doesn't that get a little confusing?"

"Never mind that," said Cooking Oil, hereafter referred to as George Two. "Who are you and what are you doing here?"

"These are the offices of Spooky TV, I assume?"

The two men exchanged a puzzled look before George One (AKA Bad Aftershave) said, "How did you find us?"

"It wasn't all that difficult."

What do you want?"

"I'm the commissioning editor for Max TV. I assume you've heard of it?"

Of course they had. It was the biggest player in the market.

"Yes, why?" George Two's curiosity had clearly been piqued.

"We at Max TV have been most impressed by the output of Spooky TV."

I've said it before, and I'll say it again. I should get an Oscar for this stuff. Two minutes ago, the two Georges were ready to throw me out onto the street, but now I had them eating out of my hand.

I continued, "The thing is, gentlemen, we're looking to introduce a late-night horror slot on Max TV. We had intended to produce the content in-house, but having seen the quality of your productions, we wondered if you'd be interested in working with us."

"What would that entail, exactly?" George Two asked.

"Assuming we could agree terms, we'd want you to produce a number of movies, which we'll run next season."

"How many titles?"

"We thought maybe four to start with. Ninety minutes each. How does that sound?"

The two guys were desperately trying to act nonchalant, but it was obvious to anyone with eyes that they were super-stoked by the offer.

"We could do that."

"Excellent."

"What sort of budget would we be talking?" George One said.

I'd been hoping we wouldn't get into the specifics. How much did one typically pay for a B-movie? I didn't have the foggiest idea, so I just plucked a figure out of the air. "We were thinking a mill."

"For four movies?"

"Each, obviously."

They were practically drooling now. "What do you think?" George One turned to George Two.

I had to hand it to them, they made a good double act. Like there was even the slightest doubt that they'd accept the offer. Eventually, after much mumbling, they both nodded their agreement.

"You've got yourself a deal, lady." George offered me his hand.

Thankfully, Mad made her appearance just in time to save me from his sweaty palm.

"Who are you?" George One spun around to face Mad. "You're trespassing!"

"My trespassing is the least of your problems." She turned back to the open door. "Come on through everyone."

The two Georges stared open-mouthed as a parade of ghosts walked into the room.

By now, it was obvious that the two Georges knew the game was up, and I was expecting them to make a run for it, but instead George One said, "None of this was our idea."

"Do you really expect us to believe that?" I said.

They both stared at me. Up until that point, they obviously hadn't realised that I was working with Mad.

"It's true," George One said. "We're innocent."

"Go on. I'm listening."

"George and I already had plans to start the TV station, and we'd intended to buy in old, cheap movies. That's when she got in touch with us."

"*She*?" Mad pressed. "Who's she?"

"Her name is Dayton. At least, that's what she told us. She offered us a way to make our own movies on the cheap."

"By using slave labour?" Mad snapped.

"Dayton told us that the ghosts wanted to come to the human world, and that they were willing to work for nothing in order to be here."

"And you really expect us to believe that you bought that nonsense?" I scoffed. "It was all rather convenient, wasn't it?"

"Maybe we're naïve, but that's exactly what we believed. At least, we did until she insisted that we kept them locked up."

"When you realised what was going on, why didn't you tell her you wanted no part in it?"

"It was too late by then. She said if we tried to back out, she'd kill us," George One said. "And we believed her. She's a very scary individual."

"I take it Dayton wasn't doing all of this for free. How much did you pay her?"

"She's taking eighty percent of the profits."

"Eighty? Wow, you two are even stupider than you look. You took all of this risk for twenty percent?"

"What choice did we have?"

I was lost for words at their stupidity, and judging by the way Mad was shaking her head, she obviously felt the same way.

"What are you going to do now?" George Two said.

Before Mad could respond, I caught her eye. "Mad, can I have a quick word with you outside?"

"Sure." Make sure these two don't go anywhere." she said to the crowd of ghosts.

They didn't need telling twice.

"What's up?" Mad said, once we were outside.

"What are we supposed to do with these two losers?"

"What do you mean? We have them banged to rights."

"Do we, though? I assumed the people running this outfit would be sups or maybe even ghosts. What can we do with a couple of humans?"

"Hand them over to the police."

"And say what? Please arrest these men because they've been ghost-trafficking? If I do that, I'll be the one they lock up."

"Damn it, you're right." Mad sighed. "What are we going to do, then?"

"Fortunately, those two geniuses in there don't seem to have realised that there's nothing we can do, so we have to use that to our advantage. We might not be able to put them behind bars, but we can still take down Dayton. It sounds like she's the mastermind behind all of this anyway."

"You're right. How do you want to play it?"

I explained my plan to Mad and left her to put part one into action.

***

Winky was still sulking.

"How long do you intend to keep this up?" I sighed.

"I don't know what you're talking about."

"I mean you and the long face. You didn't seriously expect me to buy you a card for your made-up cat day, did you?"

"Why not? I intend to buy you a Feline's Best Friend card."

"There's no such thing."

"There is now." He stopped sulking and grinned from ear to ear. "What date should it be? Next month, I think."

"You're unbelievable."

Mrs V popped her head around the door. "There's a lady who'd like to see you if you can spare her a few minutes."

"Did she say what it's about?"

"Just that she spoke with you earlier today. Her name is Rhonda Bloom."

Rhonda? Wasn't that the name of Betty's friend? "Okay, show her in, would you?"

"Hello again." She breezed into the office and shook my hand. "I'm sorry to drop in without an appointment."

"That's okay. Take a seat. Drink?"

"No, thanks."

"What can I do for you?"

"Do you remember Betty told you that I'm currently putting together a proposal for a new reality TV show?"

"Yes. The marine centre could make quite an interesting backdrop, I suppose."

"Possibly, but to be honest, I've never been totally sold on the idea."

"Betty seemed to think it was a done deal."

"Betty has rather jumped the gun, I'm afraid."

"I'm still not sure where I come in?"

"When Betty told me what you do, it suddenly came to me. This would be an ideal subject matter for the new programme."

"*This*?"

"You! The P.I. business. It would make must-watch TV. What do you say? Would you be interested?"

Oh bum!

Chapter 23

I'd been dreading this night all week. Seriously, could there be a worse way to spend an evening than watching a 'talented' pet show? The sacrifices I made for my pets went above and beyond the call of duty: Chauffeuring Winky all around town—most recently, to a quiz show and a boxing match. And it seemed like only five minutes since I'd attended Barry's art exhibition. And don't even get me started on Rhymes' poetry book.

I was running a little early, but I figured Aunt Lucy wouldn't mind. And, with a bit of luck, I might get a cake (or ten) to replace the muffin that had been destroyed by some random *fake-murder victim* guy in Coffee Games.

I'd just walked into her house, and I was about to call out a greeting when I heard voices coming from the kitchen.

"I don't think it's a good idea, Mother," Aunt Lucy said.

"She's going to find out sooner or later."

"We have to wait until we're sure."

My nose, which had been tickling for most of the afternoon, decided at that precise moment that it was time to let its feelings be known.

"Achoo."

"Hello?" Aunt Lucy shouted.

"It's only me." I went through to join them. "What were you two talking about just now?"

"The price of bunion ointment," Grandma said, without missing a beat. That woman had lying off to a fine art.

"I wasn't eavesdropping, but I heard you say something about someone finding out sooner or later?"

Aunt Lucy flushed. "I—err—we were just—err—"

"Wondering whether to tell Paloma Partridge about the price increase," Grandma interjected. "Her feet are in a terrible state, so the additional cost is going to hit her very hard."

Price increase on bunion ointment? Seriously? It was obvious that they didn't want me to know what they'd really been discussing, which made me suspect that it may have had something to do with me. But what?

I didn't want to make a scene or cause any upset, so I decided not to pursue the issue.

"What happened to Spikey?" Grandma said.

"It's Mikey, and he's okay, thanks."

"You managed to rescue him from the giant, then?"

"Yes."

"And did the sneezing powder come in handy?"

"Yes."

"Sorry, I didn't quite catch that."

"Yes, it did."

"And—?"

"And, thank you."

"Don't mention it."

I hadn't intended to.

"Is it time to go yet?" Barry came bounding into the room.

"It doesn't start for another hour." I was trying to decide whether I should have a second cupcake or not.

"I don't want to be late, Jill."

"You won't be, I promise. Have you got your outfit ready?"

"Lucy has put everything in the case for me."

"Okay, go and get it and we'll take a slow walk over there."

"Yay!" He went charging back upstairs.

"What will you be doing tonight, Aunt Lucy?"

"Actually." She took out her handkerchief and patted her nose, rather unconvincingly. "I've had a bit of a snuffle all day, so I won't be able to come. I've already told Barry and he understands."

"But what about the whist drive? I thought you were going there tonight?"

"*Whist drive*? Err, yes, that's right. I'm going to have to give that a miss."

Hmm. Very convincing. Not!

"What about the twins? They're coming, aren't they?"

"They really wanted to be there, but they have a prior engagement." She pretend-blew her nose.

"I bet they do. You three have totally thrown me under the bus."

"Are we going on the bus?" Barry was back with his case.

"Err, no. We'll walk there. Say goodbye to Aunt Lucy, but don't get too close. I wouldn't want you to catch her 'cold'."

***

The competition was being held at Candlefield Community Centre, and on the walk over there, Barry didn't pause for breath even once. Although it was nice to see him so excited, I was finding it difficult to muster the same level of enthusiasm. To make matters worse, I'd just had a horrible thought. How many pets would be taking part in this contest, and how long would it go on for?

"Barry," I interrupted whatever he was chattering about. "Do you know how many other competitors there'll be today?"

"Don't know."

"Is it just dogs and cats or will there be other pets taking part?"

"Don't know."

If you don't ask, you don't find out.

I was shocked to see the size of the queue outside the centre. It would have taken us forever to get inside, so I approached one of the wizards on door duty.

"Excuse me. This is my dog, Barry."

"I'm Barry," he confirmed.

"Hello, boy." The wizard gave him a stroke. "Aren't you handsome?"

"I was just wondering if there was a separate entrance for the competitors?"

"There is. It's around the back."

"Fantastic."

"But it's strictly for the competitors only. Not their entourage."

"I'm not his *entourage*. He's my dog."

"Sorry, missus. I can take Barry around the back if you like, but you'll have to join the end of the queue."

"Great." I handed him the lead, and watched Barry skip away.

"Was that your dog?" A female vampire asked when I joined the queue.

"Yes, that's Barry."

"What does he do?"
"Err—he dances."
"So does my Suzi. What kind of dancing?"
"Disco."
"Suzi is into break-dancing."
"What breed of dog is Suzi?"
"She isn't a dog. She's a chinchilla."
"Right? I thought the competition was just for dogs and cats."
"No, it's open to pets of all kinds."
"Have you been to one of these competitions before?"
"Oh yes, Suzi takes part in all of them. She won fifth place last year."
"Congratulations. Are there usually many competitors? I'm just trying to get a feel for how long this is likely to last."
"Lots. Last year it didn't finish until almost eleven."
"That's four hours."
"I know, and I loved every minute of it."
I was pretty sure I wouldn't enjoy *every* minute. Or any of them for that matter.
When I eventually made it inside, I discovered all the seats were already taken. It was standing room only at the back. This was going from bad to *I-seriously-want-to-cry*.

When Suzi's enthusiastic owner had said that all kinds of animals took part in the competition, she hadn't been exaggerating. I was all for giving everyone a chance, but I drew the line at the unicycling stick insect. Yes, I do realise that such a feat isn't to be scoffed at, but seriously, who wants to watch that rubbish?
Answer: apparently everyone in the community centre

except for me because when the unicyclist took his bow, it practically brought the house down.

There were other 'highlights' too: Who could forget Bubbles, the mathematical genius who was a—wait for it—goldfish. He was called Bubbles because he answered the problems put to him by blowing bubbles. Yes, it was just as bad as it sounds.

To be fair, Suzi the chinchilla certainly had the moves. If you happen to like break-dancing, that is. She too left the stage to a standing ovation.

When the MC announced that the next act would be juggling cats, I was expecting to see a troupe of felines throwing and catching miscellaneous stuff. Turned out I was wrong because onto the stage walked a giant of a werewolf wearing a scarlet cloak.

Colour me confused.

I clearly wasn't the only one who didn't understand what was going on because several people in the audience were mumbling under their breath. But then, everything became clear. Sort of.

The man opened his cloak, took out four cats from the deep pockets inside, and began to juggle them. At first, I was horrified, but it soon became clear that the cats were enjoying themselves. Rather than passively flying through the air, they were actually performing somersaults. Weird? Definitely. But no one could deny it was impressive. When he'd finished, most of the audience applauded loudly, but a few people complained that he shouldn't have been allowed to participate because they felt the talent on display was *his* and not the cats'.

Me? I didn't give a flying fig. I just wanted this torture over and done with.

I'd been standing there for almost two hours. I had a headache, my feet were aching, and I would have killed for a drink. There was a refreshment counter, but by the time I'd fought my way through the crowd, they'd sold out of everything.

At long last, it was Barry's turn to take to the stage, and despite my fatigue, I loved every second of his act. I'd struggled to appreciate Barry's paintings, but this was different. Rhymes' tuition had clearly paid dividends because Barry gave a performance that even the great Travolta would have approved of.

"Brilliant!" I shouted, as he took his bow.

I wasn't the only one who'd been impressed because the audience rose as one, to give him a standing ovation.

On the way home, Barry insisted on carrying the trophy in his mouth, even though it meant we could only walk at a snail's pace because he had to stop every time he wanted to speak.

"You should have won first prize," I said. "You deserved it."

"I'm happy with second." He clearly was. His tail had never stopped wagging since the winners had been announced.

"I don't know what they were thinking, giving that stupid goldfish the first prize."

"I thought Bubbles deserved it." Barry put the trophy down again. "Those sums were really hard. I couldn't do any of them."

"That's very generous of you, Barry."

"Are you proud of me, Jill?"

"Are you kidding? Of course I am. Incredibly proud."

When we got back to Aunt Lucy's, she and Lester were on the sofa enjoying a movie, a box of chocolates, and a bottle of wine.

"Hey, Barry." She stood up. "Is that a trophy I see?"

"I came second."

"Second to a mathematician goldfish," I said.

"Well done, boy." She gave him a hug. "We'll put this on display here unless you'd rather keep it in your room."

"I'd like you to keep it in the lounge, please. More people will see it there." He yawned. "Is it okay if I go to bed? I'm really tired."

"Of course. Off you go, and well done again."

"Did you enjoy it, Jill?" Aunt Lucy asked, after Barry had left the room.

"I enjoyed the five minutes that Barry was on stage. The rest of it? Not so much."

"Would you like a glass of wine and some chocolates?"

"No, thanks. I'm going to head home."

"Okay."

"Oh, and I'm very pleased to see you've made such a remarkable recovery from your cold."

***

I'd just magicked myself back to Washbridge when I got a call from Mad.

"Jill, I just wanted to let you know that stage one of the plan is complete."

"Fantastic. When will you need me again?"

"I've set up the meeting with Dayton, at Spooky TV, tomorrow at two."

"Did you have any problems?"

"Not really. I persuaded one of the two Georges that it was in their interest to make the call. Dayton wasn't very happy, but she's agreed to come over."

"I'll get there for about one-thirty."

"Okay. I'll get everything set up in the morning. Oh, and by the way, I also managed to persuade the two Georges that they should hand over what's left of the money they made. I'm going to give it to the ghosts who have been forced to take part in the movies."

"I bet the Georges were thrilled about having to give back the money."

"Far from it, but they weren't really in a position to refuse."

"I'll see you tomorrow."

Back at the house, Jack was in the lounge, staring out of the front window.

"What's so interesting out there?" I went and stood behind him.

"Those road works across the road. Didn't you see them when you came in?"

"Yeah. What about them?"

"They appeared this morning, but I haven't actually seen anyone working there as yet."

"You say that like it's unusual. I'm convinced they sometimes do this just for a laugh. It'll probably be like that for a week before anyone actually starts work. What are they supposed to be doing, anyway?"

"I've no idea." He stepped back from the window. "I thought I'd order in pizza."

"Because you're too lazy to make dinner?"

"It's actually your turn."

"Is it? In that case, pizza sounds like a great idea."

Thirty minutes later, we were back in the lounge, eating pizza.

"You should have taken a video of it," Jack said in between bites.

"Of Barry's dance routine? Yeah, I should have, but it never occurred to me."

"I didn't mean of Barry. I meant of the goldfish and the stick insect. That would have been really cool."

"I worry about you sometimes. Anyway, enough about that menagerie. You'll never guess what happened to me at work today."

"I wouldn't even know where to begin. Where you're concerned, it could literally be anything."

"I was offered the chance to star in a reality TV show."

"You're kidding."

"I'm not. I bumped into Betty in Coffee Games. She was with an old school friend who was thinking of making a show based around The Sea's The Limit. Then later, she came to see me and said she'd rather do a show about me and the agency."

"I bet Betty's thrilled about that."

"I'm not sure if she even knows yet."

"When do you start filming? Do you think I'll be able to get in on the act as the star's husband?"

"I don't think I'm going to do it."

"Why not? It'll be brilliant."

"It's fraught with danger. I'm already in Daze's bad books. If I were to slip up on live TV, that would be curtains for me. For us."

"I hadn't thought of that. If you were extra careful, though, it might be okay. Have you already turned it down?"

"Not yet. I told her that I needed some time to think about it."

"Fair enough. It has to be your decision." He turned on the TV. "Oh no! Spooky TV is off air."

"I might have had something to do with that. Sorry."

"Never mind." He flicked channels until he found something that caught his eye. "This might be interesting." It was a documentary about emperor penguins. "I love these guys, don't you?"

I didn't answer because I was too busy thinking about a different kind of penguin.

Chapter 24

"They're still there," Jack shouted from the lounge.

"Who is?"

"The roadworks."

"What did you expect? Did you think they'd disappear overnight?"

"There's still no one working over there."

Rather than continue to shout from the kitchen, I joined him in the lounge. "I told you yesterday, this kind of thing happens all the time. They put up the barriers and one of those tent thingies, but then they don't actually do any work for a day or two."

"You don't think it's a gas leak, do you?"

"No. If it was, they would have gone house-to-house, warning everyone. They're probably just laying cable or something."

"I suppose so. By the way, what were you up to last night after I'd gone to bed?"

"I was doing some research on a case."

"At midnight?"

"Yeah. That documentary you were watching got me thinking about the Washbridge Penguins case."

"I thought you told me that case was closed?"

"It is, but there's something about it that's still bugging me. In fact, there's a *lot* about it that's bugging me."

"Such as?"

"Why would this Royston guy spend so much money on a junior football team in which he seems to have little or no interest?"

"Maybe he's just a philanthropist. For all you know, he may donate money to a variety of causes."

"I suppose that's possible, but why did he pay me off like that? Why give me more money than I was due just to shut down the case. Unless—"

"Unless there was something he didn't want you to uncover."

"Precisely."

"That doesn't mean you have to get involved."

"Who says I'm going to get involved?"

"Are you?"

"Of course I am. I'd probably let it go if it wasn't for the fact that there are children involved. If Royston is up to no good, it may have some impact on those kids."

"What are you planning on doing?"

"I'm not entirely sure, but I thought I'd start by paying a visit to Victor Duyew, the guy who brought the case to me in the first place."

***

As I walked up the stairs to my offices, I noticed a peculiar smell—it was a bit like glue.

And that's probably because it *was* glue. There was a jar of the stuff on Mrs V's chair. She was using a brush to apply it to her desktop.

"Mrs V?"

"Morning, Jill."

"Has your desk broken?"

"No, dear, but it is rather boring, don't you think?"

"It's a desk. They're supposed to be boring." Except of course for the infamous orange dolphin desk, but that was best forgotten.

"They don't have to be boring, dear. That's where

decoupage comes in."

"De-coo what?"

"Decou*page*. It comes from the French for *cutting out*."

"I think I saw something about that when I flicked the TV onto the Craft Network by mistake. I didn't realise you were into that stuff?"

"I started about a month ago. Do you remember Victoria Crumb?"

"I don't think so."

"I'm sure I've mentioned her to you before. She's the one with the chihuahuas and the bad back." Mrs V laughed. "It's Victoria who has the bad back, not the dogs."

"Maybe you did mention her, I'm not sure."

"Anyway, I was at the fortnightly yarnie social, and I happened to mention that I was looking for another hobby. Something that wasn't yarn related. Someone suggested hang-gliding, but that didn't sound like my kind of thing. Victoria told me about decoupage, so I gave it a go, and now I seem to have caught the bug."

"Are you planning to give your desk the decoupage treatment?"

"Yes, unless you have any objections. I thought it would brighten the place up. Do you mind?"

"Err, no. I guess not."

"I thought I'd do the desktop first and see how that looks. And then maybe the drawers."

"Okay but be careful with that glue. It has a very strong smell."

"Silly me." She grabbed her handbag and took out a small facemask. "I meant to put this on earlier. I'd forget my head if it was loose."

I left Mrs V to her decoupage, and went through to my office, where I wouldn't have to put up with the smell of glue.

Or so I thought.

Winky, complete with facemask, had a jar of glue in one hand and a brush in the other.

"What are you up to now?" I sighed.

He mumbled something indecipherable through the facemask.

"Take off that mask. I can't hear a word you're saying."

"I said, *what does it look like I'm doing*? Decoupage, of course."

"Why?"

"I think we can agree that the old bag lady doesn't have many good ideas, but I thought this one sounded interesting, so I decided to give it a go."

"And you just happened to have the necessary supplies on hand, I suppose?"

"Of course not. I ordered them from Feline Crafters, using their priority delivery service."

There were times, and this was one of them, when I wondered if I was the only sane person on the planet.

"Why do you do that?" He gave me a puzzled look.

"Do what?"

"That thing you just did. That '*There were times, and this was one of them, that I wondered if I was the only sane person on the planet*' thing."

"I—err—I didn't actually say that out loud, did I?"

"No."

"So how come you know what I was thinking? Can you read my mind now?"

"No, but you're like an open book."

"Anyway, never mind that. What are you planning on decoupaging?"

"I'm not sure that *decoupaging* is actually a word, but in answer to your question, I thought I'd do your desk."

"Oh no, you don't. I don't want you and that glue anywhere near my desk."

"I won't charge you. Well, only for the materials."

"I said no."

"How about the sofa?"

"Nope."

"What can I do, then?"

I looked around the office. "If you must do something, you can do the screen."

"That's a bit boring. I thought you'd want to add a bit of spark to this place before filming starts."

"What filming?"

"The reality TV show. I hope you've had it written into the contract that I get plenty of screen time."

"There isn't going to be a reality TV show."

"Why not?"

"It's far too risky. One slip, and I'd be letting the whole TV audience know that I'm a witch."

"Just think of all the free publicity you'll be missing out on."

"Don't pretend you care about that. You're just annoyed that you won't be on TV."

"Come on, Jill. This could be your big break. Just think of all the people who started off on reality TV, and went on to have a career in show business. Have you actually turned it down yet?"

"No. I promised to let Rhonda have my answer within a

couple of weeks."

"You have to do it. If only for my sake."

Twenty minutes later, Mrs V popped her head around the door. Fortunately, Winky was working on the other side of the screen, so she didn't realise she had a competitor in the decoupage stakes.

"I didn't think you'd be able to smell the glue so much in here." She sniffed the air. "Katie and Adam Bell are here to see you."

"Send them through, would you?"

"Will do. I did offer them both one of my spare facemasks, but they said they're okay. Would you like one, Jill?"

"No, thanks."

I'd expected Katie and Adam to be downcast, but they were quite upbeat, under the circumstances.

"Deep down, I think we both knew Mum and Dad were dead," Katie said.

Adam nodded. "They would never have caused us this kind of worry deliberately. And we never bought into that story about the burglary."

"Hopefully, this will at least give you some kind of closure," I said. "What have the police told you? Are the Chases going to be charged with murder?"

"They don't think they killed Mum and Dad," Katie said.

"I don't understand. Why would they go to all the trouble of hiding the bodies, and trying to fake their disappearance, then?"

"From what the police have told us, they believe Mum

and Dad fell to their deaths while walking along the cliff path. Apparently, their injuries are consistent with a fall from height. The Chases had been ordered to install warning signs and fences after a previous fatal accident from the same spot, but they'd done nothing about it. They probably feared the caravan park would be closed down if it got out. The police are working on the theory that Norman or his wife discovered our parents' bodies, but instead of reporting their deaths, they decided to cover it up. By driving the car and caravan back to our parents' house, they hoped to divert attention away from the caravan park. The police think Mary Chase drove Dad's car, and Norman followed in his. Then he must have driven them both back."

"That makes sense. I assume they must have taken back roads to lessen the chance that they'd be picked up by roadside cameras."

"When they searched the Chases' home, they found the jewellery that had been taken from our parents' house. It wasn't worth much. I suppose they only took it to give credence to the theory that there'd been a burglary."

"What have the Chases been charged with?"

"So far, obstructing justice and preventing the lawful burial of a body, I believe. There's a chance they could face charges of corporate manslaughter too."

"None of that seems sufficient for all the pain and suffering they've put you through."

"We just want to put it all behind us," Adam said. "As soon as the police have released our parents' bodies, we'll arrange the funerals. That will give us closure at long last, and we'll be able to get on with our lives."

"We can't thank you enough, Jill." Katie wiped a tear

from her eye. "If it hadn't been for you, who knows how long we'd have been left in limbo. We may never have known the truth."

"I'm delighted I was able to help."

***

It came as something of a relief to get out of the office and away from the decoupage twins.

I'd agreed to meet with Mad that afternoon to put stage two of Takedown Spooky into action. This morning, though, I planned to talk to Duyew. Given the abruptness with which he'd insisted I drop the case, I expected him to refuse to see me, but I was wrong. When I spoke to him on the phone, he agreed without hesitation, and said I could go straight over to his place.

"Thanks for seeing me at such short notice, Victor."

"That's okay. It's not like I have anything better to do."

"I'm really hoping I can persuade you to tell me what was behind the decision to close down the case."

"I wish I knew."

"I don't understand. You must know why you did it."

"I did it because Royston ordered me to. He called me to his house and gave me a dressing down for overstepping the mark, as he put it."

"What did he mean by that?"

"He'd always given me a free hand with the Washbridge Penguins, and he let me get on with things. So when the thefts occurred, I thought he'd want me to try and get it sorted—to find out who was behind it and put a stop to it. That's why I contacted you."

"I take it that he didn't know you'd done that?"

"No, but when he found out, that's when he called me to his house and told me I had to shut down the investigation immediately."

"Did he say why?"

"No. I tried to ask him, but he told me to get out, and to make sure you were off the case by the end of the day. He said I should pay you double for your inconvenience."

"There's something very weird going on, Victor. If you spoke to him again now, do you think he might tell you the reason for shutting down the case?"

"I can't."

"Why not? For the sake of the kids, we have to find out what's going on."

"I can't speak to Royston because I'm no longer employed by him. He sacked me."

"When?"

"As soon as I told him that I'd got you to drop the case."

***

It was clear from what Duyew had told me that there was much more to the Royston case than met the eye. I felt sorry for Duyew. He came across as a genuine guy whose only concern was to do the best for the Washbridge Penguins. Being sacked like that, without a word of explanation, had hit him hard.

I needed to find out what Royston was up to, but there was no point in my trying to set up a meeting with him. I'd tried that before, and it was impossible to get past his gatekeepers and minders. That left me with no choice but to gate-crash.

If his mansion was anything to go by, the man had to be minted big time. He'd obviously invested a small fortune in security systems, but they proved no obstacle to your favourite superstar witch.

What? It's time I stopped hiding my light under a bushel. Sidebar: what is a bushel anyway?

Having used a combination of the 'invisible', 'shrink' and 'levitate' spells, I'd managed to gain access, first to the grounds, and then into the house itself. I wasn't sure if Royston was at home, but I found it hard to believe they'd maintain that level of security if he wasn't.

All I needed to do now was to locate the man himself. Given the size of the house, that might have taken a long time, had I not fallen lucky. I'd overheard one of the security guards, who was built like a gorilla, speaking into the walkie-talkie fastened to his jacket lapel.

"Kitchen, this is Secure Twelve, come in."

"Kitchen here."

"The boss wants his usual in the Grey Room. And make it snappy."

"Copy that."

The kitchen was likely to be located on the ground floor, and that would be easier to find than Royston.

Still invisible, I rushed around until I'd located it. I arrived there just in the nick of time because a middle-aged man was just coming out of the door, carrying a silver tray. On it was a cup of coffee and a bacon cob.

I quickly reversed the 'invisible' spell, and then stepped out in front of the man.

"I'll take that." I took hold of the tray.

"Who are you?"

"I've just come from the Grey Room. Mr Royston was fed up of waiting, so he sent me to see where this was."

"But we only received his order a few minutes ago."

"I know. He's in a bad mood." I made as if to walk away, but then hesitated. "This is going to sound daft, but I only started here yesterday. How do I get back to the Grey Room?"

"It's on the second floor. Wait a minute. Who did you say you are?"

That was my cue to shrink him and send him to sleep. After placing him into my pocket, I used the 'doppelganger' spell to make myself look like the waiter, and then I headed up to the second floor.

Most of the doors weren't marked, but about halfway along the corridor, I came across one with a nameplate: The Blue Room. A few doors further along, was the Green Room. Finally, at the very far end of the corridor, I found the Grey Room. There were raised voices coming from inside, so I used the 'listen' spell to hear what was being said.

"Of course Rhodesy did it!" The angry man was clearly exasperated. "Who else would it be? I won't stand for it. Do you hear me?"

"Yes, Boss."

"I want him taken care of, and I want it done today!"

"Yes, Sir. I'll give the order."

"It should have been done before now. I don't understand why you had to wait for me to come back to tell you what to do. What exactly am I paying you for?"

"Sorry, Sir, I'll get straight onto it."

Although I couldn't see who was in the room, it was a

pretty safe bet that the 'Boss' must be Royston, and he clearly wasn't happy about something.

"Hey, you!" The voice came from behind me. It was another one of the security gorillas. "What are you doing?"

"Mr Royston ordered this."

He glanced at the tray. "You'd better take it in, then." He opened the door for me, and I had no choice but to step inside the room.

This was the first time I'd seen Royston in the flesh; he was much uglier than the photos I'd seen in the newspapers. Seated behind a huge desk, he had a cigar in one hand and a knife in the other. The weaselly looking man standing in front of the desk looked terrified. I wasn't sure if that was because of the dressing-down he'd just received, or because of the knife. Probably both.

"Bring those here!" Royston shouted at me.

"Yes, Sir." He ignored me as I walked across the room. He was much too busy venting his anger at the poor weasel. "And when are those replacements going to arrive? They were supposed to be here yesterday."

The weasel swallowed hard. "There's been a delay, Boss."

"Do you know how much money I'm losing? I want them delivered today. Tomorrow at the latest."

"I'm not sure if that's going to be possible."

"I don't want to hear any more excuses. Just get it sorted!"

I'd already dawdled as long as I dared, so I made my way back out of the room.

The weasel followed, and once we were out of earshot of the room, he mumbled under his breath, "Damn stupid penguins."

"Having a bad day?" I said.

"None of your business! Get lost!"

"Sorry."

Before I left the house, I woke the waiter, restored him to full size and then wiped his memory.

Now all I had to do was to make some sense of what I'd just overheard.

Chapter 25

On the drive back to the city centre, I kept going over what I'd heard in the Grey Room. Royston had seemed particularly unhappy about someone called Rhodesy, which I assumed to be a nickname for somebody with the name Rhodes.

Royston had given orders for Rhodesy to be *taken care* of—whatever that meant—chances were, it was nothing good. Royston had also berated the weasel because the delivery of the *replacements* was running late. Based on what I'd heard the weasel say when he came out of the room, I was pretty sure that referred to the soft toy penguins, which were to replace those stolen. Stolen by Rhodesy, perhaps? Maybe that's what Royston had meant when he'd said that Rhodesy was *behind it*.

Like everything else related to this case, none of that made any sense. Why would anyone want to steal a load of toy penguins? And why would a successful businessman like Royston concern himself with something so trivial? I was obviously missing something, but what? I couldn't help but feel that the key to cracking this case was those soft toys. And I knew someone who knew a thing or two about those.

***

"That screen is looking fabulous, Winky." I gushed. "I love what you've done with it."

He stared at me for the longest moment before saying, "Are you feeling okay? Have you had a knock on the head or something?"

"I'm feeling fine. You really do have a flair for this de-coo-thingy."

"Decou*page*. Thanks. I'm quite pleased with it so far."

"Have you had any salmon, yet?"

"You gave it to me earlier."

"So I did. Would you like some more?"

"Okay." He stopped with the decoupage. "What's this all about? You want something, don't you?"

"Whatever makes you think that?" I snorted.

"Spit it out. What is it?"

"Well, now that you mention it, there is a *little* something."

"I knew it. How little?"

"I was thinking about those mini-Winkys that you made a while ago. They were so cute."

"That's not what you said at the time. I seem to remember you made me shut down my production line."

"I think you must be misremembering. Anyway, the point is, you obviously have a flair for making soft toys."

"They were pretty spectacular, even if I do say so myself."

"I agree. And with your experience and expertise, I don't imagine it would be too difficult to turn your hand to making other kinds of soft toys. Say, err—penguins, for example."

"Now we're getting to it. This is all to do with that weirdo case you're working on, isn't it?"

"Sort of. Although I'm not officially working on it any longer."

"Why do you need the toys, then?"

"Let's just say I'm doing it for the kids. That's why I know you'll want to help me."

"I hate kids."

"You don't mean that. The thing is, I need some small soft toy penguins making. Pronto."

"How many?"

"A hundred. Two-hundred would be better."

"How pronto?"

"I need them by tomorrow morning."

"*Tomorrow*?" He almost choked. "That's a joke, I take it?"

"No, I'm deadly serious."

"How do you expect me to make a hundred—"

"Two-hundred, ideally."

"How am I supposed to make them by tomorrow?"

"You were churning out way more mini-Winkys than that."

"Yes, but I'd need to retool to make penguins."

"You can do it. I have every confidence in you. Pretty please."

"It's a massive ask."

"With sugar on top."

"What's in it for me?"

"I can't afford to pay you because I'm doing this work pro bono."

"What about my costs? Materials etc?"

"I bet you still have some lying around somewhere, don't you?"

"I did put some stuff in Stu the Storage's lock-up."

"There you are, then."

"I still think I should get something out of the deal."

"What do you want?"

"How about if I do this, you allow me to decoupage your desk?"

"I—err—okay, then. But only if you deliver the penguins by tomorrow morning."
"Deal."

***

I'd arranged to meet Mad at what had until yesterday been the offices and studios of Spooky TV.
She checked her watch. "Dayton should be here in about thirty minutes."
"What exactly do you need me to do?"
"So far, all we have is the word of the two Georges, and that won't count for anything back in GT. I need you to get her to incriminate herself on camera." She pointed to the filing cabinet. "I've set one up over there, so provided she's standing next to this desk, we should capture everything she does and says."
"Right. That should be straightforward enough."
"Not necessarily. When I got George to call her yesterday, he was really nervous, and it's possible she may have picked up on that. If she did, she'll be on her guard."
"Where will you be?"
"Through the back. I'll be able to see and hear everything that happens from there."
Once Mad had left me to it, I used the 'doppelganger' spell to make myself look like George One.

Dayton made her appearance dead on time. *Dead*? Get it? Come on, this stuff is priceless.
What? No I don't mean worthless.
Tall with snow white hair, Dayton strolled across the

floor like she owned the place, but for all I knew, she might have done.

"Where's that ugly sidekick of yours?" she demanded.

"He's just nipped out for a sandwich. He might be a while because he's only just left," I said.

"I don't have time to waste waiting for that loser to come back. You'd better tell me what's so urgent that I had to visit this dump."

"Once you know why we asked you to come, you'll see it was worthwhile."

"I'll be the judge of that. Now, are you going to tell me or am I supposed to guess?"

"We had a visitor yesterday: A woman called Justine Case."

"Who?"

"Justine Case."

"That sounds made up to me."

"She's the commissioning editor for Max TV who are one of—"

"I know who they are. What did she want?"

"She's seen our movies and she really rates them."

"So now we know the woman has no taste. What else did she have to say?"

"She wants to commission us to make four movies for Max TV."

"I hope you told her we don't make movies for other TV stations?"

"She said they'd pay a million per film."

"A million? Each? Are you sure you didn't mishear?"

"Positive. That's what she said."

"Jeez, they must have more money than sense over there. What did you say?"

"That we'd do it, of course."

"Without consulting me?"

"She needed an answer there and then. It's a great deal, Dayton. You know it is."

She did. I could practically see the pound signs spinning in her eyes.

"How did she know where to find us?"

"Who cares? This is more money than we'll make in five years from Spooky TV."

"Can you two handle the increase in output?"

"Yes. Well, except—" I hesitated for effect.

"Except for what?"

"We don't have enough—err—actors."

"I sent you another two only the other day."

"I know, but if we're going to make four extra movies, we're going to need more."

"How many more?"

"At least another ten."

"Are you insane? Do you know how difficult it is for me to get hold of them? It's not like they turn up at my door and volunteer."

"I've often wondered, where do you get them from?"

"I have my people snatch them off the streets of GT, but it's not like they can do it in broad daylight. They have to wait until the dead of night."

"Thank you for sharing that with us," Mad appeared through the door behind me.

"Who are you?" Dayton took a few steps back.

"My name is Madeline, but everyone calls me Mad. Now you know who I am, why don't you tell me, is Dayton your first or last name?"

"George." She turned to me. "What's going on? Who is

this woman?"

I chose that moment to reverse the 'doppelganger' spell. "Actually, my name is Jill."

By now Dayton must have realised that the game was up, but if she did have any remaining doubts, they were quickly dispelled when Mad snapped the handcuffs onto her wrists.

***

I considered calling into the office on my way home, but in the end, I decided against it because I didn't want to disrupt Winky's production.

As I was pulling onto the driveway, I noticed that the roadworks were still there, but there was still no sign of activity. I was just about to go into the house when, out of the corner of my eye, I saw someone moving around inside the tent. Jack had been driving me mad with his constant questions about the roadworks, so I figured I'd go and see if I could find out what they were up to, and how long it would be before they'd finished.

When I called out, no one responded, but I was sure I'd seen someone moving around inside, so I pulled back the flap.

"Mr Hosey?"

"Jill. You've done it to me again."

"Done what? Why are you in here? It could be dangerous."

"There's nothing to worry about. This is my new neighbourhood watch camouflage."

"Roadworks? Seriously?"

"The man at Neighbourhood Camouflage Supplies told

me it was one of their bestsellers. It gets great reviews, apparently."

"I think he saw you coming."

"Why do you say that? It looks authentic, doesn't it? I thought it was indistinguishable from the real thing."

"That may be true, but I think you're missing the point. How long had you planned on staying here?"

"I hadn't really given it much thought. Indefinitely, probably."

"And you don't think that might strike the neighbours as a little odd?"

"I didn't think it would be an issue. I've known roadworks be in the same place for weeks at a time."

He had a point.

"Did the man at Neighbourhood Camouflage Supplies offer any kind of moneyback guarantee?"

"Yes, he was so confident I'd be satisfied that he said I could get a full refund if I returned it, for any reason, within fourteen days."

"In that case, my advice would be to take it back. Right now, while you still can."

"They did have a few other items that caught my eye. Perhaps I should do a swap rather than get a refund."

"Please make sure you give the next one a lot more thought."

"I'll do that, Jill. And thank you for your input. I do appreciate it."

***

"I can't believe it was Hosey." Jack was preparing dinner. "Whatever was he thinking?"

"He wasn't, but then this is the same guy who thought the dog poo bin was a good idea."

"That was sooo funny."

"Jack, sweetie, I know I'm not supposed to ask you about police matters."

"That's right, you aren't. So don't."

"I was only going to ask if you knew anyone called Rhodes? He might go by the nickname Rhodesy."

Jack stopped what he was doing and came over to the kitchen table. "What do you know about Rhodesy?"

"Nothing, but I heard someone mention his name today. Why? Who is he?"

"Ricky Rhodes, AKA Rhodesy, is one of the biggest drug dealers in this area. At least he was until earlier today."

"What do you mean, *he was*?"

"Someone murdered him."

"What? Are you sure?"

"Of course I'm sure. What do you know about it?"

"Nothing."

"Don't give me that, Jill. How did you come across his name?"

"Do you remember I told you that I was going to continue investigating the missing penguins?"

"Yeah."

"I paid Royston a visit, and while I was there, I heard him mention someone called Rhodesy."

"What did he say?"

"That he wanted Rhodesy *taken care of*."

Chapter 26

"I'm still not happy about this," Jack said.

Over breakfast, we were continuing the discussion (argument) that we'd started last night.

"I promise that I'll call you as soon as I know what they're up to."

"Royston is a very dangerous man. You don't know what you might be walking into."

"He may be dangerous, but I'm a witch, remember. I've been in much worse situations; you know that. If you make a move now, what have you got? A fragment of an overheard conversation, that's all. And it's not as though you can prove that conversation ever took place. What could you charge him with?"

It was quite obvious that Jack knew I was right, but that didn't make him any happier about the situation. "Tell me again what you plan to do."

"I've already told you a dozen times."

"Humour me, Jill. It's the least you can do."

"I'm going to collect the soft toys that Winky has been making overnight and deliver them to the souvenir shop. Then, hopefully, I'll find out exactly what they're doing with them."

"What makes you so sure they're doing *anything* with them?"

"I would have thought that was obvious. Why else would a man like Royston get himself in such a tizzy?"

"Maybe he's just upset because the shop is out of penguins."

"There's definitely more to it than that. Why else would he have panicked when he found out that Duyew had hired me? And, why did he sack Duyew and pay me off? If it turns out that I'm wrong, and this is all perfectly innocent, then I'll let you know, and no police resources will have been wasted. Okay?"

"You have to promise me that you'll be careful."

"I promise." I gave him a kiss. "I do wish you wouldn't worry about me, though."

"Worrying about you is my job."

***

"What do you think, Jill?" Mrs V was standing next to her desk, admiring her handiwork.

"It's—err—very yarnie-themed, isn't it?"

"I wasn't sure how to decorate it at first, but then it came to me. Why not combine my two passions?"

"It'll certainly be a talking point for clients."

"I'm glad you like it. I could do something similar with your desk if you like?"

"Err, thanks for the offer, but I'd rather not. It's Dad's old desk, and I'd prefer to keep it as he left it."

"I understand, dear. Would you like a drink?"

"No, thanks. I only popped in to pick something up."

"By the way, I've been meaning to ask, when is the replacement sign coming?"

"I spoke to Mr Tune yesterday. He's promised faithfully that we'll get it next week. I'll believe it when I see it."

"Fingers crossed, then. I don't know what that cat of yours is up to—I didn't like to look, but there's been an awful lot of noise coming from your office."

"Don't worry. I'll see to him."

Winky was lying on the sofa; he looked exhausted. On the floor in front of him was a huge pile of soft toys.

"What are these things supposed to be?" I picked one of them up.

"Penguins, as per your request."

"This isn't a penguin. It's a mini-Winky with wings and a beak."

"Technically, you're right, but no one need know that."

"Of course they'll know. It's quite obviously a cat!"

"I think you'll find that cats don't have either wings or beaks."

"These do. I thought you were going to make penguins for me. Proper penguins."

"And how was I supposed to do that in the time I had available? The tooling alone would have taken a week. Luckily for you, though, I still had a batch of mini-Winkys, so all I had to do was make the wings and beaks and sew them on. Voila!"

"You are unbelievable."

"Thank you. Even I didn't think I'd be able to manage it in the time available. Turns out I'm even more talented than I thought."

I'd expected penguins but what I'd actually got was *catguins*. The soft toys reminded me of my poor Beanie Babies, which Lizzie, aided and abetted by Kathy, had turned into monsters.

There was nothing to be done about it now; I was stuck with them, like it or lump it. Now I had to figure out how to get them to the car. It would have taken at least a dozen trips to carry them all. It would also have invited questions from Mrs V who would, understandably, have wondered where so many soft toys had come from. There was nothing for it, but to shrink the toys and slip them into my pockets and bag.

Once I got to the car, I placed the tiny soft toys on the back seat, and then reversed the 'shrink' spell.

Whoops!

I'd totally underestimated how much room all of the full-size toys would take up. They spread from the back seat into the front, pinning me up against the side window. Although I attracted a few curious looks from passersby, no one came to my aid. Instead I was forced to slowly manoeuvre my hand until I felt the door handle. As soon as the door sprang open, I along with several dozen catguins, fell out onto the ground.

Before I could drive the car safely, I had to relocate half of the stupid soft toys into the boot. Eventually, though, I made it to the Washbridge Penguins souvenir shop.

"Good morning." The young man behind the counter looked delighted to see me. He no doubt thought I was his first customer of the day. "Do you see anything that takes your fancy?" He spread his arms. "There's lots to choose from."

"I'm not here to buy anything. I have a delivery of premium penguins for you." I produced two catguins from behind my back. "I have a car full of these outside."

"What's that thing?" His sour expression was not exactly the reaction I'd been hoping for.

"The penguins you've been waiting for."

"They look like cats. With wings. And what's that thing stuck to its face?"

"It's a beak of course."

"They're nothing like the ones we had before."

"These are new. As designed by Mr Royston himself."

"Really?"

"Yes. Could you help me to carry them from the car? I've got two-hundred of them out there."

"We don't want them in here."

"I've just explained the reason for the new design."

"It's not that. They have to be delivered to the warehouse."

"Why? You sell them from here, don't you?"

"Yes, but we have strict instructions that they have to go to the warehouse first. They make the delivery to us."

"That's a bit of a weird system, isn't it? Does that happen with everything you stock?"

"No, only the premium penguins."

Huh? "Fair enough. I don't have the warehouse address with me. Could you remind me where it is?"

"Sure."

This was getting weirder and weirder. Why would Royston insist the premium penguins be delivered to the warehouse, and then from there to the souvenir shop?

The warehouse was located on a quiet country road halfway between Washbridge and Middle Tweaking. The security around the place was incredible. What exactly did they have in there? Gold bars?

"Yes?" The security guard on the gate was wearing a uniform that was at least two sizes too small for him. I was a little concerned that one of the buttons on his jacket might pop off at any moment. If it did, I didn't want to be in the firing line.

"I have a delivery of penguins for you. You're expecting

them, I believe."

"Where are they?"

Talking of buttons, this guy obviously wasn't the brightest. "The car is full of them. Look!"

"I thought you said they were penguins."

"They *are* penguins."

"They look more like cats to me."

"Since when did a cat have a beak and wings?"

"They're ugly things."

"I can take them back if you don't want them, but I understood Mr Royston has been chasing this delivery."

The guard mumbled something indecipherable under his breath, but then raised the barrier, and pointed towards the goods inwards gate.

The two men who unloaded the car made similar derogatory remarks about the soft toys, but I didn't rise to the bait. Instead, once the car was devoid of catguins, I bid the men goodbye, and made my way off the premises.

But only as far as the nearest layby.

From there, I hurried back to the factory on foot. Invisible now, I levitated over the fence and made my way back to the loading bay where the catguins were piled high. One of the guys who had unloaded the soft toys was on the phone.

"I know they weren't supposed to arrive today, but I'm telling you they're here now." He glanced around, and then continued in a whisper. "This batch are as ugly as hell. What do you want us to do with them? Okay, will do."

Once he'd finished on the call, his colleague said, "What's happening?"

"They want us to take them downstairs straight away."

"So much for my coffee break."

The two of them proceeded to load the soft toys into a large tub trolley. Once it was full, one of the men began to wheel it towards the lift, while the other stayed behind and began to load a second trolley.

Still invisible, I followed the first man to the lift, and looked over his shoulder as he entered the keycode. There wasn't enough room inside the lift for me to stand next to the trolley, so I had to climb on top of the catguins. Fortunately, my unobservant friend didn't notice that the pile of soft toys had been compressed a little.

When we reached the basement, and he started to push the trolley again, he looked rather confused—he was no doubt wondering why it was suddenly much heavier than it had been before.

In the centre of the room there was a large table, surrounded by chairs. As soon as he'd parked the trolley, I jumped out before he started to unload his cargo. He'd got half of the catguins onto the table when a door opened, and in walked half a dozen men, dressed in identical white coveralls and wearing facemasks.

Perhaps they were here to do some decoupage.

"What are these things?" One of the masked men picked up a soft toy.

"These are plug ugly!" another one quipped.

"Watch what you're saying." Warned the man who had delivered them. "I heard that Royston designed these."

That shut down further criticism.

The six men took their seats around the table. I was still trying to work out what they were doing when the door opened again, and in walked a man carrying a large parcel, which he deposited on the table next to the toys.

Moments later, everything became crystal clear.

Once I was back at the car, I called Jack and gave him the address of the warehouse.

"You'll need to move quickly. I'm not sure how much longer they'll be at it."

"And you're sure it's drugs?"

"What else could it be? They're taking stuffing out of the toys and replacing it with a white powder."

"I'd better get our people over there."

"The operation is taking place in the basement. You'll need the keycode for the lift to get down there. It's 7634."

"Got it."

"Let me know what happens, will you?"

"Yeah, I'll update you when I can."

"See you tonight."

"Okay, and Jill—"

"Yeah?"

"I love you."

Chapter 27

I would have liked to have been at the warehouse to see the police take Royston's operation down, but there was somewhere else I had to be. That was if I valued my life.

Grandma had scheduled the opening of her new beauty salon for one-thirty, which struck me as a little odd, but then she never did anything conventionally. Her other high street ventures had all been successful, some more than others. I knew it still rankled with Grandma that Forever Bride hadn't managed to displace Kathy's shop as Washbridge's premier bridal destination. Would Ever Beauty ring the death knell for Nailed-It, or would Deli be able to hold off the competition in the same way as Kathy had? Only time would tell.

It was twenty past one when I arrived on the high street, and I was rather surprised at the lack of activity. Usually, when Grandma opened a new shop, she did so with a great fanfare—marching bands, acrobats, that kind of thing. Today, though, there was nothing to indicate the shop was about to open except for the banner draped above the window, which read: Opening today - 1.30pm.

This wasn't Grandma's usual MO, and for reasons I couldn't explain, it made me nervous.

"Hey there!" Kathy was walking towards me; Peter was by her side.

"Hey there, yourself. How come you two aren't at work?"

"We both decided we'd earned a day off."

"Nice work if you can get it."

"It was Kathy's idea," Peter said. "I can't really afford to take time off."

"I didn't doubt for a moment it would be my sister's idea."

"Are you here for the same reason as we are?" Kathy gestured to the new shop.

"Yeah, I was ordered to attend. What's *your* excuse?"

"I'm dying to find out what Ever Beauty is all about. Has your grandmother told you anything about it?"

"Not a thing."

"I tried to peep through the window earlier, but she's put screens in the way so you can't see what's inside. It's all quite intriguing, don't you think?"

"Not really. I can understand why you might be keen to see the new shop, but I didn't think you'd be interested, Peter."

"I'm not. I've told Kathy that I'm going in Coffee Games while she looks around the beauty salon. Wild horses wouldn't drag me in there."

"How are the kids?"

"Okay, except that Mikey has been having nightmares."

"It's probably the excitement of moving to a new house."

"That's what I said, although why that would cause him to dream about giants, I don't know."

"*Giants*?"

"Yeah. If I didn't know better, I'd say he'd been reading Jack and the Beanstalk."

"That is weird."

"You haven't heard the weirdest part. Apparently, you're in his nightmare too. You come to his rescue every time."

"Me?" I did my best to look suitably surprised.

"That's what he says."

"Look, it's opening." Peter pointed across the road, and then he set off towards Ever Beauty.

"Pete?" Kathy called after him.

"I didn't think he was interested in seeing the shop," I said.

"He wasn't. He isn't. He told me he'd rather chew glass than have to look around a beauty salon."

"It looks like he's changed his mind."

Peter had already disappeared into the shop. As if that wasn't strange enough, another dozen men followed him inside.

"Come on." Kathy hurried across the road with me in hot pursuit.

The shopfitters had done a spectacular job, and it seemed that no expense had been spared. The left-hand half of the shop was dedicated to the sale of beauty products, divided into two discrete areas: Women's and Men's. The right-hand half of the shop had been converted into several small rooms in which various treatments were on offer: manicures and pedicures, hair removal, eyebrow threading, facials and some stuff I'd never heard of.

"I don't get it," Kathy said.

She didn't need to elaborate because I already knew what she meant. In the women's section, there was just Kathy, me and a couple of other women. But the men's section was chock-a-block, with men of all ages, practically fighting with one another to get a better view of the products on offer.

While Kathy and I browsed the over-priced offerings in the women's section, the tills never stopped ringing, and from what I could see, most of the purchasers were men.

"Hello, you two." Grandma made us both jump.
"Do you have to creep up on people like that?" I said.
"Have you seen anything that takes your fancy?"
"I might try the Wrinkle Magic." Kathy picked up the tiny box.
"Not at these prices." I scoffed. "Is there a discount for family?"
"Don't be silly."
"What's going on over there?" I nodded towards the men's section that was still ten times busier than the women's.
"What do you mean?" Grandma shrugged.
"All those men."
"What about them?"
Before I could continue with my interrogation, one of the sales assistants came over to speak to Grandma. "We've sold out of Ever Aftershave."
"Why are you telling me?" Grandma snapped. "Go and get some more from the stockroom."
The young woman scurried away towards the back of the shop.
"Not that door!" Grandma seemed almost panic-stricken. "The other one." She turned back to me and rolled her eyes. "You can't get good staff these days."

Grandma was checking how the treatment section of the salon was doing. Kathy was queueing to buy the wrinkle cream. Meanwhile, curiosity had got the better of me. I wanted to know why Grandma had become so agitated when the sales assistant almost went through the wrong door. What was behind it?
There was only one way to find out.

After a quick check to make sure no one was watching, I magicked myself to the other side of the door, to be faced with a flight of steps, which I hurried up two at a time. On the small landing there was a single door, which was slightly ajar. Unsure and a little nervous of what I might find inside, I pushed it open.

"Hi." The young woman was seated in a rocking chair.

"Hi."

"I'm Thel."

"Pleased to meet you. I'm Jill. Do you work here, Thel?"

"I suppose so, in a manner of speaking. But it's only a temporary job until I find my sisters, Pea and Aggy. You don't happen to know them, do you?"

"Err, no. I'm afraid I don't," I lied.

"You are a witch, aren't you?"

"I am, yes."

"I seem to have misplaced my sisters. I'm not sure if they're here in the human world or if they've gone back to Candlefield."

In fact, I did know her sisters. They were sirens who had lived next door to Aunt Lucy for a few days until I'd been instrumental in their arrest.

"What are you doing here in the shop?"

"I'd run out of money, and I wasn't sure what to do, but then the nice lady who owns this place offered me a temporary job."

"Did she? That was kind of her."

"It was. The work isn't too demanding, and the pay is very good."

"I see. Well, it was nice to meet you, Thel, but I really must get back downstairs."

Back in the salon, I managed to track down Grandma.

"Could I have a word, please?"

"Haven't you bought anything yet?"

"No, I haven't. A word?"

"What is it? Can't you see I'm very busy."

"In private."

I ushered her to one of the empty treatment rooms. Once inside, I closed the door so we couldn't be overheard.

"What's this all about?" she demanded.

"How did you manage to get so many men to come into the shop?"

"They're here for the extensive range of men's grooming products on offer, obviously."

"Is that really the story you're going with?"

"I have no idea what you're prattling on about, but I have work to do." She reached for the door handle.

"Hold on! I've just been speaking to Thel."

"You had no right to go up there."

"How could you do it, Grandma?"

"How could I do what? All I did was to offer the girl a temporary job."

"She's a siren and she's on the rogue retrievers' Most Wanted list."

"Fiddlesticks. Daze and her crew are just overreacting as usual."

"How is she overreacting? They lure unsuspecting men to them, and then do goodness knows what to them."

"Not in my shop, they don't. Why do you think I have her locked away safely upstairs?"

"Are you denying that she's the reason that so many men are in here today?"

"I've already told you the reason for that. It's the range of products on offer."

"Don't give me that old tosh. Peter had said wild horses wouldn't drag him in here, but as soon as the doors opened, he came charging over here. You've got that siren calling all the men on the street into the shop, haven't you?"

"It looks like I'm needed out there." She pointed to one of the assistants who wasn't even looking in our direction.

"No wonder you didn't bother with the usual promotions."

"Out of my way." She pushed past me and left the treatment room.

"What are you doing in here?" Kathy appeared in the doorway. "Are you thinking of getting your legs waxed?"

"Err, no. In fact, I'd better get going. Are you coming?"

"Not just yet. It looks like Pete could be here for a while."

"Okay, but I do have to go." I gave her a hug.

"We'll see you tomorrow, then."

"Tomorrow? Will you?"

"You haven't forgotten the Middle Tweaking carnival, have you?"

"Of course not. I'll see you then."

As soon as I was outside, I made a call.

"Daze, it's me. I know where you can find the other siren sister."

***

That evening, Jack was barely through the door before I was on his case.

"You said you'd call me about Royston's warehouse. I've tried to ring you a dozen times but all I got was your voicemail."

"Sorry, but there's been a stabbing, and I had to drop everything else."

"In West Chipping?"

"Yeah. He's not dead, but it was touch and go for a while. We've arrested his brother."

"What happened at the warehouse?"

"I wasn't there, so I only know what I've been told."

"Which is?"

"They caught them red-handed in the basement, just like you said. They arrested ten men in total."

"Royston?"

Jack shook his head.

"Why not?"

"He wasn't at the warehouse, and he doesn't own it. At least, not on paper."

"But it's his operation. You know that."

"Of course it is, but we need proof."

"So, what are you telling me? That he's going to walk away from this scot-free?"

"Hopefully not. A couple of the men who were arrested at the warehouse are high up in the pecking order. We're hoping that they can be persuaded to give evidence against Royston."

"In return for walking free themselves?"

"Possibly, yes."

"That stinks."

"I know, but unfortunately that's the way these things work."

Although it was incredibly annoying, I knew he was

right. "Did you figure out what was happening with the premium penguins?"

"We're still trying to piece it all together, but it looks like Royston was using the souvenir shop to pass drugs to his network of dealers. What could be more innocent than buying a soft toy from the club's shop?"

"Wasn't that risky, though? What if someone else had purchased one?"

"That was never going to happen. The penguins containing the drugs were kept separate from the ones that didn't. Only customers who had 'reserved' one were allowed to purchase them."

"That explains the 'premium' tag. When I visited the shop, the sales assistant told me that they had 'regular' penguins and 'premium' penguins."

"What about Rhodesy?"

"He was one of Royston's biggest rivals. It's pretty obvious that he was behind the theft from the souvenir shop. That's why he had Rhodes killed."

"What will happen to the Washbridge Penguins?"

"I've no idea, but I can't imagine Royston will have any interest in them now."

"I hope they lock him up and throw away the key. It's bad enough to be dealing drugs, but to use a kids' football team as cover for your sleazy trade is downright despicable."

"I agree. It's all pretty depressing. There was one bright spot, though."

"Oh?"

"One of the guys sent me a photo of that latest batch of so-called penguins." He laughed. "I've never seen anything quite so ugly."

"You'd better not let Winky hear you say that."

Chapter 28

As we couldn't all fit into one car, Jack and I had arranged to meet Kathy, Peter and the kids at Middle Tweaking. That arrangement also had the advantage that we might be able to slip away early if the opportunity presented itself.

"It's ages since I was here." Kathy looked down the village high street.

"The last time was when we came to that murder mystery evening at the pub," Peter said.

"That's right." Kathy's face lit up, and I knew full well what was coming next. "That was the night that Jill, the great private investigator, accused the murder victim of being the killer."

All three of them were laughing now.

"Just remind me again, would you?" Jack was wearing that smug look of his—the one I just wanted to slap off his face. "Who won that night?"

"I don't remember." I shrugged. Just then, I noticed three familiar figures walking towards us. "Myrtle's here."

"Who's that with her?" Peter said.

"Hodd and Jobbs."

"Are you joking?" Kathy laughed. "Those can't be their real names."

"They are, and I wouldn't let them hear you laughing if I were you. From what I can gather, they're ex-cons and they're as tough as nails."

"Hello, Jill." Myrtle greeted me with a polite hug. "I'm so glad you could make it."

"Myrtle, this is my husband, Jack. My sister, Kathy, and

her husband, Peter. And this is Mikey and Lizzie."

"I'm very pleased to meet you all." She turned to the kids. "Especially you two. Are you looking forward to the carnival?"

"Is there a big wheel and dodgems?" Mikey asked.

"No, but there is a hook-a-duck stall."

His face fell.

"I love hook-a-duck." Lizzie beamed.

"Sorry, where are my manners?" Myrtle said. "I should introduce my two colleagues. This is Celia Hodd, and this is Constance Jobbs."

Every time I saw those two women, they looked scarier.

"Nice to meet you all." Hodd's cockney accent was as strong as ever.

"Any friend of Turtle's is a friend of ours," Jobbs said.

Mikey was staring at the scar on Jobbs' chin, and I had my fingers crossed that he wouldn't ask her how she got it.

"You're probably all wondering where the carnival is," Myrtle said. "It's on Tweaking Meadows which is just outside the village. I thought it would be easier for us to meet here and walk down." She pointed back the way she'd come. "Shall we?"

"The village is even lovelier than I remember," Kathy said. "After we've finished at the carnival, we should stay and get dinner here. Is there anywhere you'd recommend, Myrtle?"

"You basically have a choice of one, and that's The Middle." She pointed across the road.

"Isn't that the pub where they held the murder mystery evening? It wasn't called that back then, was it?"

"It would have been the Old Trout when you were

there. After that, it was The Boomerang for a while, but it recently changed hands and name again. The current owners seem to know what they're doing, and the food is really good." She pointed at the church. "Over there is the reason we're all here today. The carnival was organised to raise funds to renovate the bells."

"Is this it?" Mikey's face fell even further when we arrived at the carnival site, and he realised it was more village fete than funfair.

And that's when I saw it.

Balanced above a giant wooden barrel full of water, was a single stool. Just the sight of it gave me flashbacks to my soaking at TenPinCon.

"They must have had that installed especially for you, Jill." Kathy laughed.

"Don't worry," Myrtle said. "The inclusion of the ducking stool was a rather controversial decision. Not everyone thought it was a good idea. In the end, it was given the go-ahead, but only after it was agreed that the 'victim' must be a volunteer."

"Who on earth is going to volunteer to get a soaking?" Jack said.

"There are a few good sports in the village who will be prepared to take a ducking for the cause."

"Would any of you like to sign up?" Charlie Cross, the retired police sergeant, was manning the ducking stool stall.

"Hi, Charlie." I shook his hand. "How is retirement suiting you?"

"It's a little boring to be honest. Still, today promises to be fun. Would you or any of your party like to sign up for the ducking stool?"

"I definitely wouldn't."

"I will!" Mikey pushed his way to the front.

"Oh no you don't!" Kathy grabbed him by the arm. "We have to drive all the way back home."

"Children aren't allowed to put their names down, I'm afraid, young man," Charlie said. "What about you, Myrtle? And you two." He was looking at Hodd and Jobbs who were both pretending to study their shoes.

"Definitely. You can put us all down," Myrtle announced without bothering to consult the other two who looked horrified.

"Excellent. That will be ten pounds each, please."

Myrtle handed over thirty pounds; she clearly didn't trust the other two to pay for the privilege of a potential soaking.

"Thank you." Charlie took the cash and handed her three slips of paper. "Put your names on the back of these, please. The draw will be made at four o'clock."

"What draw?" I was confused.

Charlie explained that the village committee had decided it would be bad form to have dozens of people walking around the fete, soaked to the skin. Instead, all would-be volunteers had to pay ten pounds to have their names entered into the draw. That would be one raffle that no one wanted to win.

Mikey and Lizzie wanted to do very different things, so we decided to split up. Jack and Peter went off with Mikey while Kathy and I accompanied Lizzie, who was desperately trying to win a teddy bear at the hoopla stall. She was already on her third attempt, but so far, she hadn't come close to getting the hoop over the bear. If I saw an opportunity, I planned on using a little magic to help her.

"You'll never guess what, Kathy?" I said.

"You've decided to put your name down for the ducking stool?" She grinned.

"There's no chance of that. A TV station wants to make a reality show based around me and the agency."

"Are you being serious? I can never tell."

"Deadly."

"That's brilliant! When do they start filming?"

"I haven't decided if I'm going to do it yet."

"Why wouldn't you? What's to think about?"

"I'm not sure it's my kind of thing. Don't you think those programmes are all a bit tacky?"

"No, they're not. I imagine they'll want to include your family, won't they?"

"That's why you want me to do it, isn't it? Because you think you'll get to be on TV too."

"Of course it isn't." She tried to look suitably indignant at the suggestion. "I just think it would be good for your business."

"I won!" Lizzie proudly held up the flea-bitten bear. "I'm going to call him Ear."

"Well done, Pumpkin." Kathy gave her a kiss. "That's a rather unusual name, isn't it?"

"It's because he's only got one of them."

"Shall I ask the man if he'll swap the bear for another one?" I offered.

"No." She hugged it tightly to her chest. "I love my Ear."

After an hour of walking around, both Kathy and I were

ready for a sit-down. Fortunately, there was a refreshment stall, which had a number of plastic tables and seats. While we rested our feet and had a drink, Lizzie tried her luck at the hook-a-duck stall, which was right next door.

"Hey, ladies, are you having fun?" Charlie Cross came and sat at the next table.

"Very much so," Kathy said.

"The weather certainly helps." I took a sip of the tea, which looked and tasted like it had never seen a teabag. "Who's manning the ducking stool while you're here?"

"Roberta Brown and I are taking it in turns."

"Have you had many sign-ups?"

"Twenty-eight when I left."

"Wow. I wasn't expecting there to be so many gluttons for punishment. Sorry, I mean willing volunteers."

"I'm just going to nip to the loo." Kathy stood up. "Keep an eye on Lizzie, would you, Jill?"

"Sure."

A few minutes later, Lizzie came over to join me. "I didn't win anything on hook-a-duck, Auntie Jill."

"Never mind. You did really well to win Ear."

"That's a handsome bear you have there, young lady." Charlie gave her an approving thumbs up.

It was almost four o'clock, so we went in search of the guys, who we found at the tin-can alley stall. Jack and Peter looked pumped, but Mikey looked fed up.

"It's nearly time to go." Kathy beckoned them over.

"Hold on," Peter said. "We've got one more round of our competition to go."

I might have known. It turned out that Jack and Peter had decided that the three of them should compete against one another. The one who knocked down the most cans over the three legs would be crowned champion.

"Okay, buddy, it's eighteen apiece," Jack said. "This is where we see who can withstand the pressure."

"Bring it on." Peter grinned.

"What about you, Mikey?" I said. "How many have you got?"

"Only fourteen." He sighed.

"You're still in with a chance." I tried to reassure him, but he didn't look convinced.

"This is it, then," Jack announced. "The third and final round. And may the best man win."

And he did. Mikey was beaming from ear to ear. Meanwhile, Jack and Peter were competing to see who could look the most disappointed.

"You did that, didn't you?" Jack whispered.

"Did what?" I said, all innocent-like.

"You used magic to make Mikey win."

"Of course I didn't. Didn't I promise not to use it unless it was something really important?"

"Yes, but—"

"Are you doubting my word?"

"No, but I don't see how I could have missed the cans altogether."

"It must have been the pressure. It obviously got to Peter too. That sort of thing doesn't seem to affect kids, though. That's why Mikey still managed to hit the cans."

"I suppose you're right."

Snigger.

We all made our way over to the ducking stool, which

was to be the final event of the day. Myrtle was waiting for us there.

I looked around. "Where are Hodd and Jobbs?"

"The cowards have done a runner, so they won't end up in the water barrel. Just wait until I get my hands on them. Still, we've done very well today. According to Charlie, forty people have put their names down. That's four-hundred pounds. Added to the rest of the takings, we should have beaten our target."

"Does that mean—?"

"Yes. The bells have been saved."

"That's fantastic. I can actually relax and enjoy this because I know I'm not going to be the one who gets ducked."

"Hmm." Kathy grinned.

"What does that mean?" I challenged her.

"Nothing."

"What have you done, Kathy?"

"I might have accidentally put your name down for the ducking stool."

"You did what? When? How?"

"While you were having a cup of tea with Charlie."

"If my name comes out, I'll—"

"Ladies and gentlemen." Charlie called for order. "We now come to the moment you've all been waiting for. It's ducking time!"

Everyone cheered—except for me. With my luck, my name was bound to come out, and if it did, I wouldn't be responsible for what I did to Kathy.

Charlie dipped his hand into a bowl and drew out a single slip of paper. "Here we have it. The name of the person who is going to enjoy a lovely dip has the initials:

J.M."

"Oh dear." Jack put his arm around my shoulder. "Still, you have had plenty of practice."

His grin didn't last for very long, though.

"Would Jack Maxwell please climb the steps and sit on the ducking stool."

On the drive home, Jack was giving me the silent treatment.

"Those trousers suit you." I laughed.

Charlie Cross had allowed Jack to dry off at his house, and he'd been kind enough to lend him a change of clothes. Charlie was of course, at least thirty years older than Jack, and several sizes larger.

"You're not funny, Jill."

"Now you know how I felt when Grandma signed me up for the ducking stool at TenPinCon."

"If you were going to put anyone's name into the draw, why didn't you put Kathy's in?"

"What makes you think I didn't?" That was easily the best twenty pounds I'd spent in a long time.

He sneezed. "I've probably caught a cold."

"Man flu, more like."

***

While Jack was taking a shower, I decided to nip over to Candlefield because Aunt Lucy had said that she thought her new neighbours might be moving in today.

When I arrived at her house, I could hear voices in the kitchen.

"You have to tell Jill," Pearl insisted.

"Yeah, it's only fair," Amber said.

This was like déjà vu, and this time, there was no doubt they were talking about me.

"What's going on?" I burst into the room. "What should you tell me?"

"It's nothing for you to worry your head about." Grandma tried to wave away my question.

"I'm not leaving until someone tells me what's going on." I took a seat at the table.

"She has a right to know, Mother," Aunt Lucy said.

"Please yourself." Grandma shrugged.

Aunt Lucy took a deep breath, and judging by the look on her face, she wasn't about to deliver good news.

"Darlene really should be the one to tell you this."

"Well she isn't here, is she? So you'll just have to do."

"Okay." Another deep breath. "About five years before you were born, your mother gave birth to another child."

My chest felt tight, and I could barely breathe. "Another? You mean—?"

"You have a brother."

"And no one thought to tell me?" I could barely contain my anger.

"There was a good reason for that," Grandma said.

"I can't wait to hear it."

"The baby was snatched from your mother within hours of his birth."

"That's terrible, but someone should still have told me about him."

"You're right." Aunt Lucy bowed her head. "We should have said something. When you first discovered you were a witch, it felt like it would be too overwhelming to burden you with any more information. And then, as time went by—"

"What? You all conveniently forgot?"

"Hold your tongue, young lady," Grandma snapped. "I know you're upset, but how do you think we felt when it happened? The wounds are still raw, even after all these years."

"Who snatched him?"

"No one knew for sure, although we all had our suspicions," Grandma said. "Suspicions that have now proven to be correct."

"What do you mean? Do you know who did it?"

"Braxmore."

"How can you know that? He's dead, isn't he?"

"Yes, he is." Grandma hesitated for what felt like an eternity. "But your brother isn't, and he wants to meet you."

ALSO BY ADELE ABBOTT

The Witch P.I. Mysteries
(A Candlefield/Washbridge Series)

Witch Is When... (Books #1 to #12)
Witch Is When It All Began
Witch Is When Life Got Complicated
Witch Is When Everything Went Crazy
Witch Is When Things Fell Apart
Witch Is When The Bubble Burst
Witch Is When The Penny Dropped
Witch Is When The Floodgates Opened
Witch Is When The Hammer Fell
Witch Is When My Heart Broke
Witch Is When I Said Goodbye
Witch Is When Stuff Got Serious
Witch Is When All Was Revealed

Witch Is Why... (Books #13 to #24)
Witch Is Why Time Stood Still
Witch is Why The Laughter Stopped
Witch is Why Another Door Opened
Witch is Why Two Became One
Witch is Why The Moon Disappeared
Witch is Why The Wolf Howled
Witch is Why The Music Stopped
Witch is Why A Pin Dropped
Witch is Why The Owl Returned
Witch is Why The Search Began
Witch is Why Promises Were Broken
Witch is Why It Was Over

Witch Is How... (Books #25 to #36)
Witch is How Things Had Changed
Witch is How Berries Tasted Good
Witch is How The Mirror Lied
Witch is How The Tables Turned
Witch is How The Drought Ended
Witch is How The Dice Fell
Witch is How The Biscuits Disappeared
Witch is How Dreams Became Reality
Witch is How Bells Were Saved
Witch is How To Fool Cats
Witch is How To Lose Big
Witch is How Life Changed Forever

Susan Hall Investigates
(A Candlefield/Washbridge Series)
Whoops! Our New Flatmate Is A Human.
Whoops! All The Money Went Missing.
Whoops! Someone Is On Our Case.
Whoops! We're In Big Trouble Now.

Murder On Account (A Kay Royle Novel)

Web site: AdeleAbbott.com
Facebook: facebook.com/ AdeleAbbottAuthor

Printed in Great Britain
by Amazon